Paul

Paul

Daisy Lafarge

GRANTA

Granta Publications, 12 Addison Avenue, London W11 4QR
First published in Great Britain by Granta Books, 2021

Excerpt from *The Scope of Anthropology* by Claude Lévi-Strauss
(Jonathan Cape, 1967). Translation copyright © 1967
by Jonathan Cape Ltd. All rights reserved.

Excerpt from *Reborn: Journals & Notebooks 1947–1963* by Susan Sontag (Picador
USA, 2009). Copyright © 2008 The Estate of Susan Sontag. Preface copyright ©
2008 by David Rieff. All rights reserved.

All possible care has been taken to trace the rights holders and secure permission
for the texts quoted in this book. If there are any omissions, credits can be
added in future editions following a request in writing to the publisher.

A CIP catalogue record for this book
is available from the British Library.

1 3 5 7 9 10 8 6 4 2

ISBN 978 1 78378 635 0
EISBN 978 1 84708 636 7

Typeset in Garamond by M Rules
Printed and bound by CPI Group (UK) Ltd, Croydon, CR0 4YY

The boldness of such an approach is, however, compensated for by the humility – one might almost say the servility – of observation as it is practiced by the anthropologist. Leaving his country and his home for long periods; exposing himself to hunger, sickness and occasional danger; allowing his habits, his beliefs, his convictions to be tampered with, conniving at this, indeed, when, without mental reservations or ulterior motives, he assumes the modes of life of a strange society, the anthropologist practices *total observation*, beyond which there is nothing except – and there is a risk – *the complete absorption of the observer by the object of his observations.*

CLAUDE LÉVI-STRAUSS,
The Scope of Anthropology

My new wife was not very talkative, she was melancholy and ironic.

PAUL GAUGUIN,
Noa Noa: Voyage to Tahiti

X = the compulsion to be what the other person wants.

SUSAN SONTAG,
Reborn: Journals and Notebooks 1947–1963

PART ONE

PART ONE

lundi

I'm sitting on a curb in the autoroute service area, waiting for Paul to arrive. The problem is, I have no idea what he looks like. There were a few photos of him and his home, Noa Noa, on the BénéBio website: one of him standing in front of the house, another posing triumphantly at the summit of a mountain. The image quality was poor though; when I tried to enlarge them his features blurred into pixels.

I check the time on my phone. It's been over an hour since I got off the bus from Paris, half an hour past the time that Paul and I agreed he would pick me up. I scroll back through our messages. He'd always taken one or two days to get back to me, and when he did so it was in fractured English, with an almost giddy use of punctuation. *We are excited to you welcome my home, Noa Noa!!* I'd told him it was fine if we communicated in French, and mentally shelved any concern about his late responses; anyone who runs a sustainable farm should not have to be glued to their emails.

The heat rising from the tarmac prickles my thighs. I stretch my legs out into the road, drawing them back every now and then as a car speeds past from the drive-through. The drivers and passengers stare straight ahead, clutching their burgers in silence. Maybe it's just the smell of the food, wrapped in papers damp with grease, but every time a car goes past my stomach lurches.

I drag my scuffed, one-wheeled suitcase to McDonald's, the service area's beating heart. The shift in light in the shaded interior feels vaguely spiritual, as if I'm approaching something sacred. I'm briefly plunged back into the moment of entering the archives in Paris each morning, the swift transition from white sun to cool, muted shade, as the unsmiling attendant buzzed me in.

Back outside with a lukewarm Diet Coke, I watch the cars move in and out of the berths, their slow dance at the drive-through. It's almost elegant, rhythmic, each member belonging to some choreography larger than itself. I think of courtly dances, their participants finely dressed and affectedly anonymous with jewelled and feathered masks, threatening a descent into debauchery at any moment. Flirtations whispered between topiaries, incests muffled by the maze's high hedges.

I remember A.B. telling me about his first intensive research project after graduating. He was assisting an Irish historian who specialised in Insular manuscripts, under whose supervision he'd spend upwards of eight hours a day hunched over miniature pages with a magnifying glass in hand. When he finally emerged from the archives each evening, he found the manuscript seared across his vision; everything was snared in the interlacing knotwork of its pages.

I look back at the cars, wondering if something similar is happening to me. No courtly dances, no masks, no topiaries. Just cars, I tell myself.

With my attention on the motorway in the distance, I fail to hear the heavy, metal panting of the rusting estate before it pulls up next to me. The car and its driver hit me all at once: I find myself caught in the teeth of a wide, full jaw filling the open window and bouncing the sun's light back to me. It's a mouth too large for the man's face, pushing out the flesh of his deeply tanned cheeks. My eyes are still in his teeth when he addresses me: 'Frances? Frances Hawthorne?'

Despite the width of his mouth, he is unsmiling. His voice is deep, and he pronounces my name in a thick accent that turns the last syllable into something like 'torn'.

'Yes ... Paul?'

He looks me up and down, brushing dark curls aside as he wipes his brow. He nods and steps out of the car. I realise I'm still sitting on the pavement as he stands over me, and I fall out of his teeth and into his shadow.

Lifting my suitcase into the boot provokes a laugh from Paul, who addresses me in French: 'How long are you planning on staying?'

I shrug and smile. We both know exactly how long I have signed up for: a week of light agricultural labour, in exchange for bed and board. After that, I will travel on to work elsewhere.

'I hate having to come to places like this,' he says, glowering at the McDonald's.

'Mmm,' I say, echoing his tone as I get into the car. 'Me too.'

A cool breeze filters through the open window. I try to relax into my seat and sneak a glimpse at Paul: he appears louche and at ease, his skin dark and thick with hairs, well worn by sun and activity. I think of the texture of some hardy and durable piece of equipment, a hessian rucksack, perhaps.

The car is not exactly dirty but it is cluttered with use: there is a layer of soil on the floor and surfaces, banana skins and apple cores on the dashboard. One of the cores is not yet brown, maybe just put down by Paul before meeting me. As if able to follow my train of thought, he reaches out and grabs it, putting it in his mouth, core, stalk, pips and all. He looks over at me as tiny flecks of saliva and apple spray into the air.

'There is too much waste in the world,' he says. 'I eat *everything.*'

We begin to speak, keeping the conversation light, the talk small. Paul speaks with an urgency that seems faintly aggressive; it takes me a couple of minutes of swimming upstream against his diction before I relax into its current.

I've always found listening easier than speaking. When A.B. and I were with his colleagues in Paris, he would talk to them and I would listen, comprehending here and there. He was often told he had a 'firm grasp' on the language, and always took this as a compliment. It made me think about the phrasing. Why 'firm'? Why did understanding have to come with so much grasping, and force?

I tell Paul I'm relieved he turned up, happy I wasn't waiting at the wrong service station. It comes out a little more effusively than I'd intended, but he doesn't seem to notice. He half apologises for his lateness before doubling back on himself with an excuse: he had errands to do on the way, something about a jazz festival.

'And you've come from Paris?' he asks.

'Yes.'

'On your holidays?'

'No,' I pause, wondering how much to say. 'I was working. In the archives. As a research assistant.'

'Oh. So you're an academic?' he says knowingly.

'No – I've only just finished my degree. But my supervisor has this research project, and he asked me to—'

'In what subject?' he cuts across me.

'Medieval history.'

'Ah.' He smiles as if some realisation has dawned.

'What?'

'I studied anthropology. It's my job to try and figure people out.'

I laugh, feeling scrutinised and unsure how to respond. I shift in my seat. The seatbelt is too tight and begins to rub the skin on my shoulder. I notice Paul is not wearing his.

'So,' he goes on. 'You're English, a medieval historian, you were a research assistant in Paris, and then – you decided to come and work on an organic farm.'

I shrug. It occurs to me how much his description sounds like an obituary.

'And what was it, out of all the hundreds of farms on BénéBio, that made you choose mine?'

'I . . .'

'Is it because of the handsome host in the photos?' He grins, eyes glinting in the sun.

I blink. He is still waiting for a reply. Why *did* I choose him? It was A.B. who'd sent me a link to the website; I think he'd refused to see me again by that point. I remember making several trips to our temporary office but he'd had the locks changed. He'd sent me the link to BénéBio's website in a short, terse email, saying that a friend of his recovering from a breakdown had done the scheme last summer, and had found herding goats in the Cévennes a 'restorative experience'.

As for Noa Noa, I remember clicking on it at random, and scrolling through the photos Paul had uploaded: the winding, lush garden; the tall, off-white house with cornflower-blue shutters and climbing vines; the open veranda with its long wooden table for making preserves and drying herbs; vistas of the surrounding Pyrenean valleys; and finally a view of a mountain from a window, taken at dawn in an almost white light. Its peak appeared to float above a valley of lilac mist.

Once I'd seen the photos, I'd closed the other tabs of

'maybe' locations one by one, until Noa Noa was the only one left.

'It was the mountain,' I tell him. 'Though I've forgotten its name. Mount . . .'

'Tagire.' He finishes my sentence with a nod. 'Mount Tagire.'

Paul tells me it is about an hour and a half's drive to his village, Lazeaux. He has been living there for a few years, although he grew up, he says, in the suburbs outside Paris.

'Not the rough ones,' he adds. 'The sleepy white ones where nothing happens and people vent their racism online.'

He moved a lot in his twenties and thirties, travelling around islands in the South Pacific, working temporary jobs in France in between to save up money. Before moving to the Pyrénées, he was a mature student in Montpellier. He tells me he fell backwards into anthropology, spending time with island tribes during his travels before going on to study them formally.

Paul the anthropologist. I imagine his gangly frame in a pale linen suit, hunched over field notes in a hut, wiping tropical sweat from his brow.

'I am a photographer too,' he says. 'I will show you my images when we get to my home.'

'I saw some pictures of the mountain on the website. It looks beautiful.'

Paul snorts faintly and waves his hand.

'They were just quick shots,' he says dismissively. 'My real practice is travel photography. I've been all over – Tahiti, Bora Bora, Tupai . . .'

'And do you still travel a lot?'

Paul looks out of the window. 'It was time to settle down,' he says, tilting his wing mirror. 'I am forty-four; I'd been travelling too long.' He smiles boyishly.

We filter off to narrower roads, leaving the traffic behind us. The route takes us higher into the hills, where the air becomes thinner, the birdsong louder and the green haze beyond the windows blindingly vibrant. The road thins down to a single lane. Each time we pull over to let an oncoming car pass, Paul grins at them, his smile unfaltering. As we go deeper into the mountains and meet fewer cars, I have the feeling that we are peeling away the outer layers of things I know and can put a name to; the familiarity of the car park feels distant.

We pass a turning leading to a nearby cathedral, Saint Pascal. Famous – amongst medievalists, anyway – for its hybridity of architectural eras, a fusion of Romanesque and Gothic styles. Maybe that was one of the reasons I chose Noa Noa; when I looked up the whereabouts of Paul's home I'd noticed its proximity to Saint Pascal and hoped I'd be able to visit. I crane my neck to follow the road, but the turning is obscured by trees.

'Have you been?' I ask, nodding at the turning.

'To Saint Pascal? Briefly, when I first moved here. But it was crawling with tourists. Plus I'm not religious. Though I would call myself *spiritual*,' he adds.

I look over, expecting to see a sarcastic expression on his face. Instead he looks gravely serious.

'I meditate,' he goes on. 'I believe there are ways to encourage the body to heal itself, ways the West has largely forgotten—'

I sneeze, interrupting him. He looks faintly annoyed. 'Sorry,' I sniff. 'Go on.'

He turns back to face the road. 'I learned a lot from my travels. I had a lot of troubles, as a young man. When I was growing up, I felt very different to everyone around me. I never felt like I belonged anywhere, or fitted in . . .' he trails off.

I realise I am nodding, though I'm not sure exactly what he means.

'But the first time I visited Tahiti,' he says, 'everything changed for me. It was like I was cut loose from everything, all this Western conditioning.' He takes a deep breath in. 'So, I went back as often as I could. And then, when they felt I was ready, I was initiated.'

'They?'

'The Areoi. Descendants of a once great and secret tribe. Their race was said to have been founded when the sun god mated with Vairaumati, the most beautiful of all mortal women. They don't usually initiate outsiders, of course, but they made an exception for me; they could see the respect I had for their ways. That's how I got my name.'

'What – *Paul*?'

'No! Noa Noa. It's one of the many faces of the god Oro. It's the name for his mad face. Mad, and . . . a little gullible.'

'Good combination.'

'Yes,' he says, laughing. 'I was out trekking with two native men. There was an inland gorge I wanted to visit, and we arrived after a few days' walking only to find the pass was half collapsed. I insisted we try, but they said I was *noa* to want to take the path and *noa* to believe I would be able to. So they camped there and waited for me, and when I came back later the next day, they said it was a miracle I had made it, but that I was completely *noa noa*. That's how I got the name.'

'I see.'

'So, when I finally decided to settle down, and found this place in Lazeaux, there was only one name I could give it.'

I adjust the seatbelt from where it's cutting into my shoulder.

'But still,' Paul says, 'I wouldn't say I am *religious*.'

Soon we pull up outside a tall metal gate. There is a distant sound of a lawn being mowed. Behind the gate, a driveway runs down past a shabby, almond-coloured house, ending in a garden that curves out of sight. The driveway is littered with footballs and lone flip-flops that appear to have strayed from the brightly coloured mountain of shoes by the back door. Our arrival prompts two yellow dogs to bound up to us, barking through the gate.

I squint at the modern house and feel confused – it looks nothing like what I can remember of Noa Noa.

'It's . . . different to the photos,' I say.

'Oh, I don't live *here*,' Paul says dismissively. 'This is Marcel's house – my friend – I just need to pick up a cable.'

He's already halfway out of the car.

'Okay. Should I stay, or—'

'Paul!' I hear another man call out. 'About time.'

A man has appeared at the back door, a small, barefoot girl clinging to his waist. He strides towards us and unlocks the gate, simultaneously unleashing the dogs. The girl squeals and tries to shush them.

'Sorry, Marcel, there was a delay on the roads,' Paul says breezily. 'Anyway, voilà, this is Frances.'

I get out of the car to greet Marcel, who stoops a little to kiss me on both cheeks. Even after a month in Paris, I'm still unaccustomed to this sudden proximity to the skin of men, and I perform the gesture awkwardly. He's not quite as tall as Paul and has lost most of his hair. But his eyes, as he steps back, are deeply set and tapered in a way that gives them a permanent smile.

'Welcome,' he says warmly, and then tries to shake loose the girl that has reattached to his right leg. 'This is my youngest, Léa.'

'Salut,' I say softly and lean down to kiss her.

Her cheek is soft and finely fuzzed like an apricot. She stares at me as I stand up.

'The cable's just in the garage,' Marcel mutters to Paul, 'but if you're not in a rush you could stay for a drink?'

Paul shrugs and looks at me expectantly. 'Sure, as long as Frances doesn't mind.'

A faint heat rises to my face. 'Of course not,' I say quickly. 'That would be nice.'

Marcel smiles and claps his hands together. 'Bon! Léa, go and get your sisters, please.'

Léa unhooks herself from Marcel's leg and shoots off into the house. Her shouts drift out into the warm air, causing all three of us to smile: 'ÈVE, LAURE, VENEZ! IL Y A UNE ANGLAISE!'

'So tell us how you ended up here, Frances.'

Marcel leans back with a glass of pastis in his hand, eyeing me steadily. We're sitting in his garden around a wooden table, shaded by an apple tree whose branches contort overhead. A thin stream runs along the foot of the garden.

Léa and Laure, who must be around six and ten, have been chattering to each other ceaselessly. Ève is a little older, I would guess early teens, and has been silent since we sat down. She turns her eyes to me now, with a flicker of what is either curiosity disguised as disinterest, or just pure indifference.

I look down at the table and repeat more or less what I'd told Paul: that I graduated at the beginning of the summer, and I'd spent a month in Paris working as a research assistant.

'Researching what?' Marcel asks.

I pause and glance at Paul. He seems to be absorbed in reading the label on the bottle. 'A manuscript. A kind of picture book, for children – we think it was used to teach them to read.'

'In French?' Marcel asks.

'Middle French.'

'And you can read that?'

'I'm learning. It doesn't have many words, anyway.'

Marcel laughs and looks over at Paul. 'Then what are you doing with this clown?'

'She saw the photos of the house,' Paul retorts. 'I *told* you they were a good idea!'

Marcel sighs deeply. 'You have no idea what you've signed yourself up for, Frances,' he says, shaking his head. 'Aucune idée.'

Paul laughs and downs the remainder of his drink in one gulp.

'Ignore him,' he says to me confidingly. 'Marcel thinks he's very funny.'

Marcel raises his eyebrows. 'Well, Frances, you're very welcome to Lazeaux.'

'Thanks.'

'We can't compete with archives but there are a few places that you might like. You know about the cathedral?'

I nod.

'And Paul's told you about the baths? Well, Lazeaux used to be famous for them,' he continues, prompted by my blank expression. 'There were thermal springs discovered not far from here, and they built a complex at the end of the nineteenth century, designed like a Roman villa. They're in ruins now, but—'

'I was going to tell her,' Paul interjects. 'It just wasn't the first thing on my mind.'

Marcel grins triumphantly. 'So what was? The story of how

we met?' He opens his mouth but pauses when he sees Paul's face. 'I can't believe it,' he says, in mock surprise, 'the one time you don't milk the hero narrative?'

Paul laughs grudgingly.

'What?' I ask.

Léa ducks beneath the table and emerges a few seconds later with a small blue flower in her hand. She begins to sing softly.

'So I was in my mid-twenties –' Marcel begins.

'Marcel is a few years older than me, as you can tell,' Paul mutters.

Marcel ignores him and continues, '– doing some volunteering in New Zealand, and I decided to travel on a little further once it was finished, to Tonga. There was no *Lonely Planet* guide back then. Or if there was, I didn't read it. Anyway, I was with –' he falters, glancing at Léa and Laure, who are busy drawing shapes on the table's surface with water, hearts and spirals that quickly vanish as the water seeps into the grain – 'I'd met a nice lady to spend the last few weeks with before coming home.'

I look at Paul, who is watching Marcel steadily with a hand over his mouth. Ève picks at her nails with apparent disinterest.

'So we arrive pretty late one night and head to a bar in the capital, Nuku—'

'Nuku'alofa,' Paul cuts in.

'Yes – anyway, then we decide we want to take a dip in the sea. Only what no one tells us is that it's practically forbidden for women to swim in Tonga.'

At this point Léa stops singing and looks up. 'You mean *none* of the girls swim, at all?'

Marcel shakes his head. 'They're not taught how,' he says. 'It's taboo.'

'And "taboo",' Paul adds, 'is actually the only Tongan word that's used regularly in Western culture.'

'Well that's just *stupid*.' Laure frowns. 'Why don't they let them swim?'

'Mais non,' Paul says slowly, laying his palm flat on the table. 'It's a *cultural difference*, and one that should be respected.'

'Encouraging women to *drown* isn't exactly respectable,' says Ève, speaking for the first time.

She leans back in her seat and concentrates on the glass of water in her hand. I wasn't expecting her to sound so self-assured.

Paul looks exasperated.

'What I was *going* to say,' says Marcel, raising his voice and spreading his hands over the table in a gesture of authoritative diplomacy, 'is that Paul – how old were you then? Twenty?'

'Twenty-one.'

'Okay, twenty-one-year-old Paul just happened to be on the beach at the time, saw what we were doing and came over to warn us.'

'How did he know you were going to try and swim?' Léa asks.

'Well for one thing, we were naked,' Marcel says. Ève's eyes flicker for a moment, and her father quickly goes on. 'Anyway, what I mean is, Paul is a seasoned traveller.'

Paul inhales deeply at this point.

'As incompetent as he may be at *real life* . . .'

'Oh, *ça* suffit!' says Paul, the smile dropping off his face as Léa and Laure collapse into laugher.

Twenty-one. When Paul was the same age as I am now he was already a 'seasoned traveller'; all I've done is follow A.B. to Paris. *But I'm here now*, I tell myself, *which is something, isn't it?* I look at Paul and Marcel, wondering if they think me as pathetic as I feel. I smile at the girls, but they smile back a little warily.

'Sorry about that,' says Paul once we're back in the car. 'Marcel thinks he's hilarious. Old friends, you know what it's like.'

I stare out at the green valley, my thoughts drifting to Léa, Laure and Ève, wondering what it'd be like to grow up here.

'Do you have children?' I ask.

Paul snorts. 'Jesus, no. I'm too much of a kid myself! I would have, maybe. But it's not really compatible with travelling.'

I nod silently; I'd guessed as much.

We fall into an easy quiet. The lane ahead of us overspills with summer growth as the late afternoon sun filters through the canopy. Every now and then I catch glimpses of settlements through the trees: grand houses dilapidating quietly in the heat; bungalows sweltering under terracotta tiles; peach-coloured pigment flaking from walls; garden chairs rusting on patios; vegetable patches tamed into grids.

'Do you like jazz?' Paul says, shaking me from the view.
'What?'

'*Jahhzz*,' he exaggerates the pronunciation. 'I ask because my friends and I – we are putting on a festival du jazz in the village this week. A concert.'

'Oh.'

'There'll be food, dancing – a lot of people will come. My friends are in a band. They've been touring all summer but are finishing up in Lazeaux.'

'Are you in it too?'

His smile fades. 'No,' he says quickly. 'I'm tone deaf, but the band are all my friends – there's Antoine, who I live with, Loïc, Manon; you'll meet them soon. But who actually lives with me changes all the time.' He blows air out through his lips and frowns, as if trying to calculate an impossibly large number. 'Antoine is an old friend of Loïc ... then there is also Béthanie, who I met a few years ago. She's staying while she figures some things out – she had a messy divorce last year.'

I nod, trying to follow the onslaught of names.

'And then,' he says, turning to me, 'there's you. Or whoever else gets in touch on BénéBio. It's been fairly quiet this summer but I don't mind; we've been really busy with the festival, and I've got an exhibition coming up ...'

'So I'm the only one?' I ask, shifting again in my seat. I was under the impression that there would be other BénéBio volunteers at Noa Noa.

'Just you! And there was only one boy before you, at the

beginning of summer. A Russian boy – lazy, useless – anyway, it means you get a room all to yourself. ' He winks.

I smile back, unsure whether to greet the prospect of labouring alone in Paul's garden with excitement or disappointment. I'd been looking forward to having some new company.

'We're nearly there,' Paul says after a little while. 'I can't wait to show you my home.'

Noa Noa is exactly as the pictures had promised: blue shutters, red geraniums, waxy-green vines curling round black balustrades. We park in the garage beneath the house, and climb the stone steps to the front door. Paul conducts me on a cursory tour of the first floor: the kitchen leads through to a mezzanine barn conversion. I instantly recognise the long wooden table from the photo I'd seen online, except in place of the jam-making equipment there is a bunch of blue flowers in a water jug. They are slightly wilted, garish against the muted stone wall and faded furniture.

'I got them this morning,' Paul says, pointing to the flowers. I return his smile and wander over to the wooden banister that overlooks the lower level of the mezzanine. It's plush with sofas, pouffes, cushions and tie-dyed throws. In place of a wall on the side overlooking the valley, a low wooden trellis runs the length of the room.

Paul appears next to me. 'This is where Béthanie sleeps.'

I stare at the wide-open view beyond the veranda. 'But . . . there's no *wall*.'

'So?'

'What happens when it rains?'

He shrugs. 'It rains. Worse things could happen. Besides, it's an original feature.'

He goes on to tell me about the conversion he'd done when he bought the property. The house was fine, but the barn had been in total disrepair; it had taken him and his friends a whole summer and autumn to renovate.

I stare at the view behind him. Just visible over the neighbour's trees is the faint blue line of the Pyrénées.

'Ah,' Paul says, following my gaze. He points to the tallest peak. 'That one there, that's Tagire.'

'It's beautiful.'

'The view's better from my room, of course,' he says. 'Maybe I'll show you tomorrow.'

I am about to say *That would be nice,* but the words stall on my tongue. Instead I say nothing, staring resolutely out at the view.

'Anyway,' he says brightly, 'you must want to get settled in.' He picks up my case and walks over to the doorway. 'Follow me.'

My room is on the same floor as the kitchen and mezzanine. No view of Tagire, but a window facing out over the lane at the top of the village. Paul says to come and find him if I need anything; there's no point getting started on any work today. I thank him, and he disappears upstairs, leaving my door open. I tiptoe after him and shut it, closing my eyes and sinking down to the floor.

A stuttering film reel of the last few hours starts playing in my mind. I realise I had not put much thought into this trip beyond working on a farm and trying not to think about A.B.; I had not been expecting someone like Paul. I think about his body, so long and thin – as though some capricious god has gone at him with a rolling pin – and the nervous thrill of sitting next to him. He seems to have done so much, to be so much of a person; the proximity to him reminds me of how I felt when A.B. first started talking to me properly. A few minutes after class at first, and then meetings in his office, the simultaneous giddiness and nausea of receiving his attention. I had been invisible but he pulled me into the light, although I couldn't bear to be seen ... And then, before I can stop them, memories from the archives flicker on screen.

I open my eyes to make the scenes stop playing, and reach for my suitcase. The last time I'd unpacked was in Paris, where I thought I'd be staying the whole summer. I pull out my clothes one at a time, shaking out the creases. I'm here now, in a village called Lazeaux, with a man called Paul and his friends. That's all I've got to think about.

'Ah, the spirit of BénéBio, with us at last!' says Paul as I enter the kitchen.

He's sitting at the table next to a large man restringing a guitar on his lap.

'Frances, this is Antoine.' Paul nods to me. 'He's in the band.'

Antoine nods gruffly in my direction. There is something

of a tamed bear about his demeanour, with eyes that are both wild and sleepily docile.

I begin to apologise for taking my time, but Paul says it's no problem. In fact it's almost time for dinner.

'We'll go to meet Béthanie and then have some food. Are you hungry?'

I realise that I'm starving. I glance at the clock on the wall. Almost 9 p.m. Paul follows my eyes to the clock.

'On mange tard ici, petite Anglaise!' he teases.

'Let's go – I'm famished,' says Antoine.

Outside, the evening is cool and clear. The last wisps of pink linger in the sky. The dogs of the village that had barked when we drove past earlier are quiet now, and the houses seem to reverberate slightly. Orange streetlights limn their boundaries, tracing outlines of shutters warped with rain and azalea leaves pushing through fences.

I follow Paul's lead to the large white house over the road. As soon as we approach the gate and close it behind us, a black Labrador runs up, leaping up at Paul's waist.

'Salut, Chet, salut, salut.' Paul catches the dog by its front paws, ruffling its ears.

The porch light outside the house at the end of the shingle driveway flickers on.

'Look what you did, Chet! You'll blow our cover.'

Chet tails us as we follow a path round the back of the house. We emerge at the top of a large, well-kept garden that slopes down to the valley. Nearby stands a bulbous structure, faintly illuminated from the inside.

'Béthanie's yurt,' says Paul, 'her pride and joy.'

And beyond the yurt, barely visible in the peri-dark, is the outline of Tagire.

'Are you coming?' Paul says, standing by the yurt and looking back at me. I can make out his features, lit up by the corridor of light cast from the yurt's interior, but struggle to read his expression. Annoyed? Amused?

'Sorry,' I mutter to cover all bases, hurrying to join him.

Inside, the air is thick with nag champa. In the centre of the yurt is a large, multi-coloured mat, covered with cushions of all sizes. Standing on a stool and facing away from us, a woman with tanned skin and cropped hair is busy adjusting the canopy of fairy lights that are strung, lattice-like, above our heads.

Paul ducks to dodge them as he steps forward.

'Pas mal, Bét,' he says, causing the woman to turn round. 'Maybe someone should put you in charge of the chapiteau.'

The woman frowns a little; it takes a few moments for me to realise that Paul is addressing his housemate, Béthanie; I misheard 'Bét' for bête.

Béthanie steps down off the stool and tugs at the bottom of the denim skirt that's risen to expose her thighs.

'Ah, Paul,' she says wearily, 'there aren't enough tents in the world to hide from you.'

'This is Frances,' Paul says, appearing not to hear her and pushing me forwards with a hand on the small of my back. 'From BénéBio. She's going to be here for the festival.'

Béthanie looks me over, unsmiling. Paul had mentioned they were a similar age, but Béthanie's features have a more weathered quality. Paul looks almost childlike in comparison.

'So you'll be a waitress on the night?' she says.

'I . . .'

'She's keen to help,' Paul says.

Béthanie raises her eyebrows. Her eyes flicker to Paul's hand, still faintly grazing my back. He drops it immediately, and reaches up to tuck in a stray wire hanging down from the lights.

'I also need help with the decorations,' Béthanie says, returning her gaze to me. 'We'll use bamboo for the entrances, and Patrice told me about some abandoned gardens we can get flowers from. I could take Frances one day this week?'

'Merde!' Paul swears. The string of lights he's been fiddling with have just swung down and hit him in the face. 'We're working in the garden,' he says irritably, rubbing his forehead.

'Every day?'

He shrugs. 'You can take her on Friday. If Frances doesn't mind?'

They both turn to look at me. 'No,' I mumble.

'Bon,' Béthanie says. 'The flowers will be fresher that way anyway.'

Another man appears behind us in the yurt's entrance. He has dark eyes and skin, with cornrows braided close to his head. 'Is this man bothering you, Béthanie?' he asks, nodding at Paul.

Béthanie grins, and crosses the yurt to greet him.

'Ciao, Loïc. Ça va?'

The man breaks into a toothy smile. His arms are raised above his head, hands grasping the pole above the entrance so that his chest thrusts into the room.

'Loïc, Frances,' Paul mutters, introducing us quickly with a flick of his hand.

Loïc's eyes travel my body like a farmer's sizing up an animal, though when they meet mine again his gaze is steady and opaque.

'Where's Manon?' asks Béthanie.

'She's just putting the finishing touches to dinner,' says Loïc. 'Everyone okay to eat in here?'

'Why not?' says Paul, clapping his hands together. 'It'll be good practice for the festival.'

Béthanie rolls her eyes, multi-coloured light stippling her face.

It's only when Paul finishes explaining how he was the first to move to Lazeaux, and that the others all followed him, that I realise none of the group are originally from the area. Since Paul moved here, Loïc and Manon have settled into the house opposite, and Marcel and his wife, Simone, relocated their family to the outskirts of the village. Various friends like Béthanie and Antoine have lodged with each of them, and are hoping to get property soon.

'We are all colonisers!' Paul giggles when I mention this.

Loïc laughs and tops everyone's glasses up with red wine. He spills a little on Béthanie's wrist, causing her to shriek and slap him on the thigh. I glance at Manon, but she smiles serenely and offers Paul another slice of charcuterie.

That's when I notice the slim band of silver on her ring finger, which takes me by surprise; I'd been sure we were a similar age.

'Loïc and I go way back.' Paul leans in to explain to me loudly, pointing at Loïc over his glass of wine. 'To our late twenties, in Paris. Mostly causing trouble.'

'It's true,' says Loïc sincerely, placing his hand on the back of Manon's neck. 'Sometimes Manon wishes we would go *back* to Paris, but she wouldn't if she knew what me and Paul got up to.'

Loïc, Paul and Béthanie erupt into laughter again.

Manon smiles and looks down. The light from above hits her lashes and casts spidery shadows over her face.

'So how did you meet?' I ask.

Loïc runs a hand over his hair, dark but with tell-tale streaks of grey. 'Manon and I?' He smiles and turns to his wife.

'I approached him,' Manon says. 'I was singing in this shitty jazz bar in the nineteenth. It wasn't great but the pay was okay; me and Maman had just moved from Rabat so it was enough for the rent at first.' She clears her throat delicately. 'Then one night I noticed a man at a table with his friends near the front. They were all jerking around but he . . . he couldn't keep his eyes off me.'

Loïc digs Manon in the ribs. 'And?' he says.

'And . . . when they left I followed him down the street.'

'Wow,' I murmur, 'that's – brave.'

Manon shrugs. 'You know when you just have a feeling about someone,' she says. 'You just *know*.'

She stares at me as if there could not be anything simpler in the world.

I feel my throat tighten, and struggle against a desire to close my eyes.

'Just wait until you hear her sing,' Loïc says, looking directly at me. 'It's completely mesmerising.'

'I can't wait,' I say at once, then regret how false it sounds. The number of phrases I can articulate are already running out; I'm afraid that my expressions sound hollow, my opinions facile and superficial. On top of that, my head is beginning to ache with the effort of speaking so much French, more than I ever have in a day.

'So how long are you with us for, Frances?' Manon asks.

'A week.'

'Ah. So brief! But you're here for the festival at least. It's the perfect end to the season,' she says, nuzzling into Loïc's chest.

'Well she can stay longer if she wants, can't she?' says Loïc distractedly, dislodging Manon's head to top up his wine glass.

'Of course,' says Paul, looking over at me. 'In fact, I insist you stay longer.'

I smile and look down at my hands. 'That would be nice but I can't.'

'*Can't?*'

Around us, the others seem suddenly alert, as if they are

really listening for the first time. The flimsy voile over the yurt's entrance billows in and out, and a cool, thin breeze passes over my ankles.

'No, really I can't,' I say, rubbing my calves to stop the chill from rising. 'I've arranged to go to another farm next week – in the Maritime Alps.'

Paul nods and half smiles. He looks somewhere between disappointed and indifferent.

'Sorry,' I add.

'It's fine,' he shrugs. 'But, you know, if you do change your mind you can always cancel on them.'

I glance at Béthanie, who is biting the cork with her teeth to make it fit back into the bottle.

'But wouldn't that be rude?' I ask.

'You worry too much,' says Paul, grinning and leaning over to top up my glass, which is already two-thirds full. 'People do it all the time.'

mardi

I wake up in a room bathed in light. A steady, early sun streams through the window, glinting off the white wooden shutters I forgot to close last night. I stretch lazily, as memories of yesterday slowly come into focus. Flashes of Paul, the drive through picturesque villages, the view of Tagire. It seems almost too good to be true; from what I've heard, BénéBio experiences are notoriously hit and miss.

I roll over and check my phone on the bedside table: 6.30 a.m. Paul said we'd start work while it's light and cool, around 7, and that he'd meet me a little earlier in the kitchen for breakfast. Next to my phone is a full cup of cold herbal tea, given to me by Paul last night after I'd declined his offer of something stronger. I'd waited for a lull in the conversation so I could leave, but Paul just kept on talking. In the end I'd had to excuse myself, and was so tired I'd fallen asleep without touching the tea.

I dress quickly and head to the kitchen, where Paul is already waiting.

'Bon matin!' he says brightly. 'How did you sleep?'

'Not bad,' I reply, stifling a yawn. 'You?'

'I always sleep well,' he says, setting things on the table. There's cereal, eggs, a large seeded loaf and jars of homemade preserves. He has already drunk half a large cafetière, and turns the handle of a ceramic teapot towards me.

'Tea for the Anglaise,' he says.

We sit down and he goes at the jams eagerly, tearing rough hunks off the loaf and smothering them thickly. 'J'adore le sucre,' he says with his mouth full, waving his knife in the air. I smile and pick up one of the jars. 'They're made from last year's plums,' he continues. 'We can make more this week, if you like?'

'That would be n—'

I break off as Paul puts a jam-smudged finger to his lips. '*Shh*. Béthanie is still asleep,' he whispers, nodding to the empty door frame leading to the mezzanine next door.

'Sorry,' I whisper back. I hadn't realised I'd been talking loudly.

I try to ask Paul how the week will pan out in terms of work and routine. I'd like to visit Saint Pascal, if there's time, and if I can structure my work shifts around a visit.

'Oh, don't worry about all that,' he says, waving the back of his hand as if swatting a fly. His voice has returned to its normal volume.

'What do you mean?'

'The main priority this week,' he says, draining his coffee mug then slamming it down on the table, 'is getting everything ready for the festival.'

'Okay.' I nod.

'So we need to make decorations and set up the chapiteau.'

'Chapiteau?'

'Yeah, chapiteau. It's like ... a big tent ... for concerts, dancing, you know?' Paul draws in the air – a large rectangle with a pointed peak. 'Anyway,' he continues, 'you've come at the right time. There's a lot to do. We'll be serving dinner to the guests before the music starts. Simone and the girls are taking care of that. We have over a hundred orders already! We thought you could help waitress.'

'Sure.' I smile, biting back disappointment. I'd been hoping to spend most of the week in the garden. 'I've waitressed loads before, at home.'

'Good!' Paul says, standing up.

'But – I mean, will we get to work in the garden too?'

'Relax,' he says. 'The garden's not going to disappear.'

I hadn't realised I wasn't relaxed. 'But the website said I should be doing five hours of work a day, in exchange for everything.'

'*Everything?*' He is smiling widely, and seems to be enjoying the confusion.

'You know what I mean. All *this*,' I say, gesturing to the breakfast spread. 'And for a bed. I mean, you've been really welcoming and I appreciate being treated so warmly but I don't want to, you know, take advantage.'

Paul laughs faintly. 'So you want me to tell you if you are?'

'Well, yes.'

'Okay. It's not going to happen, but I swear, if it does, I will.' He puts his hand over his heart in a gesture of mock sincerity.

I get up and start to tidy away the plates. Paul tells me to leave them; they can be done later and there's no point wasting the morning.

'Can you work in those?' I realise he is staring pointedly at my shorts. I look down. They're plain black cotton, with a lace trim. They're sturdy but were inexpensive; I'd bought them in Paris specifically for the trip.

'Yes – why?'

'Oh, no reason. Just that they're nice. You wouldn't want them to get ruined.'

Outside, the morning is clear and not yet too hot. Antoine is pottering around in the garage beneath the mezzanine.

'Morning, sleepy!' he calls as I yawn halfway through greeting him.

I follow Paul through to the back of the garage, to a large wooden door.

'Stand back,' says Paul, lifting up the wooden slat that keeps it in place. 'The goats always try to get out, damn things.'

He pulls the door ajar a few inches, hinged on a length of blue string. Within seconds a goat's muzzle, grey and downy, appears in the gap, nuzzling at Paul's hand.

'Get – a-way,' Paul grunts, shooing the goat back. 'See?' he says. He opens the door a little wider and motions for me to squeeze through.

I emerge on the other side, at the foot of the garden. Three goats that have been slumped in the shade scramble up to inspect me, quickly losing interest once they realise I haven't brought any food. Paul appears behind me and bolts the door.

'Well – here it is,' he says.

In front of me, Paul's garden is anaemic looking, a narrow corridor of scrubland running away from the house before dropping to another field in the distance.

Online, there had been photos of tomato plants spilling over with fruit, tall rows of maypoles trailing runner beans, and tiny lilac flowers peeking up from the undergrowth.

I struggle to reconcile the two until I realise that all the images had been cropped, giving no indication of their wider surroundings. Perhaps they weren't photos of Paul's garden at all.

'Well?' says Paul expectantly.

'It's nice,' I say, trying to mask my disappointment.

'I mean, it's not the best time of year right now,' he says hastily. 'There's a lot to do. I've been busy with my photography.'

I nod.

'We're going to build composting toilets here,' he says, pointing to his right. 'And down here are the plum trees.'

I follow as he marches ahead. The ground is hard and dry, peppered with snatches of tall grass glistening with morning dew. I watch as they're brushed aside by Paul's stride, tiny seed heads affixing themselves to the dark hairs on his calves.

'The goats belong to a friend,' Paul says. 'And it's their fault the ground's in such a state: they graze it to death.'

Just before the straggly line of plum trees that demarcates the border, we reach a large enclosure fenced in with chicken wire and wooden stakes. To my untrained eye, it's an overgrown mess: a carpet of weeds thickly lacing the ground, canes staked wonkily into bare earth.

'It's a work in progress,' says Paul, 'but there's a lot in here.'

We enter and close the gate behind us. He points to the nearest mound: a bed of mulched earth hemmed in by a low wooden border.

'This is the compost. Tomatoes and peppers will grow well here.'

He gestures to another area.

'And you see the lines there?'

I narrow my eyes. It's a struggle to pick out any kind of geometry in the green mass but I nod anyway. It looks as though no one has been in the enclosure for days, weeks even. But he's talking excitedly, obviously pleased to have someone to show it to. And I feel glad to be here, to be with Paul, learning something I never could have in Paris. This is exactly what I had in mind.

He begins to tread what must once have been a path around the beds. I follow hesitantly, trying not to trample anything that might be edible.

'These will be tomatoes and, on the canes, beans. And here,' he points to gnarled clumps at our feet, 'are courgettes.'

I follow his finger but fail to assign any of his words to the dense tangle of growth. He bends down to point out the desiccated stems of basil, coriander and mint. I make appropriate noises of surprise. He hands me a pair of gardening gloves.

'They're my pair,' he says, 'but I don't need them, scratches don't bother me.'

We begin to work steadily, hacking away at the liana creepers that have colonised the topsoil, and, I soon realise, are what made it difficult to tell the path from the beds in the first place.

'Les *étrangleurs*,' says Paul with a grimace as he yanks up a vine, festooned with white, trumpet-shaped flowers. 'They colonise everything.'

We work on and off for a few hours, taking breaks to sit in the dappled shade beneath a plum tree. I close my eyes and lean against its trunk, trying to savour the warmth of the air. When I open them again, the garden doesn't look so bad.

Béthanie prepares a quick lunch – eggs, salad, bread – and she and Antoine join us on the mezzanine. From the moment we sit down, there is an uncomfortable silence. It is such a contrast to yesterday's dinner that I can't help but think it's my fault somehow, and my responsibility to break the silence.

I ask Béthanie if she slept well and she answers in an

affirmative monotone, without looking up. I've already gone on to ask about her yurt before this registers as a clear signal not to talk to her.

'What?' she says bluntly.

Her gaze is fierce, defensive. I know I shouldn't say any more but I don't know how to backtrack.

'The yurt,' I stammer. 'Paul said you designed it. I just . . . I wondered if that's what you do. For a job, I mean.'

She raises an eyebrow and stabs half a boiled egg onto her fork. 'For now,' she says.

I look down at my plate, wishing I could sink through it.

'Typical,' Paul says, laughing out loud for no reason at all.

Béthanie looks up.

'Typically English,' he goes on. 'Rescue an Englishman from a burning building and what's the first thing he'll always say?' he pauses for the punchline, switching to a mock English accent: '*Thank you. And what do you do?*'

Antoine sniggers and even Béthanie's po-face cracks as she rolls her eyes. The tension around the table evaporates instantly. I look at Paul, feeling intensely grateful. A.B. would never have stepped in in that kind of situation. He used to let me squirm, said I needed to work my own way out of the knot.

After lunch, Paul asks if I want to see the mountain properly.

'What, today?'

'No!' He laughs. 'Well, maybe later this week, but I meant the view.'

I follow him through the kitchen, and up the tight, curving staircase. I haven't been upstairs yet, and take time to notice the photos hanging on the walls. There are views of seas and mountains, and portraits of children, naked except for bead and feather adornments.

'Yes, I took those,' he says vaguely. 'I can tell you about them later, if you like.'

He reaches a landing and then pivots to face me, pointing to the door on his left. 'If you need anything, and I'm in here,' he says, 'you can come in any time. The door should be open, but if it's not, just knock, okay?'

'Okay.'

He opens the door and I linger in the doorway; the walls are lined with maps of oceans and islands, and a single mahogany shelf runs all the way around the room, filled with trinkets: dark lacquer boxes, figures of humans and animals, wooden bowls, carved stones, fragile-looking structures woven in thread and seashells. There is one smallish, overcrowded bookcase, on top of which books are stacked horizontally. I pick out a few titles from the spines: POLYNESIAN NARRATIVES and TAHITI: AUGUST LAND. A faint smell of incense lingers in the air. I make a deliberate effort to direct my gaze around the double bed in the centre of the room.

'Sorry it's messy,' Paul says, grabbing at shirts and sheets of paper strewn on the floor. 'Come in, come and see the mountain.'

I cross the threshold and join him in front of the window.

I recognise the angle of the view from the photo I'd seen on the website; it must have been taken from this very spot. From this height I can better grasp the shape of the valley, where the river cuts through at the bottom of the village. The hill that gives Lazeaux its shape is one of five low peaks that trail the river, before opening out into fields and foot-hills. Beyond these, in the distance, the land veers up again into mountains, pale purple, biting the skyline like a row of delicate teeth. Paul lifts an arm over me to point at them, brushing my shoulder; I get a sudden whiff of sun and sweat dried on skin. I follow his finger to the flaky violet peak of Tagire.

'Of course, I had to take the best view for myself,' he says. 'It's amazing, at dawn – the clouds gather around it, the peak just poking out; it's like Mount Ronui.'

'What's that?'

'A sacred volcano in Tahiti,' he says, as if surprised I don't know. 'I'll have to show you the view at dawn sometime before you leave.'

I look out of the window to avoid eye contact. The view really *is* perfect, untouched, except for the foreground of the black curlicued balcony, the cream-coloured blossom on the vines. I can't imagine waking up to this view each day.

'I wasn't sure I wanted to live in the mountains until I stepped into this room,' Paul's saying, 'and then I saw Tagire, and I just *knew*.'

There is something so childlike about the way he says it, smiling and flopping backwards onto the bed. I'm standing between him and the window, my body half blocking the light. I pull my vest down over my hips where it's risen a little, and turn my attention to a large wooden bowl on the desk. It's dark brown, about the size of a football, with a thin, flat lip running around the edge. I reach out with my finger; it's cool to touch, and bevelled with slight grooves of use.

'You like it?' Paul says behind me. 'It's from Vanuatu.'

Vanuatu. I roll the word around in my mind, trying to place it as my finger traces the bowl's circumference.

'It's called a kava bowl,' he goes on.

'Ka-va,' I repeat, sounding out each syllable.

'It's a drink made from plant roots, and mildly narcotic. It's drunk communally, from bowls like this one, passed around in rituals, ceremonies. Usually it's only men that are allowed to drink it ... but they make an exception for virgin girls on their wedding nights.'

I automatically withdraw my finger.

'I've not heard of Vanuatu,' I hear myself say aloud.

'Oh,' he says, in that same surprised tone. 'It's in the Pacific ... south-east of Papua, west of Fiji.'

I stare at the bowl and think about all the mouths that have drunk from it, how far away it is from its home.

'Many of these,' he says, waving a hand to the objects lining the room, 'come from there. Or islands nearby.'

I follow the sweep of his hand.

'It's a fascinating culture, ordered by rank and hierarchy. There are secret societies – men only of course – where they progress through ranks to achieve power in public life – nimangki, it's called – and they acquire power in the afterlife too.'

He is talking quickly, his eyes wide with excitement as he stacks fact on fact.

'So objects like this,' he brushes me lightly as he rises to take the bowl from the table, 'are used in ceremonies to initiate boys into manhood. It has a ritual function too, but the Vanuatu employ a *purchasing* system of objects that grades each man in terms of prestige. So the more prestige objects a man has—'

'What about the women?' I ask, noticing a figure on the shelf above him. It is small and angular, roughly hacked from a dark wood. Two conical breasts jut out from its torso, and its overlarge hands rest awkwardly on its belly and pubis, forming an empty triangle.

He looks at me blankly. 'Women?'

'The women from Van . . . Vanuatu,' I press, 'you said there were secret societies – were there ones for women too?'

'Oh,' says Paul, leaning back and placing his hands behind his head as he yawns. 'Oh. Well, I'm not too sure. They're even more secret I suppose!' He gives a little laugh.

He begins to flick through the papers on his desk. I loiter awkwardly. Without the mask of conversation, I'm too aware of being in his bedroom, at his invitation. I decide to keep talking.

'So do you teach? Or write?'

He shakes his head. 'Neither,' he says, putting his hands

on his hips. 'I went to university too late, and I didn't enjoy it as much as I thought I would. I like the idea of teaching but I have too much going on here. I wouldn't feel free, you know? I am a photographer, I am a traveller – but I think, at the heart of it, I would say I am a *discoverer*. I think I'd be bored teaching. But some day, I am going to write a book.' He looks wistfully out of the window.

'Like a memoir?' I hear myself say. 'Or something more academic?'

He shrugs. 'Maybe somewhere between the two. I'll work from my journals. They're all in there.' He gestures to an old wooden chest on the far side of the room, its contents pushing the lid ajar. 'Take a look.'

I cross the room and gently lift the lid. The chest is filled with notebooks of varying size and colour, piled in disarray. I tentatively pull one out.

'It's okay, you can read it,' he says.

The one I'm holding is a little larger than my hand, with a gold fabric covering. I flick through the pages, carefully at first, and then – when I struggle to read the looping, childlike scrawl in green, blue and red biro – less studiously, moving from book to book. They are all alike: pages of notes, descriptions, drawings of figures and objects. In some parts, whole pages have been divided into columns and filled with foreign alphabets.

I glance up, just in time to see Paul's attention snap rapidly back to the papers on his desk. I return to the books. There's a pattern on the inside covers where he's attempted to mark the date and place. These must be late additions, as they are all written in the same, slightly shaky, red script. I peer at the one I'm holding – *Solomon & F— or, Tahiti? 1994(?) poss. winter 1996* – but can't make out the second word. They seem to be more approximations than dates. Each language and its attendant alphabet and history, as well as his notes on customs, costume and place, are clearly demarcated, separated from their neighbour with a thick dividing line. There are hand-drawn maps too: meticulously labelled outlines of islands and archipelagos, annotated figures and sketches.

Paul comes to sit next to me on the edge of the bed. I keep my eyes on the notebook in my hands, cradling it so that it covers my thighs. He begins to look through the books too, making little sounds of discovery as if he's reading them again for the first time in years.

'Can you speak all these languages?' I ask, turning the pages.

'More or less.' He shrugs. I notice a minute twitch in his cheeks, as if gills are flexing beneath his skin.

'Wow,' I murmur, glancing back at the impenetrable markings. They look infinitely complex; I can only labour my way through Middle French with several dictionaries to hand, but Paul seems to be able to move fluidly between languages and cultures, by a kind of natural talent. I begin to feel ashamed of my institutionalisation; why hadn't I found my own way like Paul? Why had I followed A.B. so blindly?

He shifts slightly. The mattress bows in the centre and our

bodies veer closer. I become aware of a dry, savoury smell, somewhere between salt water and wood-shavings, emanating from his body.

I reach forward for another book, keeping the first firmly covering my thighs. We read for a few minutes longer, and then Paul tosses the one he's been browsing into the chest. The bed squeaks as he stands up.

I close the book in my lap and begin to hurriedly place the others back into the chest, sensing I've outstayed my welcome.

'It's fine,' Paul says, gesturing for me to stay put. The sunlight hitting the side of his face makes him look like a Byzantine icon: dark eyes and hair stencilled on gold. He places the book back into my hands. 'Please,' he says. 'Take your time – I'd like for you to read them. I'm just going to take care of some things downstairs.'

I realise as I sift through the pages that I'm not used to handling manuscripts whose authors are still living; I have to stop myself from overanalysing the images and notes. They're just notebooks. And clearly not personal, otherwise he wouldn't have let me read them. But I get the sense that they hold the key to something, that if scrutinised in the right way they'll reveal some essential truth. About Paul's nature, but somehow more than that too, some vital mystery, the outline of which I can't yet discern.

There's a shuffle from the doorway. 'Sorry, I forgot these.' Paul reappears and snatches up a set of keys from the desk. He hesitates in the doorway for a moment, looking back at me.

'You look good there,' he says, 'in the light.'
I am unsure what to say.
'Thanks—'
But he is gone.

mercredi

The next morning, we've not long started in the garden when the car horns start blaring. Far off, echoing through the valley.

'What is it?' I ask.

Paul looks as confused as me. I almost think we've imagined the noises, until they start up again, sounding from the other side of the hill. It's only then I realise how quiet the day has been otherwise, unnaturally quiet, as though even the birds have slept in.

We carry on working, but I soon become aware of something other than the noise: a throbbing sensation that feels as though it's coming from the ground itself.

'Can you feel that?' I ask.

Paul frowns.

'Yes, but I don't— Ah! Of course,' he says, with a little sigh. 'What is it?'

'It's the Tour. I forgot that was today.'

'What tour?'

'The Tour de France!' Paul says. 'I meant to tell you yesterday. It's due to pass through Lazeaux around noon – Agnès next door says it hasn't come through this way for over a decade.'

He jumps up to crane his neck through the line of plum trees.

'So they'll take that road, you see?' He points to the hill that obscures the next valley, and traces the road that skirts the side of the house, just under my bedroom window. 'There'll be a great view from that side. Especially your room,' he says, grinning. 'It's a big deal. People will come here from the next town to watch. Do you follow the Tour?'

'Not really,' I confess.

'Ah,' he says. 'Then it's just a coincidence. I was beginning to think they might have followed you here!'

I laugh along, unsure what he means.

But as we return to the task of liberating vegetation from the liana's chokehold, it strikes me as a strange coincidence too. As if the village of Lazeaux – or Paul's very home – is emitting some sort of magnetism, pulling far-flung strangers to its core.

The sun creeps higher in the sky as we work, pushing the day towards noon. Paul is crouched a little way away from me; I notice drops of sweat clustered on the back of his neck. The Tour is getting palpably closer; car horns blare from the other side of the hill and the mysterious throb is now discernible as the beat of generic Euro-house. Snatches of auto-tuned vocals cut through the valleys.

A flash of red catches my eye: a car rounds the corner of the hill with a speaker mounted on its roof. It broadcasts commentary in a fuzzy male voice, unintelligible over the music.

We stop working and lean over the fence to watch as the car passes. It's soon followed by a flotilla of vehicles, each tugging a platform stage behind them, emblazoned with logos of various sponsors. On one float, someone in a giant red M&M suit waves; on the next, four women in lurid bikini bottoms and cropped T-shirts printed with corporate logos dance around speakers installed in the centre of the stage.

As the flotilla nears the village, the commentary and music merge into a wall of noise. It's so loud that it masks the sound of the helicopter that appears over the hill, surveying the procession rolling beneath it.

It's like a medieval carnival of fools, dropped in from a dream sequence; I'm about to remark on the strangeness of it when Paul comments bitterly, 'Vultures,' before turning to spit on the ground.

'Who?'

'Them,' Paul half shouts over the music, pointing at the bikini-bottomed girls. 'All this crap is the promo-team that drives out ahead of the cyclists. It's just companies and money, totally *soulless*. You have to be stupid to enjoy this kind of thing.'

I say nothing, thinking about the *mésalliances* of the

medieval carnival, the world turned upside down through the marriage of opposites: pure and impure, young and old.

'*You* don't want to go and watch, do you?' Paul asks pointedly.

We are interrupted by a call from the other end of the garden. Marcel is walking towards us with Léa behind him, skipping and waving a tiny orange flag.

'What are you doing back here?' cries Marcel. 'The whole village is out in front of your house!'

'Everyone's there!' cries Léa breathlessly. 'And look what I got!' She waves the flag passionately. '*And* they were throwing sweets and these hats!'

She unrolls a cylinder of starched white fabric that turns out to be a visor, its peak printed with a slogan in gothic script.

'The ladies were throwing them,' she says.

'Sell-out,' Paul says to Marcel with a grin.

'If you want to be a purist that's fine, but don't drag Frances down with you,' says Marcel teasingly, shooting me a con-spiratorial look.

He takes the visor from Léa's hands, shakes it out and places it on his daughter's head, gently weaving her ponytail through the gap at the back.

Paul's smile thins.

'I wasn't stopping her,' he says, frowning. 'She can go if she wants.'

Paul and Marcel look at me expectantly. I suddenly feel dizzy; the sun is too hot on my face.

'Sure,' I begin. 'I mean, I don't mind. If we need to keep working in the garden it's fine.'

'It's hot,' says Marcel quietly, glancing from me to Paul. 'Have you given Frances any sun cream?'

Paul shrugs. Something brushes lightly over my knee. I look down and see Léa crouched to the ground, tickling my legs with her flag.

'Why don't you both come and have a break?' Marcel is saying.

'Please, Frances?' Léa pouts.

I crouch down and tickle her back with a long stem of grass. She shrieks and runs off down the garden.

'Come on!' she says. 'We're missing loads already!'

I follow, feeling relieved; she is so much easier to please than Paul or Marcel.

Léa runs ahead of me, through the garage and out onto the road in front of Paul's house, thronged with the village crowd. On the other side, elderly men and women have installed themselves on garden chairs beneath parasols. Léa spots her sisters, and runs into the arms of a woman in a fuchsia sundress who must be Marcel's wife, Simone. She tucks a strand of wavy brown hair behind her ear, waving at me as Léa turns round to point in my direction. I watch them embrace for a moment, then turn back to fetch my camera.

'Frances!' Léa's shout rises above the roar of the crowd. 'Quick, they're nearly here!'

I don't need the urgency in her voice to know they're close.

The flotilla is thinning out, and will soon leave the road clear for the cyclists. The helicopter whirs.

Just inside the door, I collide with Paul. I apologise instantly.

'Steady,' says Paul, grinning. 'Here, I thought you'd need it so I took it from your room,' he says, handing my camera to me. 'A basic model, but safe, traditional.'

Before I have a chance to respond he brushes past me and sprints down the steps to join the crowd.

I follow dazedly, losing sight of Léa and her family. I look around, straining to see Paul, and eventually spy him crouching at the foot of the grass verge by his driveway, looking through an enormous camera that, from this angle, entirely obscures his head. I watch him for a little while, feeling invisible in the swelling crowd. Paul repositions himself every now and then, recording it all. The camera looks unwieldy but organic, like an overdeveloped part of his body.

In the space of a second, Paul lowers the camera from his face and looks directly at me. I turn away instantly, embarrassed to be caught staring. I raise my camera over my face, pretending to take a photo of the floats. I hold it there as the hot plastic becomes clammy against my skin, until I hear a voice in my ear and feel a touch at my elbow. It's Paul.

'I'm going upstairs to take pictures of the bikes,' he says. 'It's too busy down here. Want to come?'

I follow him into the house as he bounds up the stairs. We reach the first-floor landing and Paul carries on; he turns round and holds up a hand when I try to follow.

'No, you stay down here,' he says breathlessly. 'I'll go upstairs. Then we can compare photos from different heights!'

I step into the guest bedroom and crouch down to balance the camera on the windowsill. Within seconds, a flash of metal glinting in the sunlight comes speeding round the hill: the first of the cyclists. I move slightly to try and perfect the angle. All the bikes are now in sight; I am just about to take the first shot when I hear a voice call my name from above.

It jolts me out of position; I look up and see the big black eye of Paul's camera lens, angled down at me. The shutter clicks several times, impossibly fast.

He mutters something I don't catch before aiming the camera back at the road. I turn back too, but by the time I reposition my camera the bikes have already sped past. I'm too late; I watch through the viewfinder as the cyclists disappear around the next bend. I snap a couple of shots anyway; when I scroll back through them they are mostly blurry shots of trees, which I delete immediately.

I hear Paul bounding down the stairs.

He bursts in, asking excitedly, 'Did you get any?'

'Not really. Did you?'

'Take a look,' he says triumphantly. He stands next to me and holds the camera as far as the neck strap will allow, though I still have to lean in to see. His T-shirt is damp and I can smell the sweat cloying on his skin.

'What do you think?' he says.

He seems pleased, but it's hard to tell whether or not the

photos are good; they're in focus, but unremarkable. How interesting can photos of men on bikes be?

'They're good,' I say.

'I might be able to sell a few,' he murmurs.

When he flicks to the next photo, I recoil instantly. It shows my face upturned with a smile, my head floating free from my body, decapitated by the side of the house.

'T'es belle, non?' he says.

I stare at the photo in confusion. When Paul took the photo I'd felt surprise, swiftly followed by mild irritation at missing the bikes. But the girl in the photo shows none of those things: her smile is serene and untroubled.

The sound of someone clearing their throat comes from the doorway.

'I hope I'm not interrupting?'

Paul jerks back in surprise. An older man with pinkish skin and white, wispy hair steps into the room.

'Ah, salut, Patrice,' says Paul. 'Pas du tout. Come and meet Frances.'

The man sticks out his hand in the same moment that I step forward to kiss him on the cheek.

'Anglaise?' he asks. We both laugh at the confusion.

He's a generation or so older than Paul, but despite his age there is something shy, boyish about him. He asks Paul if he got any good photos; I notice his eyes are a pale forget-me-not blue.

'Not too bad,' says Paul. 'They went so quickly, though, it was hard to get a good angle.'

Patrice nods. 'And the crowd was so busy. I tried but people kept pushing. It was too much.'

Paul shrugs.

'I've actually come to ask your opinion on something.'

'Yes?'

'Just a couple of landscapes I've been working on – they're back at mine. I don't want to say too much. I wondered if you had time to drop by, sometime this week? I need another eye.'

Paul exhales heavily. 'I don't know, Patrice. I'm really busy, what with the festival and this BénéBio stuff . . .'

Patrice watches Paul intently, though Paul seems reluctant to meet his gaze.

'Patrice is also an artist,' Paul explains.

'I drive the school bus. But in my other life I'm a frustrated, undiscovered painter.'

His smile is sad, self-deprecating.

'And a revolutionary,' Paul jokes, clapping him on the back. The gesture seems freighted somehow, establishing distance as much as intimacy.

'Hardly,' Patrice says, looking embarrassed.

'Mais si,' Paul goes on. 'Patrice used to be an activist. Back in the day, in Paris. N'est-ce pas?'

Patrice looks at me apologetically. 'I organised some demonstrations, wrote an article here and there. Nothing world-changing,' he explains quickly.

'That's why he's always trying to improve us,' Paul says. 'None of us are progressive enough for him!'

'That's not true—'

'Ça va, Patrice. I'm only teasing.'

Patrice smiles weakly. There is something tense about their exchange, but I can't place it. I become aware of the buzz of the crowd drifting through the open window, pooling into the lull in conversation.

Paul clears his throat. 'Bon. I should go and get some pictures of the crowd before it disappears.'

He leaves, and my first instinct is to follow him out of the room. Instead I stay put, smiling politely at Patrice.

'Do you mind –' he begins slowly, in heavily accented English, '– do you mind if we speak in English? I don't have many chances to practise.'

I begin to reply in French and then catch myself, laughing. 'Of course not,' I say. It's been days since I spoke English; the sound of my own voice is at once strange and familiar, like driving past somewhere I once lived.

Patrice begins to explain that he's always painted; he stretches his own canvases and works mostly in oils and acrylic. Recently, he has begun painting on furniture.

'But I lack peers,' he says. 'I'm in touch with only a few artist friends, and they stayed in Paris after we graduated.'

'Is that where you studied?'

Patrice nods. 'At the Beaux-Arts. It was a crazy time.' He smiles. 'Someone mentioned to me you've just come from Paris too. Are you studying there?'

'No. Well, I was studying, in England, but I finished just before summer. I was in Paris for a research project; my supervisor he – he needed an assistant for a manuscript he's researching.'

'How interesting,' he says thoughtfully. 'What kind of manuscript?'

I falter for a few seconds; it feels so strange to be speaking English, to be the one answering questions.

'It's probably not that interesting,' I say quickly.

'Please,' he says. 'It can be a listening exercise.'

'Okay, well, we know it's fifteenth century, though we don't have exact dates. We don't know who the patron was, either, but it must have been commissioned by someone with money. The point of it seems to have been teaching children literacy.'

'It's a children's book?'

'Yes – like an alphabet book. There are a few pages for each letter, full of illustrations – it's incredibly beautiful.'

'I didn't know those kinds of books had been around for so long,' he says.

'We didn't either. But I suppose it makes sense; there's a theory about the oversized initials in medieval texts being used to helped children learning to read.'

'Fascinating, fascinating.'

'I'm sure it's not for the majority of people.'

Patrice shrugs. 'The majority of people aren't to be trusted.'

'But you need them for a revolution?'

He closes his eyes. 'I knew I wouldn't get away with that. But I'm an old man now. I'm allowed to be less idealistic.'

*

Later that day, Paul ushers me into his room and indicates where I should sign on the forms sent to him by BénéBio. 'We should have done this yesterday,' he says distractedly.

I become self-conscious about my handwriting as he watches me sign my name; my fingers momentarily lose their muscle memory and I end up skipping a letter in my surname. I have to strike the whole thing through, and print it again clearly outside of the allocated box.

Paul steps in and holds the paper up to read. 'France's,' he says teasingly.

'What?'

'Your name,' he says. 'It's funny. Like me being called England's.'

I laugh awkwardly, looking around the room for distraction. I notice something glinting in the light by the doorway. It looks like a bunch of red bangles studded with white beads, hanging from a hook set high on the wall.

'What are those?' I ask, moving towards them, away from Paul.

I reach for the bottom loop and slip my wrist through gently, feeling its fragility as the beads graze against my skin.

'They're bat's teeth,' he says, coming to stand behind me. I unhook the loops and let them hang around my wrist. They're heavier than I'd expected, and I notice the beads have a curious milky sheen. 'From Papua New Guinea, a traditional form of currency.'

'This is money?' The ornamental thing becomes strange with the weight of function.

'There are around five hundred teeth per coil,' says Paul. He reaches for my wrist and holds it in one hand, running a finger over a blunted tooth with the other. 'So these would be traded between islands for goods or alliances. Feathers and shells were used in the same way.'

I stare at the teeth, a slew of questions snagging on the tines. Who made them? How were they attached to the twine? For a moment, my wrist looks snared, in the process of being devoured by a helix of gaping mouths.

'They're – actually *quite* delicate,' he says, frowning.

My pulse lurches as he takes my hand; I realise a second later he is simply removing the coils from my wrist. I apologise instantly.

'It's not a problem,' he says, placing them back on their hook, furrowing his brow. 'They're just very fragile.'

I look back at the teeth, wondering out loud if they should be in a museum.

'Sure,' Paul snorts. 'I'm sure they'd gather dust nicely there.'

He begins to look through one of the drawers on his desk.

'Here,' he says, turning around to present me with something. 'If you like the bats' teeth, you might like this. It's from the same place. You can wear it if you like.'

I look down at the thing in his hand. It's a bracelet, woven from a coarse, khaki-coloured fabric and trimmed with short brown feathers. The word *TEHURA* has been sewn across it in blue and maroon beads. It strikes me as ugly, though I am touched by the gesture.

'It's nice,' I say, taking it from him. '"Tehura", what does it mean?'

Paul puts his hands in his pockets.

'It means ... beautiful, or precious ... something like that. Somewhere between the two.'

He smiles at me, and I look down at the bracelet, aware that he is waiting for my reaction. How to convey that I appreciate the bracelet, but I'm not assuming it's a gift, and definitely not a romantic one? I awkwardly slide it over my wrist and turn my palm upwards, rotating the bracelet so that *TEHURA* signs the inside of my wrist.

'Perfect,' Paul says.

Suddenly I remember what the bats' teeth reminded me of, something from the first ever class I took of A.B.'s: *Icon and Allegory 2A*. We were focusing on chthonic imagery, and the apocalypse page of a particular manuscript had featured something called a 'hellmouth': a giant stone serpent head spouting flames, engulfing the dancing bodies of sinners. A.B. said the hellmouth was a common motif in medieval imagery and could take many forms: stone, flesh, sometimes the head of a monster. The accompanying text often described the hellmouth as beautiful or sweet-smelling, enticing good Christians into the jaws of sin.

I must be frowning because Paul says, 'What is it?'

'I was thinking ...' I falter, wondering how 'hellmouth' would translate into French.

I attempt it literally, mentally adding 'l'enfer' to 'la bouche', frustrated by my heavy-handed grasp of the language.

'I was thinking, it reminds me of . . . of a mouth,' I burble, 'you know, the red, when it's stretched out – it's like a throat – and the bats' teeth . . . they're like a jaw.'

I cringe. It was not what I had wanted to say at all. But Paul smiles warmly, his eyes glazed over with a look I can't place.

'Wow,' he eventually murmurs, 'incroyable.' His smile almost swallows the word. 'Incroyable.'

'What is?'

'The way you think,' he replies. 'It's so . . . *creative*.'

The same burning sensation spreads over my face. The affirmation feels good, but for all the wrong reasons: I hadn't even said what I meant to say. But still I roll the word over in my mind, incroyable, daring to believe that he means it.

'I would be so lucky,' Paul's saying, 'to have someone like you translate my book.'

I smile, but I'm not in the room any longer. I'm in a fantasy where Paul and I are trekking through an unfamiliar jungle on one of his expeditions, me hanging back while he walks a few paces ahead, dictating observations while I scribe them down. *Here is a receptacle of history*, he says; *over there is the lie of the land*. I feel safe walking in his shadow. I never have to worry about the horizon; I just follow his footsteps, watch him banishing chaos as he goes.

jeudi

It's barely 8 a.m. when, after a quick breakfast, Paul and I get ready to set off for the market in Bouéry. Paul has lent me a bike. It couldn't say 'girl' any more clearly: sprayed lilac and painted with blue flowers. A large wicker basket is tied to the front with ribbons, lending it an air of top-heaviness. I can tell by looking that it's several sizes too small.

'Try it!' Says Paul, offering me the handles.

'I think I'm too big for it.'

'Just *try.*'

Reluctantly, I hop on the bike, and immediately feel too low to the ground. Meanwhile, Paul mounts a bike with a high, slender frame. He makes an elegant loop of the driveway then pulls up alongside me. There is a marked difference in our height.

'It's the only women's bike we have,' he says. 'But I can ask Patrice or someone to drive you—'

'No, no it's fine,' I say. 'I can ride it.'

The road to Bouéry is anything but direct, winding over hills and snaking through valleys as if undecided about its destination. There are few cars on the road, which I'm grateful for – less for the threat from traffic than for the lack of witnesses to a journey I find faintly humiliating.

Paul glides past me while I pump at the pedals furiously to keep up. He is soon far ahead and I grow resentful of the distant speck of his head, peering round every now and then to check my progress.

At one point I lose sight of him altogether, and eventually crawl around an uphill bend, breathing heavily, to find him waiting with an expression of total tranquillity.

'Have you tried changing gear?'

'Yes, but they don't seem to do anything.' I pant, trying to catch my breath. I glance down and see layers of rust caked around the chain. 'How old *is* this bike?'

Paul shrugs and looks away. 'I don't know. Bét used it last summer and it was fine.'

I'm concentrating so hard on keeping up with Paul that it's only when we reach the hilly outskirts of Bouéry and dismount, my basket rattling over cobblestones, that I glance over my shoulder and take in the view. Behind us, the green hills seem to fold and unfold as a living, supple mass. There is something empty-looking about the horizon, and I realise I have already become accustomed to the Pyrenean skyline, to the jagged crest of Tagire.

The narrow streets of the town wind between houses whose shutters and latticed windows yawn open to the cool morning, and geraniums spill over terracotta pots. The flowers are beautiful until I get too close and the fragrance makes me nauseous.

We rest our bikes against the side of the church. There's no need to lock them, Paul says. The street is empty, but reverberating with the hubbub of the market somewhere nearby. Paul tells me there's something he wants to show me.

I follow him out of the sun and into a narrow alley between the houses. The market fades from earshot, hushed in the shade of the buildings. He glances round every now and then to make sure I am following; he seems to be enjoying the suspense.

A few moments later a voice calls out his name. We both turn to see a young girl leaning out of a ground-floor window a few paces behind us.

'Paul!'

'Ciao, Magali.' Paul waves.

He doubles back and the girl leans further out of the window to offer him each of her cheeks in turn. She is young, probably ten or eleven, but already has a womanly face, her long dark hair hanging devoutly down beside her widely-set green eyes.

'Where's Maman?' Paul asks.

Magali pouts and glances at me. In less than a second I feel as though she's looked me all over and judged me – as what? Uninteresting? Unattractive? Her eyes slide back to Paul.

'She's washing her hair. But she saw you through the window and told me to return this.'

She holds up a book with a violet cover. The yellow-lettered title reads *LE CAS POUR DUALISME*. Paul makes a murmur of recognition and takes it from her.

'Ah!' he says. 'Fantastique. And did she enjoy it?'

Magali shrugs with cool indifference. 'She barely looked at it. I read some of it though.'

Paul smiles. 'And did you understand it?'

'Bits.'

'I'm not at all surprised. You'll have to come round and look at my books sometime. Would you like that?'

A smile flickers on her face before she straightens it back into a pout, a hint of red lingering on her cheeks. She looks over at me again.

'This is Frances,' Paul says. 'Une Anglaise. She's volunteering with me at the moment.'

Magali tosses her hair. We kiss. She seems uncannily self-possessed.

'Bon, well, we should get going.' Paul claps his hands together. 'I'm going to show Frances my exhibition. Have you seen it?'

Magali nods.

'And did you like it? I could take your photo sometime too, if you want. You could be in my next exhibition.'

Magali smiles shyly before running out of view, breaking her precocious composure.

I fall into step next to Paul as we carry on down the alley.

'Magali's mother is a curious woman,' he says, under his breath. 'Always interested in learning, but never has the dedication to do anything with it. Her daughter is another story though; she's a very gifted child.'

A breeze comes up the alley. I become aware of a lump in my throat and wonder, bewildered, if I am about to start crying.

The alley opens onto a wider street, where the walls are peeling and the terracotta troughs cracked and emptied of plants. Paul stops in the middle of the road as a few people pass us on their way to the market.

'What is it?'

'*There!*' He sighs impatiently, and points to a shop across the street. 'Go on, take a look.'

I cross over. The windows are filled with photos in dark wooden frames, propped on shelves draped in dark blue velvet. It's a bit tacky: patterned fabrics and feathered ornaments hang from hooks either side of the window, along with a display of carved instruments and large, leather-bound journals. I cast a quick eye over the photos and recognise a few from Noa Noa: portraits of children in tribal dress, various family scenes and landscapes. Beneath the photos, the journals are weighted open and I clock Paul's elaborate, looping handwriting.

The clarity of the images sharpens as a shadow falls over the glass.

'Well, what do you think?' Paul says from behind me.

'They're great,' I say tentatively. 'Really great.'

He murmurs something I don't quite catch, though his excitement is tangible. He explains that the gallery belongs to a friend of his, who offered him the space for an exhibition. As he speaks, I notice the show's title, announced by way of a poster Blu-Tacked to the window's interior: *EXPOSITION D'UN GRAND VOYAGEUR: PAUL GAUILLAC.*

Paul continues to talk excitedly about the photos, telling me how each one came to be taken, interrupting himself periodically to embellish the details.

One image shows a girl, of around five or six, naked from the waist up. She looks out of the photo with a sense of total calm, even detachment.

'This girl belonged to the family I lived next door to,' Paul says, running his finger over the glass. 'Every morning, I would leave my hut, and find little presents just outside the entrance: mangos, taro, fresh pandanus leaves. Then I would hear her giggling and she would be peering out from behind a tree . . .'

His voice trails off, and a glazed, faraway look comes over his face. 'But we were not far from the faré amu – a separate hut for eating – so I suspect some of the "gifts" might have been stolen. She became very attached to me.'

I look back at the image, trying to imagine the girl leaving gifts for a younger Paul. And whose permission had he asked to take her photo? Hers, or her family's?

'If there *is* a theme here,' Paul continues, 'it's a celebration of difference, of childhood. These instruments,' he points to the wooden objects resting softly on the velvet, 'are used for all kinds of occasions. There is such richness and ... *vitality* ... in the music and dancing of these people – it moved me. We've almost totally lost it here in the West. I wanted to find a way to celebrate it, make it present.

'So,' he cries, stepping away from the glass, 'this is my exhibition. The space is not perfect for it, as you can see, I would ideally like to have a little more hanging room, *and...*' he looks derisively at the run-down, empty street, 'a location with *slightly* more footfall. But, I'm taking the exhibition on tour, so it's good practice, at least.'

'On tour?'

'Yes – there is a festival next week for slow travellers. They invited me to make an exhibition of my photos.'

'Slow travellers?'

'Travel by foot or bike or hitchhiking, or ... basically anything except by plane. It's like a pilgrimage, except it doesn't have to be religious. I have some friends who walked from one side of Europe to the other with their one-year-old son.'

'So would you ever take a plane?' I ask, thinking uneasily of the flight to Paris I took a month ago.

Paul grimaces. 'God, no. Why do that when you can hitchhike?'

'But what if you're going somewhere really far away – like when you went travelling?'

'What about it?'

I detect – although I'm not sure – a warning tone in his voice.

'I just meant – how did you get to the South Pacific other than flying?'

He shrugs. 'Well I flew, of course. But that was in the early nineties. No one knew about carbon emissions at that point. *Obviously* I wouldn't do that if I were young now. I'd get a boat.'

He looks away, seemingly done with the conversation.

I turn back to the window display, looking from the photos to the instruments, to the looping notes of Paul's journals. There is something uneasy, unsettling about it all. The children and families in the photos are clearly all aware of having their photo taken, so that can't be it. If the display is meant to be a celebration, why do all the images and objects feel so lifeless?

But Paul's done a degree in anthropology, I tell myself; he must know what he's doing.

As if he has heard the debate going on in my head, Paul says, 'I consider it important, you know – to open people's eyes. There are so many towns, like this one, where people have never left, don't know there's a whole *world* out there. At least here, when they walk up their own street on their way to the boulangerie, they will see these pictures and think about something bigger.'

Of course, I think. Of course Paul has thought about all these things and found, somehow, a way to resolve them. He smiles at me and I smile back. I feel the knots of doubt begin to uncoil from my body, and an urge for Paul to take me by the hand and show me the way through.

'Come on, let's get to the market,' he says.

I tell him to lead the way.

'Don't you want a picture of me?' Paul adopts a playful, hyper-masculine pose, one foot placed triumphantly on a rock, balling his hands into fists at his hips, titling his chin up in a sneer.

'Get out of the way,' I say, laughing. 'It's the view I'm after.'

Before leaving the market, Paul suggested we take a different route home. It's mostly downhill this time, though we've pulled over at a high point so that I can get a few photos. I watch through the viewfinder as Paul breaks position and disappears from the frame. I take a few shots of the green fields that undulate gently towards Lazeaux, and a few of Bouéry, where buildings dapple the hilltop like a speckled egg.

I turn round, and search in my viewfinder to locate Tagire. It's not long until I find its peak, rising highest and sharpest from the frenetic blue line of the Pyrénées. I hear another series of clicks, and spin round to see Paul's camera directed at me.

'Non, non, reste-là!' he says, as I flinch. He checks something on his screen. 'Just pretend I'm not here.'

I turn to face the landscape, away from his lens. I feel serene. The air is warm on my skin and the sky void of clouds. The unfiltered sun seeps evenly through the valleys, outlining each detail against the horizon. The hour or so we spent at the market passed in a blur. I recall the smell of the fish stalls in the shaded market hall, the jellied eyes of the fish sprung open in perpetual vigilance. The sellers' calls to passers-by were too rapid for me to understand and became instead a refrain that orchestrated the swell and flow of the crowd.

I cannot remember exactly where we went, what we bought, or anything Paul said, but his body was a constant presence ahead of me in the crowd. I found I had attuned myself to his movements, a signal I could receive and follow even when the reception became strained. Only now, away from the market, I remember the moments leading up to it: the encounter with Magali and my doubts about Paul's exhibition. Those events seem to belong to another morning, to a different pair of people altogether.

I glance back at Paul, who is fiddling with his camera. He seems so sure, so self-contained.

'We should have a picture together,' he says, motioning with his camera, 'so we can remember you being here.'

'But there's no one to take it.'

Paul perches the camera on a rock by the side of the road. 'Quick!' He jumps back excitedly. 'The timer's on!'

I freeze as he puts his arm around me and we pose for the camera; I am too aware of suddenly being pressed against his body, of feeling his pulse. I fear that my body is betraying me, as if this new proximity to my skin allows him to read my thoughts. Soon a red light flashes on the camera's face.

Paul steps away and retrieves the camera. 'Ah!' he exclaims, looking at the display before showing me. It looks as if I've been cut out and pasted next to Paul. 'You look happy,' he says.

I squint at the picture, trying to see the person he sees.

'I am,' I say as the sun beats down on my face. 'I am.'

The lane takes us through a valley dense with trees. Eventually we emerge by the river at the foot of Lazeaux. Paul gestures to the other side, where ten or so men are gathered, hanging a sheet of white tarpaulin between two poles of the still-skeletal structure.

'They're setting up the chapiteau for the festival,' he says.

They pause to watch us cross the bridge. At least half of them have taken their shirts off, and as we get closer I recognise Loïc and Antoine, with a layer of blond fuzz on his brown chest.

'About time!' someone calls as we approach.

Loïc stands halfway up a ladder; I can just make out the definition of his body, shining with perspiration.

'Ah, how idyllic,' Loïc coos. He holds up his hands to frame us in a crude impression of a camera, moving his index finger to imitate the shutter. 'Don't they just look like the image of happiness?'

The men laugh. My heart begins to thud.

'*The – image – of – happiness*,' Loïc repeats, sounding out each word.

I meet his eyes and a heat flares in my cheeks. Paul is grinning sheepishly as if he's been caught out. I'm suddenly possessed by a desire to scream but instead I look down and feel powerfully resentful towards my bike, covered with flowers and ribbons, towards the skirt that rides higher than my leggings. I see the moment through their eyes: Paul the older man; me, something else . . .

I half hear the men exchanging gloomy prognoses that a storm is forecast for the day of the festival. They've been working on adding extra support to the chapiteau.

'So do you think she'll hold for the party?' asks Paul. 'La tente?'

'Should do. Unless she has a breakdown.' Loïc sniggers.

Somehow, I mobilise my feet on the pedals and turn my wheel sharply away from them, cycling as fast as I can.

Paul calls after me in surprise. I pretend not to hear him.

As soon as I'm out of sight, I fling the bike away from me and burst into hot, pathetic tears. *So stupid*, I think. *I'm so stupid.* I look up and notice a dog has appeared at the gate of the driveway across the road, a large brown Alsatian, panting and pushing its nose through the wrought-iron bars. I'm not sure how long it's been watching. From around the corner, the sounds of men laughing echo over the river and the hot, dry stones.

After a while I walk up to the house. It's only when I flop down on the bed that I realise I have climbed one more storey than I needed to; I've come to Paul's room, not mine. I stare at the mountain through the window. The room is dark, filled with the kind of shade that gathers in houses on hot days; the edges of furniture and objects become blurry, threatening to shapeshift at any moment. Vestiges of sandalwood in the air. I can hear the men – Loïc and the others – calling to each other. I catch myself straining to hear Paul's voice amongst them, but I can't distinguish it.

I look over at his notebooks lying where I left them on top of the chest. I pick one up and skip to a page at random:

MASTICATION OF KAVA ROOT:

Roots not mature or ready for drinking until 5+ years of age. Traditional preparation involves human mastication of kava root; pounding or stripping optional but less effective. Customary to select virgin boys or girls of tribe for mastication; believed sexual purity essential to quality of kava.

Also desirable: clean mouth, strong teeth and jaws. Fibres chewed until soft pulp.

N.B. mastication attempted – unsuccessful. Root v. tough.

The sound of feet on the stairs disturbs my concentration. A few seconds later Paul appears in the doorway, smiling and a little out of breath.

'I was trying to find you.'

I nod and look back down at the book.

'Are you bored, or something?'

'Bored?' I look up, surprised. 'Why would I be bored?'

Paul shrugs. 'I don't know – maybe you don't like it here.' He wanders to the window. 'Or you want to be around people your own age.'

I close the notebook, keeping my finger inside as a place marker. Paul turns his back to me and places his hands on the desk, gazing, I assume, at Tagire.

'Maybe you are missing your friends,' he says. 'Or your boyfriend.'

I stare at his back for a couple of moments. It is still and silent as the mountain.

'I don't have a boyfriend,' I say simply, effortlessly. It sounds truthful, and I suppose, in a way, it is. How would I even begin to explain A.B.?

He flexes his fingers, drawing the knuckles back and in, like a cat.

'Me neither,' he says. 'A girlfriend, I mean. I suppose I am still looking for someone. For my goddess.'

He extends the end of the word, its sibilance rattling around the room. Ma déesse. I don't answer. He moves to turn round and I look down at the notebook, pretending to be absorbed. In my peripheral vision I calculate how far away he is from me, the distance to the door.

'So why didn't you tell me about the manuscript?' he asks in a sharper tone.

'What?'

'The manuscript you were working on in Paris. All that stuff you were telling Marcel. Patrice mentioned it too. Why didn't you tell me?'

'I – I don't know,' I say, truthfully. 'I didn't want to bore you with it.'

He sighs. 'Look at me.'

My heart is hammering in my ears. I look up at him but I can't see his features; his body seems as amorphous as the furniture.

'You can tell me anything, okay? You could never bore me. I just feel pretty stupid when you talk to my friends about things before talking to me.'

His gaze bears down on my face. I mumble an apology – he's clearly hurt. He stays a few moments longer, then excuses himself, saying he has things to do.

I sit in the empty room, reeling with relief and – what? Exhilaration? I run through what just took place. A thousand things, and then their opposites. Everything and nothing. I look around, as if the books, maps and statues will act as witnesses, will offer their own account of what happened.

Suddenly I feel panicked and want to leave. I'm almost out of the room when I realise I've left Paul's notebooks in a circle around where I have been sitting. I tidy them into the chest. Paul has taken such good care of me, I realise. He's been so generous and welcoming, and all I've done in return is act ungratefully. I must be the worst volunteer he's ever had. I run my finger over a notebook's silver binding, making a mental note to apologise to Paul for my behaviour, the next time I see him.

vendredi

The next morning, Paul isn't at breakfast, ready to start work in the garden. It feels strange to break our routine, even though Béthanie had already asked if I could help gather flowers for the festival today. When we're nearly out of the door and Béthanie calls up the staircase to Paul, I realise I'd been counting on seeing him. I step out into the bright day feeling jittery, convinced his absence is related to something I've done or, worse, failed to do.

Béthanie and I spend the morning working our way through the village's abandoned gardens, hoisting ourselves over peeling wrought-iron gates of houses which, Béthanie assures me, are uninhabited. The buildings went to seed a long time ago: ivy scaling their caved-in walls, branches poking through smashed windows. It feels good being outside, feeling the stems brush against my calves, imagining the texture of the air filtered by the plants around us.

'It's such a waste,' she says, treading the path ahead through the waist-high growth, hacking at swathes of weeds. She seems to know exactly which flowers to gather and where from. Her backpack is already filled with bright red trumpet blooms. 'But all the better for us. No one else is going to enjoy them.'

As we work, I become aware of wanting to do well, wanting her to approve of me. We don't talk much but I watch her discreetly, picking only the flowers she selects, and treading a path parallel to hers. I mirror her gestures: the short, choppy movements she makes with her arms; slipping the secateurs into my back pocket like she does.

At one point I notice a clutch of grass seeds clinging to her hair, and reach up to brush it off. She slaps my hand away instantly and looks furious. Then, it passes, and her expression becomes one of faint irritation and embarrassment. I step back, a little stunned. 'Sorry,' she says shortly, avoiding my eyes. After that we carry on in silence.

'Merci,' says Béthanie as a stout middle-aged woman emerges from the bar's interior with two large glasses of red wine. She puts them down on our table and loiters for a few minutes, speaking rapidly with Béthanie. I smile at her but she doesn't look my way; I focus instead on the flower heads drooping out from our bags.

The village square is growing dim with the onset of evening, shade rising from the gutters and doorways to join the creeping vines and drainpipes that scale the houses. The terracotta chimneys remain untouched, lit like beacons. At the other side of the square a thin, elderly man appears and begins to cross slowly, limping heavily and leaning on a stick. When he reaches us, he ducks his head at Béthanie who nods and mutters salut as he disappears into the bar.

When our glasses are nearly empty, Béthanie asks if I want to see the abandoned baths. She stands up and slings the rucksack over her shoulder, flowers jostling against her neck.

'The springs dried up in the fifties,' she says. 'But I know the way in.'

We cross the square and make our way down a narrow street that opens out again into a large forecourt. At its far end, the entrance is set into a low-lying Roman peristyle, its paint peeling. A narrow colonnade runs its length. The steps are cracked, with weeds growing through the stonework, and the windows are messily nailed over with planks of wood. On the boarded-up door is a crude graffitied outline of a hunched figure, the word 'nympho' sprayed in orange across its body.

'Quel dommage,' Béthanie says as she runs her hand down one of the columns.

For a moment I hear another word: 'damage'.

'Why don't they restore it?' I ask.

Béthanie snorts. 'With what money?'

I follow Béthanie along the colonnade. At the far end is a large, circular tower with a domed roof. Béthanie walks round the back, where bricks have been broken and pulled away to make a rough entrance.

'I hope you're not claustrophobic,' she says as I squeeze through the gap after her. 'Watch your step – there's a drop in the middle.'

Inside, I press myself against the wall as Béthanie flicks on her lighter and I wait for my eyes to adjust.

The room is octagonal, each wall lined with fading murals of classical figures. They must have been painted at the end of the nineteenth century, when Marcel said the baths had been built.

The panel directly opposite me depicts a young girl dressed in a simple white smock; blonde curls flare out from her head like a halo, and her arms hang demurely at her sides. She stares straight out above me. I turn to follow her gaze and see it leads to a tiny window above my head, too high to see through. Beneath the girl is a scroll emblazoned with the word *PYRENE*, the edges just nudged by her bare toes.

Béthanie is crouched down in the centre of the room where the floor drops away to darkness below. 'The springs were down there,' she says. 'So this was a kind of steam room, I think. I've seen an old photo with a ladder leading down through this hole.'

I ask Béthanie about the painting of the girl.

Béthanie glances round at me. 'Pyrene? I'm not the person to ask.' She sighs. 'You'd be better off talking to Patrice. He's an encyclopaedia for that kind of thing. Or then again,' she mutters, almost inaudibly, 'maybe ask Paul. It's more in line with his interests . . .'

'What interests?' I ask, trying to sound casual.

'Forget it,' she snaps. 'Come on, I'm tired. We'll have to cycle home in the morning if we stay much longer.'

I follow her back out into the cool air. The evening has thickened since we were last outside; semi-darkness now cloaks the buildings around the forecourt. Just before we leave, I look up at Pyrene's window and turn to follow her line of vision. In the distance, barely perceptible in the overlay of our gazes, is the dark peak of Tagire.

When Béthanie and I get back to Noa Noa, the lights are on in the mezzanine, and voices seep out into the cool evening.

'A meeting of the elders,' Béthanie remarks drily as she leans our bikes together. 'Deciding the village's fate.'

We creep inside and pause in the doorway leading to the mezzanine.

Huddled around the far end of the long wooden table, Paul, Loïc and Antoine are engrossed in conversation. Loïc, who seems to be doing most of the talking, leans forward on his elbows, speaking rapidly with a grave expression on his face; Antoine is slumped back with his legs splayed open, frowning and picking at the label of a wine bottle. Paul sits at the head of the table, nodding insistently at whatever his friend is saying.

Béthanie nudges me. 'It's like the Last Supper, non?' She lets out a snort and stumbles from the door frame, laughing.

Loïc stands up in alarm at the noise, knocking his chair to the floor with a clatter. 'Do you have to be so childish?' he exclaims, but he is already smiling as he sits back down.

'You just looked so serious,' says Béthanie, catching her breath. 'I couldn't resist.'

'It's a festival meeting,' mumbles Antoine, without looking up from the wine bottle.

'Ah,' says Béthanie. 'And what about dinner? Have you already eaten?'

Paul and Loïc exchange glances. Paul shrugs and gestures to the baguette ends, cheese rinds and wine dregs strewn across the table. 'Kind of.'

Béthanie sighs. 'It's like having three children. I'm starving and Frances hasn't eaten either – will all of you eat if I cook something?'

There is a rumble of assent around the table. I catch Paul's eyes before following Béthanie into the kitchen.

'Merci, les femmes!' the men call after us.

Béthanie sets to work quickly, cracking a whole dozen eggs into a large bowl.

I open the fridge and hunt through the salad box, trying to salvage any of the wilting organic leaves that have not yet turned to slime.

'If there's one thing I learned from having a Spanish husband,' I hear Béthanie say from the other side of the kitchen, 'it's how to make a good omelette.'

I keep my eyes down as I sort the soggy leaves from the just about edible. It's the first time she's mentioned her ex-husband.

'Did you live together in Spain?' I ask.

'No. In France.'

I chop a salad onion, brimming with questions. How long were they married for? What led to the break-up? I sprinkle the onion over the leaves, hoping to disguise their limpness.

'And was he a chef?'

Béthanie swears as the hot oil jumps up and burns her. 'Non,' she says, sucking the back of her hand.

'What did—'

'Please, Frances,' she says wearily, 'I'd rather not talk about it.'

I blush instantly and look down at the salad. 'Of course,' I murmur by way of apology.

'Magnifique,' exclaims Loïc as we set the food down on the table. Béthanie takes a seat next to him, while Antoine makes space for me next to Paul.

'You know, Frances,' Paul says as Béthanie begins to serve the tortilla onto plates, 'before Bét came, I lived like a pauper.'

Béthanie shushes him dismissively, smiling.

'It's true!' Paul says. 'I used to just forget to eat. In the daytime, anyway.'

'It's impossible to *forget* to eat,' says Antoine.

Paul shrugs. 'I suppose it's a hangover from travelling, you don't always know where your next meal is going to come from, you get used to going for long periods without—'

'What he means, Frances, is that he gets all his calories from alcohol,' Loïc cuts across him. Laughter erupts around the table as Paul smiles, raises his glass to Loïc in admission and downs the remainder of his wine.

By the time I next look at the clock, another hour has passed. The drink and company warm my cheeks and I feel relaxed, following the talk easily and occasionally joining in. Béthanie's omelette is surprisingly sweet, and the salad, despite its elderly leaves, tastes fresh.

'I forgot to say,' Paul says with his mouth full, looking at me, 'we decided today. We're going to climb Tagire the day after the festival. You're coming, of course. There's no way we can let you leave Lazeaux otherwise. It's a rite of passage.'

I smile tentatively.

'It's easy as anything,' Paul says. 'Léa did it last year when she was, how old – four?' He directs the question at Antoine, who shrugs and helps himself to another slice of omelette. Loïc watches him lift it to his mouth disapprovingly. 'Marcel *did* have to carry her some of the way, but—'

'Marcel is very kind, but I don't think he will carry Frances up the mountain,' quips Béthanie.

I laugh faintly to disguise disappointment; the day after the festival is my last day in Lazeaux, when I'd been hoping to visit the cathedral.

I meet Paul's eyes and for a few moments everything around us blurs, flickering in the candlelight. The flames hit his features from below, darkening the stubble on his upper lip and exaggerating the shadows around his eyes.

'It's late,' I hear Béthanie murmur and light up a cigarette. Her voice is distant, like a radio playing in the next room.

Paul is still looking at me with a look I can't place. I smile breezily and get up to clear away the plates.

'You've been an angel,' Loïc says, leaning back so I can reach his plate. 'You can stay for good!'

Béthanie rolls her eyes and saunters to the stairs that lead down to the lower tier of the mezzanine. She leans on the banister and looks back at us.

'Night, boys.' She gestures to me with her cigarette. 'Frances, get some sleep – we've got serious work to do tomorrow.'

I nod, and take the plates into the kitchen and start washing up. A few moments later Loïc and Antoine stumble in. We quickly kiss goodnight while I hold my dripping hands over the sink.

Minutes pass with no sound from the mezzanine. I try to focus on the washing-up, try not to think about Paul, who is still in the next room.

Soon, I am aware of someone entering the room behind me and lingering at the end of the kitchen table. It might be Béthanie, on her way to the bathroom, but I know without turning around that it isn't.

'Don't worry about those,' says Paul, slurring slightly.

'I'm nearly done,' I say, keeping my back turned.

Silence falls, heavy and total. I resist its weight, searching my mind for something to say, something light and conversational and buoyant. I am sure that as long as we keep talking, everything will be fine; Paul will stay on the other side of the room and I will finish the drying up and go to bed; tomorrow I will wake up and we will be with other people all day. I will dance with Léa and Laure and Ève at the festival;

84

and then the next day, when we climb Tagire, I'll ask Patrice about the mural of Pyrene; maybe there'll even be time to visit the cathedral on the way home; and the day after that, I will thank Paul for having me and for being so welcoming. I'll leave Lazeaux for good, and Paul will be a fond memory. Or maybe we'll stay friends, and I'll come back to visit every summer. Watch Léa and Laure and Ève grow older. Paul and I will write to each other sometimes, send postcards, maybe he'll post jars of jam at Christmas.

Paul clears his throat and sets his glass down on the table.

I still can't think of what to say. I concentrate on the circular movement of my hand and the tea towel over the plates.

'What's wrong?' he says.

I keep my eyes on the plate, noticing its hairline cracks, even though the surface looked smooth a few moments ago.

'You haven't been yourself this evening,' he says. 'I can tell.'

'I don't know,' I say, thinking of the trip with Béthanie. 'I keep upsetting people without meaning to, like earlier, with Béthanie—'

Paul laughs, short and sharp. 'Béthanie is always upset – don't worry about her.'

'And you?'

'Me?'

'I thought I'd upset you, yesterday. You seemed annoyed or something – I don't know.'

Another laugh. 'You're very perceptive until you're myopic, Frances. Upset is the opposite of how I feel.' He takes a step towards me. 'Well, I suppose I'm upset about the fact that you're leaving.'

I laugh, staring at the wall. The sound is hollow and my face feels like stone. I try to move, turn around, but my feet won't lift. It's as if they have sprouted roots in the kitchen lino, grown down through Noa Noa's foundations. Slowly, I pivot on the spot, plate and tea towel in hand. I look at Paul's face and find I'm unable to look away, even though it's painful; it's like staring directly into the sun.

'I have been so happy since you arrived,' he says. 'It's been a dream.'

I laugh again, unsure if I should thank him, or reciprocate. The breath catches in my throat and I feel a little dizzy; I push back against the counter to steady myself.

'I think *you* have been happy here, too,' he says. 'Haven't you?'

I concentrate and manage to form a single word: 'Yes.'

'Meeting you has made me realise that I have lived too long like a monk, here in Lazeaux. Maybe,' he says, 'maybe I have been waiting too long for my goddess.'

'Maybe,' I echo.

'Maybe it's you?'

'Maybe.' I am stuck on repeat.

Paul takes a step closer. 'Coquine,' he says, smiling, baring his teeth. 'Coquine, you have been teasing me the whole time.'

He is close now, and reaches out to take the dish. I can see the dense thickets on his forearms. My hands drop to my sides. Numbness comes, with a strange relief in giving in to it. I calmly reconcile myself to the possibility that I might never move again.

'Maybe you think I am too old?' he says.

Maybe. Coquine; the refrain plays in my ears.

'But then, you're *different*, Frances. You are older than people your age. Just like I was, then. You and I are the same. We are old souls.'

The hem of his T-shirt brushes my skin as he takes my face in his hands. Then he is kissing it and his mouth is a dry cave closing over mine. He pushes into me, hard against my thigh.

'It was fate that brought you here,' he's saying. 'Fate brought you to me.'

I close my eyes, and find, to my surprise, that I have left the room. I am somewhere dark and warm, a cinema perhaps, and a film is playing. It's a nature documentary, one I watched with A.B. in Paris. The camera zooms in on the spindly green legs of a praying mantis, brandished like razors in an ambiguous gesture. The narrator explains in a deep and lulling voice that, contrary to widely held knowledge, it has been disproven that the females of the species are given to consuming the male after the sexual act. Recent studies show that in the preceding decades of laboratory observation, it was in fact the blinding brightness of the strip lights used to monitor the insects' movements that caused high levels of stress hormone to be produced in the female, which ultimately triggered her panicked performance of sexual cannibalism. Subsequent periods of observation in natural lighting further proved the hypothesis.

I open my eyes and crash back into my body. Paul is still kissing my mouth, his tongue probing over mine. He moves to my neck and murmurs something. It comes in and out of earshot. Ma déesse, ma déesse.

I wriggle a little. He moves his head back to look at me. There are dark wheels spinning in his eyes.

'Coquine,' he says, 'come to bed.'

samedi

When I wake up, I am alone in Paul's bed. A hazy glow filters through the voile half covering the window, and I can hear music somewhere in the distance. I stretch and notice something tacked to the ceiling above my head: a large paper map of an island. Tahiti, or Vanuatu? I don't recognise the shape. Thick lines of highlighter pen are drawn over its surface, with words scribbled next to them that are too small to read. I'm surprised I hadn't noticed it until now, but then last night it had been dark, and before that I'd had no reason, while in Paul's room, to look up.

There's a thickness to the air, almost humid, and the sky is muted and grey. I approach the desk and see the Kava bowl has been moved to the centre, weighting down the small note tucked beneath it. I remove it and read, in Paul's familiar scrawl: *Mon amour, it was so hard to leave you sleeping. I have gone to meet Loïc and the others to help with the chapiteau. I*

will count the hours until I see you again. With impatience, P.
I screw the letter up and then think better of it. I get dressed
and stuff the note into my pocket, dawdling in front of the
maps and wall hangings, the carved figures on shelves. I
avoid looking out at Tagire, though I feel its form, eye-like,
watching me as I move.

I hear Béthanie call for me downstairs and realise, with the
beginnings of something like nausea, that if she goes into my
room she will see my empty, undisturbed bed. I leave Paul's
room and hurry down the stairs to meet her standing outside
my door.

I blurt something about using the bathroom upstairs.

Béthanie regards me for a few moments. Has she noticed
I'm wearing yesterday's clothes? 'We're due down at the
mairie,' she says flatly. 'Be ready in five minutes.'

I slip past her into my room, closing the door behind me. I
stare at the unwrinkled bed, my heart pounding in my ears. I
fluff up the pillows, disturb the sheets of thick calico. Just in
case, I think. I pull off my T-shirt and throw on a new one,
looking around the room for other signs that might betray
my absence. I take Paul's note from my pocket and smooth it
out on my thigh. It's heavily creased, and the clamminess of
my hand has smudged the ink, though I can still make out
the words. I hesitate for a few moments over where to put it,
then slip it under my pillow.

'Patrice says it's been empty for at least a decade,' Béthanie
tells me as we hurry downhill to the old mairie. The air

outside is close, and moisture begins to pool in the small of my back before we are halfway down the street. The heat appears to have a soporific effect on the village too; the dogs are nowhere to be seen, while the houses' still-drawn shutters look like sleepy, unopened eyes.

The bursts of music become louder as we get closer to the river, and I become aware of a queasy feeling in my stomach. When the shouts of the men by the chapiteau come into earshot, I am so sure that I'm going to throw up that I stop for a second and double over, clutching my middle.

Béthanie marches on a few paces before she notices. 'What's wrong?' she calls. There's a familiar expression on her face, the frown she'd given yesterday if the flower I'd chosen to cut was in fact a weed, or if I missed my step through one of the abandoned jungles and grazed my leg.

'Nothing. I'm fine.'

'Come on then.' She frowns. 'Manon's mother is in charge of the food. She's probably been there since the crack of dawn.'

We turn onto a dusty driveway, our feet crunching through old pine needles. For a few seconds the river and the white body of the chapiteau come into sight, before disappearing behind the hedgerow. Outside the mairie, Simone is unpacking boxes from the boot of a car. Ève lingers on the steps of the portico, arms folded across her chest. Laure is absorbed in braiding her younger sister's hair – Léa stands ramrod straight with her nose to the wall.

'Sorry we're late,' calls Béthanie, causing Simone to look up and smile.

'We've just arrived ourselves.'

'And Manon?'

'Inside. With her mother.' Simone raises her eyebrows pointedly. 'But she'll need to escape at some point to practise with the band.'

'Then we'll provide cover,' Béthanie mutters. Simone giggles and shushes her, glancing at the girls. Léa and Laure chatter away, unawares.

'Ève, come and help us with the boxes,' Simone calls. Ève wanders over and glowers into the boot. The largest box is marked *CARCASSES DE POULET CONGELÉES 50 KG*, and is soggy at the edges where moisture has made dark stains on the cardboard.

'Chicken juice. Disgusting,' says Ève as Simone and Béthanie heave it out of the boot and squat to take opposite corners, depositing a third corner into Ève's reluctant hands. The three of them waddle towards the door.

Just before disappearing inside, Béthanie calls over her shoulder to me. 'Bring the vegetables, will you?'

As soon as we are all assembled before her in the kitchen – Béthanie, Simone, Léa, Laure, Ève, Manon and I – Manon's mother sets about assigning us tasks. She is an enormous, unsmiling woman. Her eyes bulge out fiercely beneath the ochre-coloured pashmina pulled low over her forehead, and a plait of long grey hair snakes down her back. She asks my name and kisses me brusquely on the cheek.

The morning passes quickly and bleeds seamlessly into the afternoon. Léa and Laure work on the floor, squatting over a large vat of water, Léa passing carrots for Laure to peel, while Béthanie, Ève, Simone and I form a production line of chopping. Behind us is another vat of hot water, in which the chicken carcasses are set to defrost. Manon's mother deals with the chickens, holding each one by the legs and shaking it dry, before dismembering it with a few economic chops of her knife on the counter thickly coated in white flour. Each time she does this it generates a little powdery cloud that drifts over the room.

We work in silence, more or less, though I wish there was more chatter to distract me from the ache in my stomach. I can't tell whether Béthanie knows or suspects where I slept last night, and if she does, whether she lets on to Simone while I break to use the bathroom.

At some point, Manon disappears to practise with the rest of the band, and we soon hear her voice, distant but amplified, broadcasted from the chapiteau. The rest of us work steadily on, and when I do exchange a few words with Béthanie and Simone, mostly to discuss the next stage of the cooking, their expressions are inscrutable.

Not long after Manon's departure, there is a crunch on the gravel outside. My insides clench to a fist and I stare at the doorway, sure that Paul will walk in any second. Instead Loïc appears, topless, leaning in the doorframe.

'Salut, les femmes,' he says coolly.

'Put it away,' Béthanie says, slapping at his chest with a tea towel. 'What do you want? This is a women-only zone.'

'Yeah, no boys allowed,' quips Léa, looking up from the vat of floating bald potatoes.

Loïc glances down at her in mock surprise. 'Oh really? I had no idea. And what will happen if I stay?'

Léa runs her finger in a circle around the surface of the potato water, making a whirlpool. 'I will give you some potion from the cauldron ... and turn you into a *FROG*!' she shrieks, flicking water in Loïc's direction. He jerks out of the way, laughing.

'Enough!' Manon's mother barks, glowering at Loïc. 'We're busy. What do you want?'

Loïc bites back a smile. 'We need a cable from Paul's garage, but we can't spare anyone from the chapiteau. He said you know which one it is.' He nods at me.

My heart hammers. 'The one he borrowed from Marcel?'

Loïc shrugs. 'Must be. Just bring it down quick as you can, okay?'

'Wait a minute!' calls Manon's mother to Loïc's disappearing back.

He reappears in the doorway.

'What?'

'You can't just come in here and order us about. She's doing an important job. Send one of the girls instead.'

'I'll go!' Léa cries, jumping up. 'I know which one it is.'

Loïc shrugs apologetically as Léa rushes past him. 'Sorry, Frances, I thought you'd get early release.'

Manon's mother's frown deepens.

'I don't mind,' I say. 'Whatever's easiest.'

Loïc nods slowly as if something is dawning on him. 'Incroyable,' he says, turning from me to Béthanie. 'Incroyable. Why is it Frances knows how to be amenable but the rest of you are so stubborn?'

Before Béthanie can reply, Loïc vanishes. What did he mean by 'amenable'? Images from yesterday flash through my mind, of the men working on the chapiteau as Paul and I arrived on our bikes, mine stickered with flowers, ribbons streaming, girlish. The sound of their laughs as I retreated, the hot stones warmed by the sun. A familiar lump rises in my throat.

The storm that has been dryly bristling all day finally breaks. The downpour is sudden and torrential, ushering the guests straggled over the banks of the river inside the chapiteau. Everyone apart from Ève, Laure and I, who ferry plates of food back and forth. It's hard not to skid on the grass as I walk, slopping chicken stock over the sides of the plates. Soon my hands are streaming with the orange liquid and I utter strings of apologies as it drips onto the white paper tablecloth in front of the guests. My hair and clothes are plastered to my skin but I resist touching them, fearful of spreading orange everywhere. I silently pray that Paul, wherever he is, can't see me.

When I return to the mairie, Manon's mother scolds me, pointing to the bright coins of liquid splattered down my front. Simone takes stock of the situation and comes at me with a wet sponge.

'It won't budge,' she says, dabbing forcefully. 'This is potent stuff. I had a feeling this might happen so I brought a spare.'

She leaves and reappears a few moments later with another shirt made of soft white lace. She peels the stained T-shirt over my head and helps me slip on the new one. It smells faintly of lavender and talcum powder, familiar and alien at the same time. I feel like a child being dressed for my first day at school, and as she tugs it down around my waist, I don't want her to let go of me, wish I could slow the moment down and make it last indefinitely.

She tucks a strand of hair behind my ear.

'There,' she says, stepping back to admire her work.

'Jolie!' Léa cries. 'You look like you're going to get married!'

I follow Simone out to the back of the chapiteau, where she counts the guests under her breath.

'Have the band eaten?' she breaks off to ask.

'I don't know.'

'They'll probably be out by the van,' she says. 'Loïc is very superstitious about being seen before performances. Why don't you go and check?'

Outside, the rain shows no sign of abating. I hunch over the plates to try and protect them from the worst of the downpour, squinting to make out the dark shape of the van parked a short distance away.

As I approach, I see the seats at the front are empty and the lights are off. I call out, kicking at its side in place of knocking. No response. I am about to leave when I hear a thud from the other side. I hang back, waiting for another sound to confirm the first. Nothing. The plates weigh heavy in my hands; the couscous has begun to swim.

I go to check round the other side.

They don't see me at first. Manon is pushed up against the side of the van, her bare legs hooked around Loïc's waist; his jeans are loose around his thighs. They are thrashing together like some sea creature washed up on shore. I stand there for what feels like minutes, taking in the dark lacerations on Manon's legs, from her feet up to where her dress is hoicked around her hips.

But it must be only seconds before Manon's head snaps around. A dark slit atrophies her face as she sees me and begins to laugh. Loïc opens his mouth and I can make out only the palest parts of his face: teeth and eye-whites. Their bodies still moving as if they haven't seen me at all. Each second is waterlogged. I become aware of the wetness over my feet, a compound of rain and chicken stock, sluicing grains between my toes: the plates' contents have slipped out of my hands.

'Quoi?' Loïc slows to a halt and throws his hands up. Manon is no longer laughing.

I reach down to retrieve the plates from the faintly steaming grass. 'Sorry. Sorry.'

Then I turn and hurry back to the chapiteau. From the

other side of the van comes their laughter. I stride through the wet grass, and their sounds are soon swallowed by the rain.

Back inside, the chapiteau is transformed. Antoine and a few men I don't recognise are disassembling the tables and chairs, and the crowd is on their feet, softly inebriated, chattering as they're herded about like semi-tranquilised cattle. I resist looking around for Paul. It's too loud to make out anyone's words; I see only a sea of mouths firing rapidly, the sounds detached from coherence. Béthanie emerges from the throng and approaches me.

'There you are. Where did you go?'

She looks down at my top and frowns. I follow her gaze and see the rain has turned Simone's white shirt partly see-through.

'I can go and change—'

'There's no time,' she snaps. 'The band are almost ready to start; we need to take everything to the kitchen.'

I follow her back outside. The rain has eased off a little and the clouds are beginning to clear. I stack the plates together, and a crescent of moonlight, almost liquid, appears on the topmost face. An amplified voice stutters out from the chapiteau as we make our way over the grass, soon followed by the band's soundcheck and bursts of broken cheers from the crowd.

When we reach the kitchen, Manon's mother takes the plates from my hands and places them in the sink without a word. I watch them slide into the hot, foamy water.

'Your feet!' Béthanie remarks to me on her way out.

I look down, and see that my feet are cut to ribbons, latticed with tiny, dark slits, just as Manon's legs had been. I lift one foot to the light in horror, and see that the marks are not cuts after all but blades of wet grass, stuck to my skin. I almost laugh with relief.

'Faster, Frances!' cries Léa, 'faster!'

I smile and feel her small fingers tighten around my wrists as we spin round and round. Everything becomes kaleidoscopic, colours shaken loose from their shapes. A small space has been cleared to make room at the side of the stage, where only those who are either too old or too young to care about being seen are dancing. Next to us, Laure takes turns being twirled underarm by Simone and Béthanie, and several older women are swivelling and twisting in time to the music, faint lines of perspiration glistening on their upper lips.

The music has been going for over an hour. Earlier, I found myself dawdling as I cleared up in the kitchen, anxious about going back to the festival. But as soon as I stepped inside, Léa and Laure appeared in front of me, each taking one of my arms, and pulled me to the chapiteau and in through the crowd. It was hot and writhing with life like a forest floor. On stage, the band was in full flow: Manon in the centre, midsolo, with Loïc behind her, straddling a double bass. Antoine stood to the side, on guitar, while two men I didn't recognise played piano and saxophone. Manon's body became tense as the melody built; it was as if the note was an orb of energy growing inside her, waiting to release itself high into the air before bursting over the crowd.

I feel awkward at first, but soon abandon myself to dancing giddily, gleefully with the girls. There's something safe about it, as if by dancing with them I become one of them – a child of whom no one expects anything. It is so tiring having a woman's body. I'd like to slip right out of it and shrink back down to a child's size.

'There's Paul!' Léa cries, pointing to the edge of the crowd. He's on a chair, crouching, a camera directed towards the crowd raised over his face. As a photographer, he's mastered the art of blending into the background, but the disguise is ruined by what looks like a white sarong tied around his waist.

'What's he wearing?' I ask Léa.

'I can't remember what it's called,' she says. 'He always wears it to parties.'

The rhythm builds; Léa and I move frantically to keep time and I lift her effortlessly into the air. When she jumps back down she is flushed, the strands of hair shaken loose from her ponytail, framing her face like a halo. We whirl faster and faster as the song builds to a crescendo. I shut out images of the plates on the grass, the cuts on Manon's thighs, the wet blades clinging to my feet. Only Léa stays in focus, grinning. Suddenly it's the end of the song: the instruments cut out and we break apart, panting, clapping along with the crowd.

Antoine picks up the saxophone and begins a slow, sultry solo.

I notice Paul hovering at the edge of the crowd. I purposefully look away, but feel his gaze hit the back of my neck like a guillotine. Then he is right next to us, asking Léa if he can have a dance with the beautiful lady.

'It'll be your turn when you're big enough,' he says, winking at her.

She skips off and throws her arms around her father's waist.

'Nice shirt,' Paul says, offering me one of the two cups of dark wine in his hands. I take it, and down the whole lot in a few gulps. He raises his eyebrows. He plucks a red trumpet flower from the decorations and tucks it behind my ear.

'You have been hiding from me, coquine,' he murmurs. 'I've been thinking about you all day.'

I smile and shake my head. He takes my hands and pulls me in close to dance. His body is flat and bony; I think of the sketches in his journals of bisj ancestor poles – totems of slender, elongated figures standing on each other's shoulders. The topmost figures, I remember, straddled large, ornately carved wooden phalluses, curving into the sky at forty-five-degree angles.

I am aware of eyes on us from all sides, and feel suddenly exposed to something that dancing with Léa had shaded me from.

'What does it mean, "coquine"?' I ask, clutching at conversation.

'Hmm?'

'"Coquine". You keep saying it.'

'Do I?'

I look at the stage behind him, where Antoine's black brogues are roughly parallel to my eye level.

'It's a kind of shell,' he says. 'A seashell.'

I nod, not knowing what to say.

'Do you like my pāreu?'

'Your what?' I struggle to hear us both over the music.

Paul grins and gestures at the white garment tied around his waist. 'My pāreu. It's traditional festive dress, a gift from a friend from Temoe.'

'It's cool.'

'You know,' he says, as the music builds to another climax, 'I had always dreamed that I would end up with a woman from another culture. But in fact, you're—'

The saxophone is so loud that I miss the last word.

'What?'

'PERFECT,' he yells, just as the music cuts out. 'YOU'RE PERFECT!'

His last words ring in my ears. Those standing nearby titter, followed by catcalls from further into the crowd.

'Bravo,' says Loïc, speaking into the microphone. The crowd laughs in response as Paul grins self-consciously. He turns back to me and swoops in, lifting my chin, closing his mouth over mine.

I close my eyes, remembering childhood logic: *if I can't see them then they can't see me.*

The last thing I see before I do so, over Paul's shoulder, is Béthanie. She's standing at the edge of the crowd, no longer dancing, watching us. There's a strange look on her face that might have begun as a scowl, but has fractured into something else. She turns her back and, when I open my eyes again, is gone.

Outside the chapiteau I almost collide with Patrice, who's sitting on a bench by the entrance.

'Sorry,' I say. 'I was just looking for Béthanie – did you see her?'

'No.' Patrice shakes his head. 'I just came out to get some air.'

I join him on the bench and look up. The sky overhead is almost clear, a few straggly clouds drifting across the moon. The scent of wet grass rises freely through the air, mingling with the smell of sweat and cigarettes that's gathered in my hair. It's a relief to be outside. I'd extricated myself from Paul with the excuse of finding Béthanie, but really I just wanted to get out.

'Do you know about geomagnetic reversal?' Patrice says, interrupting my thoughts.

'What?'

'Geomagnetic reversal. Every half million years or so the Earth's magnetic poles reverse, completely flip.'

His face is turned up to the sky, and stray light from the chapiteau falls across his face, making his moustache flicker orange and gold.

'It hasn't happened in a while,' he says, pausing to scratch his neck. 'We're due another.'

Hazy recollections of poles and magnetic fields drift through my thoughts, addled by the cheap wine. I can only summon a sequence of objects used at school: oblong magnets half red and half blue; vertebrae-like models of DNA with detachable helixes and bases, half the parts missing. I look up at the sky and almost expect to see a giant helical coil drilled through the firmament, turning like a corkscrew into the Earth.

'It sounds dangerous,' I say, imagining disasters, apocalyptic scenes. 'Would we survive it?'

'Most likely, yes. We wouldn't really notice it at all, other than our navigation devices, mapping and the like, going haywire.'

'Oh,' I say, suddenly fearful. Of what I don't know. It is not particularly cold, but I notice that I am shivering. I pull the trumpet flower, hot and wilted, from behind my ear.

'You are having a good evening?' Patrice asks.

'Yeah. Kind of.' The petals come apart in my hand. I look up to see Patrice looking at me, his eyebrows knitted together in concern.

'Are you leaving?' I ask before he has a chance to question me.

He chuckles. 'Yes. I've lasted longer than I thought I would. I came mostly to support the boys. It's good that they put something on like this. Good for the village . . .'

'Who are all these people anyway? All the guests?'

'All sorts.' He shrugs. 'Mostly locals. A lot of them complain, you know, about Paul and his type – but they have to admit it's good to do these things. Of course, when I was young there were dances and the like, but—'

'What do you mean, "Paul's type"?'

'Oh, nothing really. I've never found stereotypes particularly helpful. As I said, it's a good thing, what they're doing with the festival. And it makes it more fun for visitors too. Like you. Are you enjoying being here?'

I nod automatically. 'It's not exactly what I expected, but everyone's been very welcoming.'

Patrice lets out a little laugh. 'You were expecting farmers.'

I laugh too, trying to ignore the shrivelling feeling in my gut. Tomorrow is my last day in Lazeaux, when everyone is going to climb Tagire. But the prospect of going along as Paul's – what? Guest? Lover? – is unbearable.

Before I know it will happen, I am asking Patrice if he will take me to Saint Pascal the next day.

He looks at me in surprise. 'Aren't you all climbing Tagire tomorrow?'

'The others are. But I'm afraid of heights.' The smoothness of the lie surprises me. 'And I won't get a chance to see the cathedral otherwise.'

'No. No, of course.' He nods. 'I understand. Let me think. I could come by in the morning, say ten?'

The knot in my stomach loosens a little. 'Great.' I grin with relief. 'Thank you.'

'Not a problem,' he says, getting up stiffly from the bench. 'In which case, if you don't mind, it's long past my bedtime.'

He steps forward to kiss me with an awkward, adolescent jerk of the head; I'm reminded of the boyishness that struck me when we first met. He turns to leave, walking towards the bridge and the cars parked on the far bank. I watch his back recede across the dark field.

I slip off my sandals and walk through the waterlogged grass leading down to the water. The river has swelled with the storm, and as I tread it runs cool over my feet, swirling around my ankles.

I glance back up at the glowing shape of the chapiteau. It's illuminated from within like a bulb, a thin membrane encasing the hot filament of the crowd, as if it's bodies, not instruments, conducting the music. Bodies opening and closing, taking in grains and meat and wine and beer, letting out slurs and jokes and propositions. I have the strange impression of observing another species. The marquee's shape calls to mind a drawing in one of Paul's journals, under the heading *CASTRAL DOMESTICITY*, Paul's notes on nomadic peoples who live their entire lives in tents. But unlike Paul, I can come to no conclusion about the culture I see. The longer I stare at the chapiteau and try to determine its outline, the hazier it becomes, looking less like a structure and more like a living, breathing entity.

The current calls my attention back to the river. I look down and see nothing but opacity; the trees leaning from each bank meet overhead in a canopy of artificial night; the water too dark for reflections. I let my knees sway a little, wishing that I were light enough to be carried downstream.

dimanche

Patrice's red car is covered in painted flowers: white and yellow daisies with looping green stems. It looks like a couple of six-year-olds have gone at it in art class, and I can't help but smile.

'I painted it myself,' he says as I get in. 'But it could do with a new coat soon.'

The engine judders to life and we pull away from Noa Noa, onto the lane the cyclists sped along a few days ago. I turn to look into my bedroom window as we pass, wondering if Paul is still in there, twisted in the sheets.

It's a bright, clear day. There is little to indicate the storm of the night before. Patrice hums softly and tells me we should be at Saint Pascal within the hour. The green hills fall softly in the distance, fading into blue with a shimmering white outline.

I feel numb to the tranquillity of the landscape. As soon

as I told Paul this morning of my plans for the day he began to sulk, and I felt immediately that I had betrayed him, that my decision to come with Patrice amounted to a kind of mutiny.

'Why didn't you just tell me you didn't want to go?' Paul had demanded, lying next to me in bed. 'Why did you go to Patrice?'

I hadn't been able to answer. I'd felt so awful that my first thought had been to call Patrice and cancel the trip.

When I didn't reply, he changed tack. '*Everyone* is going to Tagire,' he murmured into the nape of my neck, running his fingers over my spine. 'I thought you wanted to see the mountain?'

I was turned to the wall so he couldn't see my face. My lips throbbed, feeling raw and bruised; I must have been chewing them in my sleep. 'I do,' I said, tensing. 'But I'd really like to see the cathedral too – remember I asked—?'

'Fine,' he snapped, withdrawing his fingers.

I rolled round to look at him. He was staring straight up at the ceiling, arms pinned stiffly to his sides. I studied the dim trace of his profile, the shadow thrown by his jaw, the stubble like dark sediment. He had looked carved from stone in that moment, in the calm repose of some noble, anonymous effigy, weighted down by time. Then his jugular gave an involuntary twitch and the spell was broken. He was alive after all.

It occurred to me then that Paul might be angry, and the realisation came with a certain thrill. I apologised gently.

'No, *I'm* sorry,' he said, softening. 'Of course if you want to go to the cathedral you should. I will miss you, that's all.'

'But, like you said, everyone is going. You won't be alone—'

'I just wish you were staying here longer,' he interrupted.

He'd rolled over then, his eyes glossy with excitement. 'Why don't you? You could just stay.'

'For the summer?'

'For good! This could be your room, and—'

'What about work?' I'd asked, laughing.

'What work?'

'How would I make a living?'

Paul's expression snapped from quizzical to dismissive. 'I thought you said you didn't know what you wanted to do.'

'Yes, but—'

'So stay here while you decide. Or we could go somewhere together, travel . . .'

'Where?'

He shrugged. 'Anywhere. Where do you want to go? I've learned more from travelling, and from living here, than I did studying. You have your *whole life* ahead of you – you don't always have to do what's sensible.'

I hadn't known what to say so I made some kind of joke, indicating that I knew he wasn't serious. All the same, I began to imagine what life would be like in Lazeaux, an endless summer of bike rides, festivals and long, wine-filled evenings. But then I hit a brick wall: Paul would be there too. I didn't know if I wanted that any more than I wanted to run back to Paris, to apologise to A.B. about what had happened in the archives.

I wriggled down to the edge of the bed and said I was going to have a shower.

'Frances,' he called, grazing his hand against my leg as I passed. There was a pleading look on his face. 'I just don't want to lose you, now that you're here. Promise me you'll think about staying?'

I stared at him for a moment or two, feeling like I was under water. Until then things had seemed relatively simple; whatever happened with Paul would be cut off by my leaving at the end of the week. That date was a marker in time, a clear exit route. But his wanting me to stay turned that certainty into a tangle of possibilities. How could I explain to him that it was painful to be given a choice? Making it to the next farm was the only certain thing in my future; Paris was out of the question, and back home I could only sleep on my mum's sofa for a few weeks at most. But what if Paul was right? What if I'd be happier if I stayed here, rather than listlessly follow the course A.B. laid out for me?

I told him I'd think about it.

Later, when I stepped out of the shower and stood in front of the mirror in the tiny bathroom, I realised I'd left the tap in the sink running the whole time. I turned it off and took a deep breath. I stared at my face but my features were unrecognisable, as unfamiliar as the chipped olive-green tiles framing my reflection.

*

Patrice asks if I mind taking the longer, more scenic route. We pass through field after field of sunflowers. He doesn't ask about Paul or the festival, and I am happy to avoid the subject. Instead he talks a little about his family, and asks about mine. I'm slow to answer his questions at first, as I realise I have become unaccustomed to giving any account of myself beyond details pertaining to the immediate present. I tell myself this is mostly to do with the novelty of speaking another language; I just haven't found a way to express myself yet.

Patrice is single and childless, though when he was young there had been a boy in Paris, Michel, who he had fallen madly in love with, and seen on and off during his thirties. 'But, you know,' he says, 'it wasn't meant to be. It wasn't easy being gay, then, and I wasn't as brave as him.'

He mentions a grown-up nephew, Jérémie, who's recently moved out of the area.

'And you?' Patrice says.

'Hmm?'

'Your family.'

'There's not much to tell. I'm from a small town in Dorset; my mum's a receptionist.'

'No siblings?'

'Just me.'

'And your father?'

The sunflowers' faces are hidden from view, angled towards their common point of observation. A field of diligent spectators. 'I don't know,' I say. 'He left before I can remember.'

'I see. I'm sorry.'

'It's fine,' I blurt awkwardly, half resenting his sympathy. 'Really. It's just a fact. Like the sky being blue.'

Patrice nods and the conversation tails off. A few minutes later he motions at the sunflowers and asks if I know the story.

I shake my head. He begins to tell me a tale from Greek mythology, about a water nymph called Clytie who falls in love with Apollo. My eyelids begin to droop as he explains how Clytie stood on the bank of the river, without moving, eating or drinking, craning her neck to watch the parade of the sun god cross the sky. But Apollo paid her little attention, and after many days she looked down and found she had taken root, her limbs grown down into the earth to find water and nourishment. But her head was still turned up to the sun, following its every movement. She had become a sunflower.

As Patrice speaks I see Paul again, his body coming towards me in the kitchen, his hands cupping my face, his voice rustling the plants outside the window.

When I open my eyes again, the interior of the car seems darker than before, filled with shadows, and the green stalks outside are drawn like bars across the window.

'Who's Pyrene?' I ask, suddenly remembering.

'Who?'

'Pyrene. There's a mural of her in the abandoned baths.'

Patrice nods. 'Ah, that's right.'

'Béthanie said to ask you about it.'

He clears his throat and checks the rear-view mirror, although we haven't passed a single car all morning. 'I've probably forgotten half of it,' he begins. 'Pyrene was the maiden that the Pyrénées were named after. She was a daughter of the King of Gaul. Hercules passed through the kingdom on one of his quests – I forget which one – and the princess, Pyrene, offered him the customary hospitality: meat, wine, a place to sleep. But Hercules was so consumed by lust for her, and fuelled by wine that he ... well, he violated the code of hospitality.'

'What code?'

Patrice looks uncomfortable. 'She became pregnant.'

'Oh.'

'Anyway, Hercules carried on with his quest, and Pyrene ended up giving birth to a serpent. She was afraid of her father's wrath, as you can imagine, so she ran away to the woods, where she eventually went mad, bawling and babbling to the trees about what had happened. In the end she got ripped to pieces by wild beasts.'

'God. That's horrible.'

Patrice nods, grimly. 'Hercules found her corpse on his way home, and was overcome with grief – too late – so he set about building a tomb for her from stones in the forest. And the stones became mountains, which became—'

'The Pyrénées.'

'Exactly. They taught us this in school.' He gives an incredulous laugh. 'Can you imagine?'

I shake my head.

Turning back to the window, I see the sunflowers are gone, replaced with fields of low, straw-coloured crops. I try to remember what the mural of Pyrene had looked like, but the details evade me; at what point in the narrative had she been depicted? She had seemed young, angelic, the vision of beauty. It must have been before the encounter with Hercules; or maybe in the days immediately after, before she found out she was pregnant? On top of that, I am unable to remember if the golden curls of her hair were in fact tiny serpents baring fangs and forked tongues, or whether that is an embellishment I've added in light of Patrice's story. And then, as if the wind changes halfway through my thoughts, Pyrene's features become irreversibly fixed: a medusa crossed with an angel.

'There she is,' Patrice murmurs a little while later, 'the cathedral.'

On the horizon, the outline of Saint Pascal looms into view, crowning a hill that rises sharply from the green fields lapping its base. The spidery outlines thicken as we approach. The image of the high fortress walls is so medieval that I half expect to see a moat at the base and heraldry draping the walls; but encircling the mound there is only a lush garter of trees.

We drive slowly through the town and park at the foot of the hill. Patrice goes to pay for a ticket and I look up at the cathedral emblazoned against the skyline. Flanks of angular buttresses stream from its sides to join the raw rock face below. They look like jets of water, petrified in time.

'They call it a cloister in the sky,' Patrice says, rejoining me.

'See how the walls are hewn from the hill rock?' I follow the line his finger traces around the ramparts.

We begin a meandering ascent on foot, entering through the sloping arch of the medieval gate, and climbing up through winding, cobbled alleys. On the main street, half-timbered houses are packed tightly together, their ground floors converted into cafés and souvenir shops. I peer in as we pass, and see that they are mostly empty.

'It used to be a famous pilgrimage destination,' Patrice says. 'Being so close to Lourdes. But now they have to cater for tourists more than pilgrims.'

I nod, wondering which term is more applicable to Patrice and me. I glance down passageways that siphon off the main thoroughfare. Signs of everyday life sidle into view: washing lines strung between windows; a girl sitting on a step outside a back door, called inside by a female voice; hand-painted signs advertising studio opening hours of potters, jewellers, artisans.

Patrice keeps up a running commentary about the population of the town and its local politics; 'The rent is becoming unbearable,' he says, pointing to the top floor of a house with particularly ornate latticed windows. 'I knew an academic who lived there, once, an historian. But she had to move; it became too expensive.'

The tiny lozenges of glass are neat and opaque. I try to imagine the unnamed woman's life, living so close to the object of her research. How it would be to open her kitchen windows and take in the shape of the cathedral each morning. And then, Paul's voice: *You could just stay . . . this could be your room . . .*

Throughout the climb, the cathedral is barely visible above the rooftops. But the houses thin out as we reach the summit and emerge onto a large forecourt. We step into the shade of the tower and gaze up at its body, looming rigid and airless over the square. All activity seems frozen in its purview; the sounds of the street fade behind us.

'I remember now; the tower is the oldest part. Romanesque, I think,' I say to Patrice.

'You've studied the architecture?'

'Not really,' I shake my head. 'I mean, it was in a lecture once. I prefer manuscripts.'

A child's voice echoes out over stone; a small boy with wild blond hair is running over the forecourt, chased by a man and a woman in matching lime-coloured fleeces.

Patrice doesn't seem to notice them. 'I think I prefer buildings to books,' he says. 'You can go inside them for one thing. They have atmosphere.'

'But they're also unreliable,' I say. 'Don't you feel a room changes each time you step into it?'

Patrice reaches up a hand to touch the stone, its sharp angle eroded to a curve. 'You mean depending on the season? Or time of day? Or that someone religious will experience the cathedral differently to an atheist?'

'Kind of. But it's something to do with scale as well. You can't be inside and outside of it at the same time, but if you're writing about it or trying to be objective you have to pretend you are. At least with a manuscript, you know you're always outside of it. It's . . . more contained.' I was about to say 'safer', but stopped myself.

Before I can add anything else I realise that I've just regurgitated, more or less, one of A.B.'s lectures I sat through earlier in the year. It was not long after he'd invited me to join him in Paris but had told me to keep quiet about it until after graduation. Not that there was anything wrong with it, he'd said, but discretion helps keep hassle to a minimum. I'd sat through the slides with a secret, silent thrill.

'I am always struck by the brusque utility of Romanesque architecture, its fusion of parochial defensiveness with a burgeoning language of ecclesiastical aesthetics. It takes a great deal of imagination to isolate the style in time, disentangling it from an evolutionary view of architectural development, its naivety seen as paving the way for the elegance and finesse of Early Gothic styles, whose slender spires and intricate mouldings would characterise the shape of devotion in the centuries to follow. Such a disentangling is especially difficult here, where the styles themselves have become joined in mortar as well as chronology.'

It's not until Patrice touches me lightly on the shoulder and suggests we go inside that I snap back into the present. I realise it had not been A.B.'s voice delivering the lecture in my head but Paul's.

Patrice heaves open the door. I have a fleeting impression, as I step over the threshold and my eyes adjust to the muted, candlelit interior, that my foot won't touch anything solid, and will instead plunge through limitless space.

Patrice hands me a leaflet from a table nearby. The information confirms, more or less, what we have already spoken about, and the title repeats Patrice's phrase, 'a cloister in the sky', in an archaic, floriated font.

We set off in different directions around the space, passing each other occasionally. Patrice lingers over the larger-than-life-sized paintings on the tomb's panels, and in the treasury, a hush falls over us both as we gaze at a single chainmail glove that seems to be woven from gold, impossibly fine and slender.

Later I crouch down to make sketches of the grotesques on the misericords that hide, troll-like, beneath the choir stalls. They are not dissimilar to some of the marginalia adorning the pages of the manuscript A.B. and I had worked on, and make memories surge through me: the thrill of being 'chosen' when he asked me to join him in Paris; waking up next to him for the first time, feeling so tentative next to the unknown territory of a man's body, so different to those of boys I'd slept with.

When one of us eventually thinks to check the time, we've spent more than two hours inside. We take a brief break in the cloisters overlooking a valley that Patrice tells me is filled with ancient Pyrenean oaks. I glance down at the treetops but find their uniformity unremarkable. No one is around but we continue to talk in hushed voices, sharing the half baguette and bunch of grapes that he produces from his bag.

'If the cloisters were on the other side,' Patrice says, brushing crumbs off his front, 'we'd be able to see Tagire from here.'

He leans over the edge to try and peer as far around the apse as possible. 'Strange to think that they're all up there, now. They might be pointing to us and saying the same thing.'

I look out at the trees guiltily, the bread suddenly feeling thick and claggy in my mouth.

'We can leave if you've had enough?' says Patrice, misreading my expression.

I swallow and shake my head. I am in no hurry to get back.

We look out over the slopes of the valley thick with green oaks. From the height of the cloister they look like a soft carpet, as if I could step onto them and run all the way to Tagire.

Back inside, a group of schoolchildren is midway through a tour. A woman with bobbed hair and a fawning smile shepherds them along as they run their hands over the pews' wooden carvings, making excited squawks. The sounds arc high into the stone firmament and fall back in warped echoes that the children look stunned to hear, as if they are being addressed by ethereal doppelgangers. They soon trundle outside.

As the quiet is restored I notice something dark and bulbous mounted on a wall on the far side of the nave. I cross over, my sandals clicking on the cool stone, to a lozenge-shaped shield of rusting metal. I step closer, only to realise the shield is actually the cadaver of a large crocodile, mounted upright on the wall. Its snout faces downwards, blackened head higher than eye level, jaws parted, skin pulled taut over its skull.

'They stuffed it with an iron rod down the middle,' says Patrice, appearing beside me. He traces a finger in the air downwards over the crocodile, as if in benediction. 'That's how they got the body so straight.'

Patrice is right; the entire body is eerily erect. Rusting iron belts around its middle and back legs secure it to the wall.

'Why is it here?' I step forward, pressing my body against the wall and tilting my neck back until I am directly beneath it, gazing up into its jaws. Inside, I can see nothing except two small drops of light that filter through the hollowed sockets.

'According to folklore,' Patrice says, 'the crocodile was sent by the devil. It terrorised the region for years, hiding in rivers, waiting for human prey. Some versions say it would only eat the flesh of virgin girls.'

A chorus of screeches indicate that the schoolchildren have re-entered the main space. I step out of the crocodile's jawline.

'So when the beast was finally caught, they brought the body here to be exorcised, and strung up in the house of God.'

'But how did it really get here?' I ask. 'Stories aside.'

Patrice shrugs. 'That *is* how it got here, partly. Myths are important. We're not far from Lourdes, after all. But there are other stories, that the dead body was brought back from the Crusades as some kind of trophy.'

'Or warning?'

'If you like.'

I pull my jacket over my shoulders and look up to the windows, where dust dances in shafts of light.

By the time we get back to the car, afternoon has slipped into evening. I chat on and off to Patrice, trying to ignore the liquid feeling of dread rising in my throat as we get closer to the village. Eventually the car eases round a hill, and then the lights of Lazeaux come into sight.

A week's worth of conversations, glances and accidental touches swim in my mind. It feels like the events of my time here have been out of my control, a succession of waves breaking over me.

We pull in and Patrice leaves the engine running. The village is still and quiet. Lights are on in the mezzanine. Someone – Paul, Béthanie, maybe Antoine – is home. The seconds tick by. I think about unbuckling my seatbelt, but my hands remain clasped in my lap. I slowly realise I don't want to get out of the car.

'Do you mind if we sit for a while?' I ask.

He reaches out to readjust his wing mirror. 'I'm due at Marcel's for dinner in half an hour, but—'

'I only need a minute.'

He switches the engine off and says amiably, 'Strange to think you're leaving tomorrow. Where are you going again?'

'First to Nice by car share, and from there two buses up into the mountains.'

'The Maritime Alps? It's beautiful there.'

'The village sits on top of a mountain,' I tell him, remembering the pictures I'd seen online. 'Called Malmot. The farm's on one side of the slope, with polytunnels, animals—'

'A real farm then,' he says, laughing. 'Unlike Paul's. Well, I'm sure you'll be missed here.'

Outside, the evening is segueing into night. I stare at the patch of darkening sky framed by the wing mirror. A bat swoops across, so quickly I wonder if I've imagined it.

'Patrice, can I ask you for some advice?'

'Of course,' he says. 'About what?'

'Well, I wonder if I should just stay here instead of travelling around.'

'What about the farm near Nice?'

'I could cancel it.'

'Why would you want to?'

'I don't know. Well, Paul said I could just stay if I wanted to, and I don't know if I'm ready to leave yet.'

'It's not really my place to say anything . . .' he trails off, bringing his hand up to rub his brow. The orange light shimmers over his skin, appearing to snag on the hairs on the back of his hand.

'But since you asked my opinion, I think it's good for you to carry on with your journey, as intended. Who knows, the next farm might be even better?'

I nod silently, hearing only the residue of Paul's words: *it was fate that brought you here. Fate brought you to me.* What if the next farm was awful, and I tried to come back, and he'd changed his mind? What if I was no longer welcome?

I look past Patrice to the window, where the sky is darkening.

'How do they know when it's time?' I say.

'Who?'

'The magnetic poles. Last night you said they flip every half a million years. I was just wondering how . . . how they know when it's the right time. To change. Or stay the same.'

'I wish I knew.' He shrugs. 'It's not exactly clockwork, but it must be some kind of internal trigger.'

'Like an instinct?'

He hesitates. 'I suppose you could call it that.'

I am about to ask more when he shifts in his seat and says, 'I'm sorry, Frances. I'd like to stay and talk but I'm due for dinner.'

I quickly undo my seatbelt and hop out of the car.

'Good luck with your travels,' he says, as the engine stutters into life. 'I'm sure you'll have a wonderful time.'

Once his car fades from view and earshot, I hear voices coming from inside the house. I creep up the steps and open the front door a crack. It's Paul and Béthanie, though they're in the kitchen, out of sight.

'It's the same thing again, Paul,' Béthanie is saying. Her voice is tired and exasperated, as though they've been arguing the same point for hours.

Paul groans. 'It's nothing like that. And that was just once—'

'Just once? Jesus, Paul, why can't you be honest?'

'There's nothing to be honest about! I don't have to answer to you.'

Béthanie says something I don't catch.

'You're imagining it, Bét,' Paul says, sounding annoyed. My heart is pounding in my ears, almost drowning out their conversation.

I think I hear Béthanie crying.

'I just thought you were better,' she says, in a strange, cracked voice.

Paul says something stern that I don't catch, and then Béthanie makes a sound of defeat.

'Fine,' she says. 'Well, I don't want to be here.'

I hear keys being snatched off the table, and then footsteps. I pin myself against the wall as I realise she's going to come out of the front door and walk right into me. I watch the door open millimetres from my face, grateful for the fig tree's leaves that hide me from view. She stands on the step for a few seconds, breathing in and out with deep shudders. I hold my breath as she wipes the wet from her face and walks down the steps, out of the gate and into the village.

I find Paul in the kitchen, staring darkly at the tablecloth.

He looks up sharply. For a moment, neither of us speak.

'Did you hear any of that?' he asks.

'Not much. Just enough to hear that she was upset.'

He nods slowly.

'What were you talking about?'

He says nothing, a watery smile spreading across his face. I count three, four, five empty wine bottles on the table.

'Come here, coquine,' he says, holding out his arms.

I hang back.

He yawns and begins to rub his eyes. 'It was nothing important. Béthanie just gets upset sometimes. She's very temperamental.'

He beckons me again but I stay rooted to the spot. 'I want to know.'

'Okay, okay.' He sighs. 'She was upset because of you. There's nothing going on,' he hurries to add. 'We got drunk together last Christmas, had a little kiss – nothing more, trust me, she's not my type. Anyway I think she's still a bit hung up on it. Since the divorce. She hasn't exactly got anything else going on, so . . .' He trails off.

I run over his words. They make sense in light of how Béthanie's been with me all week. But something's still off. I try to dredge up the conversation I'd just overheard; Béthanie had seemed annoyed at him for something he wasn't admitting to.

'You haven't got anything to worry about, coquine,' Paul says, stepping towards me.

My face feels like it's on fire.

'I feel guilty.'

He laughs. 'Why?'

I stare at him. About Béthanie, if he's telling the truth; I hadn't known she felt like that. It makes me feel like a character slotted into a plot I don't want to play out. Me the usurping daughter, her the – what? Tossed-aside mother?

'Don't focus on bad energy,' Paul says. 'Not when there's

so much good to go around.' He's close enough now to pull me to him. I can smell the wine on his breath. But it's easy to let myself be taken. He leans down and says, 'It's our last night together, coquine. Let's not spoil it.'

lundi

We set off early in the morning. Paul drives me as far as the out-skirts of Montpellier. From there he'll head north to the slow travel festival, and I've arranged a car share going east to Nice.

'Won't they mind you arriving by car?' I tease.

Paul grins. 'Don't worry, I'll park outside of town and walk in.'

We've spent a lot of the journey laughing. Now that I'm leaving, I feel light and at ease with Paul, and quietly wonder if my decision to leave was the wrong one. But as we trace the green lanes leading back to the main road, even my doubts seem too much effort to commit to.

Just outside of Montpellier, we pull into the motorway lay-by where I've arranged the pick-up. It's hot, the sun streaming in through the open windows. Once we stop, Paul turns and hooks an arm over the back of my chair, unleashing a wave of his scent: dried sweat, incense.

'It's not too late, coquine.' He sighs deeply and plays with a strand of hair at the back of my neck.

I stare at the dashboard. It's still littered with banana skins and nutshells, although this time it doesn't strike me as being messy. I look at the clock on the dashboard; we're a few minutes early.

'Frances?'

'Mmm?'

'You'll come back, won't you? You'll come back to me.'

His hand comes to rest just above my knee.

'I—'

A horn blares from the car behind. Paul checks the rear-view mirror and swears.

'That must be him.'

Paul nods, looking pissed off. I feel a rush of silent relief. We get out and Paul takes my suitcase from the boot. I am suddenly anxious to leave, muttering platitudes about being grateful for his hospitality, wishing him luck at the festival. The door of the car behind us opens and a man in sunglasses steps out.

'Bye—' I begin, but Paul grabs me to him, kissing me hard on the mouth. He doesn't let go for what feels like a long time.

When he does, I don't look back. I wheel my suitcase over to the car behind us, feeling like some item passed between the two men.

PART TWO

lundi

It took most of the day to get to Nice. The autoroute was thronged with people heading south for vacations, and we were often at a standstill. Olivier, the driver, seemed friendly enough, though the opaque black sunglasses he wore throughout the journey gave him an aloofness that counteracted our physical proximity. It turned out he was a single divorcé; his two young daughters lived with his ex-wife outside Nice. For the past twelve years he'd worked as a freelance business consultant, although a lot of the work had dried up since the financial crash, he told me, so he'd started car-sharing to bring in a little extra cash.

He was quietly curious about where I'd come from and where I was going. I told him about BénéBio, that I'd come from a village called Lazeaux and was on my way to another called Malmot, in the Maritime Alps. He'd heard of neither. It was exciting to tell someone about Lazeaux for the first time, to hear how it sounded as a story. I began to gush about the village but soon struggled to convey a sense of it; everything made it sound cultish, rarefied.

'So, it's like a commune?' he asked.

'No, I mean everyone lives near each other, and they share things. But it's more about time I think. Slowing down, having time for little things . . .'

I looked out of the window, at the straggly plants growing in the centre of the motorway.

Olivier laughed to himself. 'I'm sure we'd all live like that if it were possible.'

'What do you mean?'

'Someone's got to be paying for it. I take it they don't work, these BonBio people?'

I thought about it for a few moments.

'Well . . . Patrice drives the school bus, and Paul sells his photos, sometimes—'

Olivier sighed heavily. 'I thought as much.'

'What?'

'It's a fantasy,' he said simply. 'The rest of us live in the real world, and we have to pick up the bill.'

'It's not like that,' I said, feeling stung. 'They're good people.'

But something in his words rang true. Lazeaux *had* seemed dreamlike. Collecting flowers with Béthanie, the preparations for the festival; it had seemed so idyllic in its simplicity.

Olivier cleared his throat. 'So that was your boyfriend who dropped you off?'

'No, that was Paul,' I replied. 'He was my host.'

I internally kicked myself for not lying. Olivier raised his eyebrows but said nothing.

The rest of the journey was punctuated with long stretches of silence. I felt defensive, and gave only blunt answers to Olivier's questions. He'd burst the bubble of the past week too suddenly, and now the outside world was rushing in, complex and hostile.

Beyond the autoroute the earth was arid and yellow, yielding only the scrubby plant life Paul had told me was called garrigue. The land flattened out, rising occasionally to blunt plateaus and shallow crags.

'It's nothing against you,' Olivier said at one point. 'Those types just piss me off.'

'What types?'

'These pseudo-eco-warriors. Who probably go back to their plush flats in the périphérique come winter.'

'But you don't know they're like that. And just because they live differently, and care about the environment—'

Olivier snorted.

I considered for a moment. Their whole lives – Paul's for example – were geared around sustainability; weren't they?

Olivier said he had something to show me. With one hand on the wheel, he unclipped his phone from its holder and began scrolling through photos before handing it to me.

It was hard to know what I was supposed to be looking at. The image showed two large sacks resting on a beach.

They were filled to overflowing with empty plastic bottles and boxes.

'That's about a week's worth,' said Olivier, tapping his card against the reader as we stopped briefly at a tollbooth.

'Of what?'

'Junk. From the sea. My flat's not far from the beach and come summer it's always full of tourists. *City types*,' he said, with contemptuous emphasis. 'They don't know how to treat a place. So after work sometimes I head down to the shore with empty potato sacks. They're the sturdiest. I collect all the rubbish on the beach, then I dive down to get all this junk off the seabed. The next day, I recycle them.'

I looked at the image, then up at Olivier to see if he was joking.

'Sometimes I find treasure too. If you keep going ...' he gestured at the phone.

I swiped on to a series of his findings: hundreds of coins and dirty fragments of jewellery; the single rusting blade of a propeller. It was hard to reconcile the bounty of Olivier's hobbies with the bland stock image I'd had of him before. I felt vaguely guilty, and something like admiration began to stir. I swiped to a close up of a brooch and used my finger and thumb to zoom in. I could see he'd tried to clean it up but the grooves were embedded with dirt, making the motif indiscernible.

'I got a good price for that one,' he said, leaning over. 'Great condition.'

He explained how he had a friend at a university who found buyers for the objects.

'What about museums?' I asked.

He smiled. 'And have them confiscated? They don't thank you for finding these things. It's a choice between the black market or leaving them for the next person.'

I slotted the phone back in its holder. The satnav returned to the screen, showing the route to Nice. It said we were only a few hours away, traffic allowing.

At the next service area we pulled over. There was a McDonald's, a shop selling souvenirs, sweets and drinks, and a large boulangerie from which the smell of freshly baked bread wafted over to the car park. As we got closer, Olivier pointed to the name of the boulangerie, the word 'PAUL' emblazoned in enormous white letters.

'Look!' he said. 'Your host is still with us.'

'Host' – the word sounded somehow different in Olivier's voice. I must have heard it a hundred times in the past week, but never in its Catholic sense, as I did now.

We stepped over the threshold. The boulangerie was dark inside, black walls and furniture. The white letters of 'PAUL' bounced off every surface. I felt a little dizzy. The display cases were lit up from within, as if the baguettes, pastries and rows of buns were glowing with divine light.

Despite my protests, Olivier insisted on driving into the city centre to see me safely onto the bus. We drove past the Jardin Albert I, which boasted clipped lawns, palm trees and ornate and fluted fountains, and was flanked by streets of expensive-looking bistros and boutiques. The pedestrians milling around seemed moneyed and well groomed, clutching purchases and speaking loudly into their phones, or walking side by side in mannered silence. No one seemed to know each other or attempt a greeting. It was a city of strangers.

'Holiday crowds,' Olivier murmured, reading my mind, as we slowed down at a pedestrian crossing.

There was nothing unusual about it – it was the same in Paris, or any other city. But after Lazeaux it seemed remarkable; I felt tangential to the city's tastes: too poor and itinerant to partake in its pleasures.

Olivier spotted a parking space. I quickly scanned my travel notes for the next leg of the journey. My hosts were a couple called Artur and Valerie; all I knew about them was the location of their farm high in the Maritime Alps. I'd need to take two separate buses to get there, arriving around 11 that evening, when Valerie had said she'd meet me in the village square.

We pulled up next to a four-star hotel called l'Étoile Anglaise. Olivier handed me my case from the boot, and I thanked him for bringing me to the city centre. It had been unnecessary, after all; most car shares specified pick-ups and drop-offs at the outskirts only.

Then he leaned in. 'Time for a coffee before you catch your bus?'

The sudden proximity caught me off guard. I saw myself doubled in his shiny lenses.

I tried to decline politely but felt dizzy. Maybe I'd stood up too quickly, after so long in the car. Olivier had his back to the low sun, eclipsing his features. I had the sudden impression of talking to a rock face.

'I don't have very long,' I said. But he'd already leaned over my travel papers and pointed to when the bus was due – an hour from now, underlined in green.

I felt too tired to protest. Loïc's words from a few days earlier bounced around my head: *Frances knows how to be amenable.*

I bought a ticket as I boarded the bus and took a seat at the back, forgetting the driver's face instantly. The route went back through the city centre, past the boutiques and hotels and English bars, back along the promenade past the cool evening sea. I realised I was watching anxiously for Olivier's car, and berated myself for the things he had managed to extricate from me before I got on the bus: a photo taken against the yellow parasols of the café we sat in, a mobile number I'd only remembered to fake after the sixth digit.

The bus route went northwest of the city. We drove through a large valley, tracing the meander of a wide, mostly dried-up river. The land either side was sparsely dotted with disused warehouses, agricultural nurseries and pépinières. After the boutiques and bistros in Nice, this sudden dereliction and decay came as a shock. The other passengers were mostly older women, who I presumed were local to the villages and hamlets we passed through. They gazed silently out of the windows, sun-aged and liver-spotted, departing in clumps of two or three when their stops came.

The mountains that loomed either side of us were too tall to be seen from the bus windows. Instead they cast shadows, darkening the valley. Further inland, we began to trace the foothills on the western side of the valley. The bus was almost empty when it eventually stopped outside a crumbling hotel.

'Ici pour Malmot!'

I stepped out, and watched the bus pull off and disappear around the corner. The hotel was abandoned, or perhaps closed for repairs. Other than the faint lights of Nice flickering in the distance, there was no sign of civilisation. According to the timetable, the bus to Malmot was only a twenty-minute wait. I sat on the gravel, as the sky grew dark around me. I checked my phone, unsurprised to find I had no signal.

The time that the bus was due came and went. Perhaps Valerie had sent me an outdated timetable, perhaps there was no bus into the mountains tonight, perhaps I would be stranded until morning. The doubt solidified into grim certainty. Unseen things flew through the air and landed on my skin, and I was half grateful, half resentful for the susurrating cicadas, giving form and rhythm to my fears.

Sitting there reminded me of waiting for Paul before we met. It seemed unthinkable that there'd been a time I hadn't known Paul, hadn't known who I was waiting for. I rocked back and forth between the two moments, before Paul and after, wondering what he was doing. It occurred to me that if I'd stayed with him in Lazeaux I wouldn't be alone on the hillside in the dark.

Minutes passed like slow hours. By the time I heard an engine, trundling far off at the foot of the hill, I felt that I had grown another body entirely, one suffused with the emptiness of the valley and the coarse, fragrant garrigue.

The bus was actually more of a minivan, driven by a large man with a cloud of white hair. As he opened the door I saw he was wearing a blue Hawaiian shirt. The buttons were pulling at the front over his belly, and the pattern shone garishly in the light pouring out from the cab. He greeted me and helped load my case into the back.

'Just you?' he grunted.

'Yes.'

I saw him pause and take stock of my accent. 'American?'

'English.'

I thought I could smell alcohol on his breath. He moved lightly, and hummed under his breath as he got back in the driver's seat and started up the engine.

The darkness kept me from seeing how high we'd climbed. We were still driving at an incline, and I could see only the road ahead lit by the headlights. It was worryingly narrow, with tight curlicue bends. I caught the driver's eye in the rear-view mirror.

'Relax,' he said. 'I can do this journey in my sleep.'

I held his gaze, disbelieving.

'Seriously,' he went on. 'I've done it twice a day, up and down the mountains, for the past twenty years. Haven't missed a day. Not for rain or snow!'

'And it's okay in the dark?'

I saw his silhouette shrug. 'No bother. Sometimes it's dark in the morning when I drive the other way, back down from Malmot.'

'Why so early?'

'Why do you think? For work. There's nothing to do up here. Everyone works in Nice, or nearby. But it's a two-hour ride, each way.'

I checked my phone. Still no signal, and nearly 11 p.m. Valerie would already be waiting in the square.

'You here to volunteer with Artur and Valerie?' The driver called from the front.

'How did you know?'

He laughed. 'Why else would you come all the way out here?'

The man chattered away. By coincidence, it transpired that Malmot was soon to stage a music festival, jazz and other things. The men had already begun to erect a chapiteau in the village square. But I was due to leave the day before the festival began. In all honesty I was relieved to be missing it; it would have stolen from the novelty of the festival in Lazeaux.

'You should change your dates, if you can,' he said.

'I can't. Maybe if Valerie and Artur had given me notice—'

'Ha,' he grunted. He met my eyes in the mirror then looked away. 'They keep to themselves, that's all.'

I tried to press him but he wouldn't say any more on the subject. I changed tack and asked how he'd become the sole driver on such a perilous route. He said he used to be a driver in the army, and that his first posting as a young man had been in Tahiti.

My heart made an irregular thud. I leaned forward. 'Tahiti?'

'Yes, have you been?'

'No, but—'

'It's paradise.'

'Even as a soldier?'

'Especially as a soldier! I think of it every day – the girls, the booze, every evening dancing – you've never seen such a beautiful place.'

I stared out of the window, my thoughts drifting back to Paul. Maybe he and the driver had been there at the same time? Had they been friends, drinking partners? Outside, the clouds had almost cleared, and the moon begun to give back some light and shape to the valleys. In its shapes I saw overlays of imagined Tahitian landscapes; hadn't Paul said that he was always reminded of the island, by the sight of Tagire at dawn? We rounded the side of the rock face and a small cluster of lights came into view straight ahead.

'There's Malmot,' said the driver.

Judging by the distribution of its lights, the village appeared to teeter precariously on top of the mountain, as if it might fall into the darkness beneath at any moment.

'Is anyone waiting for you?'

'Yes – Valerie said she'd be in the square.'

It was now 11.30. I felt bad for keeping Valerie up so late. As we pulled into the square, the driver spoke again.

'Okay, this is you. I'm Francis, by the way.'

I looked up sharply. 'Me too. With an "e".'

Francis made an amused noise.

'See you on the way back down, Frances with an e.'

I hadn't expected Valerie to be so childlike. She was sitting on the rim of the fountain in the centre of the small square, hugging her legs to her chest. When she stood up to greet me she seemed even smaller, with a boyish body and cropped brown hair. She looked incredibly tired. She nodded to Francis as he backed out of the square, and indicated for me to follow her. We walked along a dark, deserted street, then for a long time down a bumpy dirt track. Valerie shone a torch in front of our feet to light the way.

My broken suitcase bumped along noisily beside us. Valerie eyed it and said she would have brought the truck if she'd known. She asked about my journey offhandedly. I thought about telling her that Francis had been late, but didn't – she hadn't asked in a way that implied interest in the answer. After several minutes a few lights came into view. Dogs began to bark as we approached. Another light flickered on and two collies appeared, the outline of a building behind them.

'That's the house,' Valerie said, flicking the torchlight. 'Come meet us there for breakfast in the morning.'

She turned to walk in the opposite direction, lighting up grass and stones. 'You sleep out here.'

I followed her feet and the torchlight downhill to a small stone outhouse. She opened the wooden door with a creak and flicked on the light. The collies rushed in around our legs. The interior consisted of one long room with three single beds and a small chest of drawers. One of the beds was made up with sheets. Valerie pointed to a shower and toilet behind a curtain at the far end.

'Any questions?'

I looked back at Valerie. There were deep lines around her eyes that belied how childlike she'd looked from afar. I shook my head.

'Okay. We'll eat around half seven. See you in the morning.'

She shooed the collies out and closed the door behind her. I watched the torchlight bouncing in bright drops, back the way we'd come.

mardi

Early the next morning I was woken by the sun on my face, teasing through the thin curtains. I stared groggily at the unfamiliar ceiling. Outside, the birds were in full flow. I rolled out of bed and dressed quickly for a day of work: canvas shorts and an old vest. I checked my watch: 7.15 a.m. A little time to explore before breakfast.

I stepped out onto the stone ledge and took in the view. On the slope closest to me was Valerie and Artur's farm, where crops and polytunnels filled the wide verges carved out of the hillside. Below that, the valley was criss-crossed with dry yellow fields. In the far distance, mountains rose against the skyline in deep blues, white clouds nipping at their peaks. I looked again and realised the white peaks weren't in fact clouds but snow, sprinkled on the blue and grey rock like icing sugar.

I thought briefly about Tagire – its lilac peak seemed a

paltry spectre in comparison. I stood still a while, breathing in the warm, honey-like air. A faint breeze whispered up from the valley and lifted my hair. Two thoughts dovetailed in my mind: the first, a wish that Paul was here to take charge and show me what to do, and the second, relief that he wasn't. I squinted at the sun. It was climbing quickly; by mid-day it would be too hot to work.

I made my way up to the house, stepping over rocks in the uneven path. Piles of junk were strewn through the grass as high as my knees, rusting husks of disused machinery and scraps of old furniture. The house was a bungalow, squat and earth-red. The collies lazed outside in the sun. They rushed up to me, and I fussed over them until Valerie came out holding a cafetière, a thin smile on her face.

She gestured for me to sit at the wooden picnic table set outside the porch, overlooking the valley. I sat so I could see the view, then moved round, embarrassed, to a seat facing the house when she shook her head.

'Did you sleep?' she asked, sitting across from me and staring out at the valley.

'Yes, thanks.' I noticed she hadn't said 'well'. 'And you?'

She nodded. Her mouth became so small it almost disappeared. She poured coffee into three glazed earthenware cups.

'It's stunning,' I said, turning round to indicate the valley. She nodded again and lit a roll-up. I watched the stick-insect figure of a farmer begin to drive a tractor through his field, far below.

We sat a while longer, sipping our coffee. Valerie gazed

in an unfocused way at the mountains in the distance. She seemed able to ignore my presence at her table with such well-practised ease that I didn't feel uncomfortable or an inconvenience to her, more like a stock character, temporary and nonspecific. I wondered how many other BénéBio volunteers had sat where I did now.

After a few minutes, a man stepped out of the bungalow. He was tall, tanned and muscular, with sandy, shoulder-length hair. He held a baguette in one hand, and used the other to cover his mouth as he yawned, eyes closed. He only clocked my presence at the table when he opened them.

'Salut.' He nodded brusquely as we exchanged names.

He sat down at the end of the table and tore a hunk off the baguette. Valerie handed him a newspaper. The round glasses perched low on his nose offset his shabby T-shirt. He looked about a decade younger than Valerie, who, I thought, as she tore a tiny portion of bread from the baguette and passed it to me, could be an older relative.

He scanned the newspaper then looked up at me.

'You with BénéBio?'

'Yes.'

'English?'

'Yes.'

He nodded slowly, chewing in silence.

'Where's Lili?' asked Valerie.

Artur shrugged. He muttered something to Valerie that I missed, and they proceeded to have a conversation that was too rapid for me to follow. I picked up the odd word: market, valley, morning, weekend. I chewed the dry bread and looked out at the view, trying not to compare the meal with the morning array of jams and pastries at Noa Noa. When I turned back round, Valerie was looking pointedly at Artur, who was absorbed again in the newspaper. Valerie tapped the ash from her cigarette into a little ceramic dish.

'She'll be late for school.'

Artur sighed and stood up, unhooking his legs from the table. He disappeared inside, calling Lili's name. I remembered what Francis the bus driver had said the night before: *they keep to themselves.*

'Come on,' Valerie said to me. 'I'll show you around.'

The sun was already hot on the back of our necks. I followed Valerie between beds of chard and courgettes, through the polytunnels dense with tomato vines and aubergine plants. The humidity was dizzying after only a few seconds, and Valerie advised me to keep a bottle of water on me at all times. I noticed where the heat had concentrated into two red blotches on her cheeks.

We walked on, Valerie pointing at the herb beds, the fruit trees heavy with apples and plums, the chicken coop. The latter was a large enclosure with scratchy dry earth, plastered with feathers and chicken shit. There was a little wooden hut for them to sleep in at night. Valerie showed me how to open and close the door by pulling on an old blue rope.

She explained my duties, and the pattern of each day. We'd

work in the morning from 8 until lunch, and then again in the evenings once it was cooler. In the afternoon I was free to do as I pleased, but she recommended I didn't attempt anything too ambitious in the heat.

I didn't unpack until later in the afternoon. There was a stale smell coming from my suitcase, so I kept the door open to air it out. I tried to shake the wrinkles from my clothes but they seemed deeply ingrained; I folded them away again with the same creases. I took out my camera and flicked back through some of the photos. Blurry Tour de France cyclists, gangly Paul on the return from Bouéry, shots of the girls in our waitress outfits for the festival.

I noticed it when I went to put my camera back in the suitcase: a bag made of pale pink voile, which I'd never seen before, nestled among my clothes. I pulled it out and undid the strings, tipping the contents onto my palm. A flurry of dried rose petals, and the bracelet I'd seen in Paul's room: coarse and khaki with feathers and beads. The word *TEHURA* in a rough font. I stared at the bracelet. Paul must have snuck it into my bag – but when?

I was so distracted that I jumped at the sound of a knock. Artur was standing in the doorway.

'It's cooled down a bit,' he said. 'We're going to get another hour of work in before dinner.'

I nodded. Artur was looking quizzical. I became aware then of the bracelet in my hand, the rose petals strewn over my lap.

I tossed the bracelet into the suitcase and got to my feet. 'Where are we working?'

It wasn't until dinner that I met Lili, who'd got home from school at some point in the afternoon. Valerie and I had made a warm salad, and now that everything was laid out she lit a few tea lights and called, 'Lili! À table!'

We sat in the same positions as breakfast. Lili appeared a few moments later. She was around nine, with skin as dark as Artur's and sun-streaked hair streaming from a centre parting. She had a long face and looked incredibly serious, like some kind of child saint. She walked over and kissed me on both cheeks, before sitting down next to her mother.

Valerie lit a roll-up and told Lili to start eating because it would get cold and that Artur would come up when he was ready.

'But where *is* he?' Lili whined.

'He's fixing the crates for market. You *know* how busy market day is.'

Lili said nothing and began to pick at her food. Valerie smoked and ignored her plate altogether. Artur finally turned up five or ten minutes later, emerging from one of the paths leading down into the garden.

'You've started,' he said as he sat down, more as a statement than a question. He took off his glasses and used the hem of his dirty T-shirt to polish the lenses. I glimpsed the groove of his hipbone and looked away instantly.

Valerie stubbed out her cigarette. 'It was going to get cold. We called you.'

'I didn't hear.' He reached for the salt and pepper.

After that we ate in silence. Artur ate mechanically, aggressively, as if to make a point. The candles flickered gently in the breeze; threads of blue cloud began to streak across the skyline. The bright spot where the sun had been, just above the snowy peaks, turned dull.

'Oh I almost forgot,' Valerie said, addressing me. 'We're going away for a few days. For a family wedding. Near Nice, en bas. We'll be back at the weekend.'

Valerie, Artur and Lili all looked at me.

'Okay.' I tried not to sound too surprised. 'When are you leaving?'

'Probably tomorrow, around dinner time. The day after that is market day so we'll stay with friends and go from there. We meant to tell you sooner but, you know, the date was set after we knew you were coming.'

I nodded. 'So . . . will you leave me a list of things to do?'

Valerie gave a small smile. 'No. You can do whatever you like.'

I tried to smile back. The prospect of a few days alone on the farm didn't fill me with excitement.

'As long as you feed the chickens.'

I nodded.

'And the dogs.'

'I don't have school tomorrow,' said Lili. 'I can show you the way up to the village, if you want?'

I smiled. 'I'd like that.'

'There's a ruined castle on top of the hill. It's cool.'

She grinned and looked down at her food, as if embarrassed. The table went quiet again. Valerie looked furtively at Artur, the ghost of her smile still visible. Artur looked back. Their looks were impossible to read.

mercredi

Next morning, I woke up to find the sky had changed overnight. Instead of sun there was a low-hanging greyness, and everything bristled with the static of an oncoming storm. It was uncomfortably hot. Valerie and I worked quietly picking green beans, packing them into the plastic crates they'd be taking to market the next day. We spoke little; Valerie was clearly used to working alone or maybe with volunteers who talked among themselves and were happy to leave her in peace. I was lost in my own thoughts too, thinking about Paul and Lazeaux. I'd put on the bracelet that morning, as if it would somehow keep me company.

After lunch, Lili sprung up from the table and announced she'd be taking me up to the village. She marched off towards the scrubland behind the bungalow.

'This is the quick way,' she said. 'Grown-ups never use it.'

I followed, wondering whether I counted as grown-up in Lili's local cosmology; if I wasn't her and I wasn't Valerie, I must be something vaguely in between.

The quick way was barely a path, and I wasn't as nimble as Lili, whose feet easily found a way between the thorny bushes and loose shingle. Her long hair rippled over her back, and I saw that one section had been braided with lime-green thread. There were pink and orange beads at the bottom that clicked as she clambered up. After a few minutes she began to pant loudly and un-self-consciously, dog-like. I asked her about the braid and she said she'd got it done on holiday, in Ibiza. An old woman had braided it, and she'd made Lili sit between her legs. The woman smelled bad and it was weird to sit there, Lili said.

By the time we reached the road, I was panting too. We turned round to look at the view. The bungalow was small beneath us, barely halfway up the slope leading down to the valley. The sky was still thick and overcast. In the distance a dark cloud brooded over a hill, rain lashing down in columns beneath it. But here it was dry for now. We trudged up the road towards the village.

The road led to the square where Valerie had met me from the bus. Around the old stone fountain in its centre stood the scaffold skeleton of a chapiteau, smaller than the one in Lazeaux. There must have been about twenty men in the square. A few stood on stepladders, fixing the frame, but the majority sat on chairs, shaded by the one stretch of white canopy already in place. The rest of the fabric lay in bundles at their feet. They sat too far away for me to tell if they were talking, but they had noticed our arrival, and were now looking over. I felt uncomfortable in an indistinct way, and protective of Lili. I started to shepherd her away when a voice called out my name.

I turned round with a sinking stomach. Francis the bus driver was strolling towards us with a huge smile on his face. He was wearing another Hawaiian shirt, this time jade green. We kissed and I began to introduce Lili, but it transpired they already knew each other; Francis occasionally drove the bus she took to school in the next village.

'So, Frances with an e. How is the farm?' He seemed excitable and expectant. There was a band of sweat beneath his hairline.

I suddenly felt very tired.

'Fine,' I said, wanting to steer the conversation away from me. 'How's the chapiteau?'

Francis looked back over his shoulder. 'Oh, not bad. We'll get there. It's hard work, and the weather's not good today. But we should have it ready for next week.'

I raised a hand to cover my eyes, peering at the structure. Hadn't the chapiteau in Lazeaux been erected in two or three days flat?

'Who's "Tehura"?' Francis asked, slurring slightly as he pointed to my wrist.

I followed his gaze to the bracelet Paul had given me. 'Oh this? It's not a name. It's – it was a gift from Tahiti.' I dropped my wrist to show it to Lili, who wanted to see. 'It means "precious", or "beautiful", I think.'

Francis snorted loudly. 'Well maybe,' he said with a dismissive shrug.

'What do you mean?'

'Maybe it meant that once. But Tehura is a girl's name, in Tahiti. About the most common one you'll find.'

I stared at him for a few moments. His eyes were clouded, and this time I could definitely smell alcohol on his breath. I looked over at the other men and saw the empty bottles strewn around their feet.

'Are you sure?'

Francis nodded. I found myself struggling to keep focus. I saw the movement of his head as if through mottled glass.

'Bye, Francis,' I heard myself say. 'I promised Lili she could show me the castle—'

Not long after we'd reached the ruins, the weather broke. The sand-coloured stone spotted with rain, and soon darkened all over. Lili led me to the highest point of the hill. Behind us, the village veered away down the hillside. On every other side was a sheer drop to the valley floor.

I squinted through the rain. The cloud was low overhead, limiting visibility. I couldn't see the mountains in the distance, but could just make out long, dry lines snaking over the land below. Sparse bushes were scattered either side of them and I realised they were dried-up rivers, like the one we'd followed on the bus from Nice.

Through the thick air we saw a bolt of lightning. I felt Lili shiver beside me.

'Come on,' I said. 'Let's go back.'

Lili nodded. On the way down I asked her about the ruins. They hadn't been much to look at, a few crumbling walls and evidence of doorways. There'd been no visible attempt to preserve them, no information placards or heritage signs. Lili didn't know anything about the castle, who had lived in it or when.

'But in summer, all the boys camp in it and tell ghost stories to each other.'

'Do you go too?'

She shook her head and shot me a look full of disdain. In that second I saw Valerie's face. But Lili knew her voice had given her away. It had been wistful, and full of longing.

That night I lay awake, restless. The dogs stayed up barking for what seemed like hours. They'd been tied to long leads overnight so they couldn't get far from the bungalow, but with enough give for them to strain and howl at the dirt track leading to the village.

They'd been quiet when Artur, Lili and Valerie left for the wedding. But from the moment I turned my light out and tried to sleep, they went berserk. At first I thought they weren't used to being left alone. And then, as I drifted in and out of sleep, I began to be gripped by fears. Maybe they were barking at intruders? At someone who knew I was here alone? When I thought about my circumstances in an objective way, my vulnerability dawned on me for the first time, but only as an impersonal, distant matter of fact, as if I was a character in a story, whose situation represents their symbolic isolation: alone in a foreign country, on the side of a mountain without mobile reception, in a small stone hut with a rusty bolt on the door. Soon I began to resent Valerie and Artur for leaving me alone, for treating the character in their charge so poorly.

Every few minutes the dogs would fall silent and I'd go numb with relief that whoever it was had gone away. Then the barking would start up again with renewed intensity. I stared at the moonlight dappled on the wall. I heard rustling noises outside, or thought I did. I became convinced that someone was watching me through the window. My heart began to bark like the dogs. I looked at my watch. It was around 3 a.m. Had I slept at all? It occurred to me that I needed a weapon. Yes – in case I needed to protect myself. I stumbled around the room, not wanting to turn the light on in case it called attention to me. But the room was bare; I couldn't find anything.

Then I remembered the rusting piles of junk outside. There'd be something useful there. But I'd have to go outside. I paused, agonised, then decided it was worth the risk. I unbolted the door, trying not to make a sound. Moonlight flooded over me as I stepped onto the porch. The grass was bathed in its strange light, but it seemed safe, for now. I groped around in the junk piles for a few minutes, not knowing what I was looking for. And then I found it. What felt like a scaffolding pole, about the length of my arm. I practised swinging it through the air. It was heavy, but not difficult to raise above my head. It would do. I tiptoed back inside and bolted the door. I threw myself onto the bed, leaping from the floor to the mattress the way I had as a child, in case there was someone underneath that would grab my ankles if I got too close.

jeudi

In the morning, I woke up dazed and hot. My head was thick with disordered sleep and the comedown of adrenaline. I rolled over and felt something hard and cool against my skin. The scaffolding pole. The events of the night before came back, and in the morning sunlight they seemed almost funny. Had I really been so terrified that I stumbled around outside looking for a 'weapon'?

I showered and dressed, wandered up to the house and fed the dogs and chickens. On the bench outside, I had a little breakfast and sat facing the valley, a basin slowly filling with sun. It was still early, and the day seemed to stretch endlessly before me. I made a loose plan of going up to the village, maybe seeing if I could find a path into the mountains. The dogs sauntered over then lay down to snooze at my feet. I envied them for not needing a plan at all.

I checked my emails before leaving. Valerie had said I could use the internet while they were away, so I turned on the switch she'd shown me in the living room, behind the ancient desktop. It flickered slowly into life. The bungalow had an inert, stale feel to it. Maybe it was the rounded, burrow-like corridors, the thin netting in place of doors, or the way the walls crumpled into the mountain at the back of the house. In Lili's room it was especially bad, the back wall so uneven it seemed the rock face was pushing through it.

Artur and Valerie's room, facing the valley, was the largest and had the best light. The walls were a pale strawberry red, with matching net curtain where the sun cast a pink grid over the duvet. Two bookshelves were filled with old paperbacks and silver-framed photos. Everything was covered in a thick layer of dust. I noticed a stack of notebooks by the bedside table but had no desire to open them. I vaguely wondered which side of the bed was Artur's and which side Valerie's. The house didn't seem alive in the way Noa Noa had. It was just a background, refusing to come into focus.

In my inbox were the usual bank statements and newsletters; dross from sites I hadn't unsubscribed from; a few messages from friends who I hadn't got round to telling why I'd had to leave Paris. Nothing from A.B. – but what had I expected? It seemed I hadn't missed much during my week off-grid.

I scrolled absently for a bit then checked my junk folder, just in case. The page opened up. Nothing was out of place. And then, sandwiched between an offer on Rolexes and discounts on Viagra was an email from Paul, with an empty subject line. My whole body was alert as I clicked on it.

Coquine, how are you? I miss you. The slow travel festival is good. Seeing friends, lots of music and dancing. I am busy with visitors to my exhibition most of the day, but so far I've only sold postcards. I keep thinking I see you in the crowd. You'd like it here. There's a family of eight who have cycled from Seville, and last night there was a film screening about a pregnant couple that walked from Lyon to Jerusalem. It took them nine months, and the woman had the baby when they got there. The female body has always amazed me but now I have more respect than ever. Anyway, my love, I must go. Keep in touch.

Paul.

(P.S. Did you find the present?)

I re-read the message several times. Hours seemed to pass before I logged off, shut down the computer and returned to the sun, feeling sluggish and restless at the same time. I'd been excited to discover the message but reading it had had the same anti-climactic effect as having no message at all. It wasn't enough. The sun was scorching. I hung back under the porch's shade, slipping one foot out of my sandal to draw a spiral in the dust with my big toe. One of the dogs wandered up to me sleepily and began to lick it. I looked down at the collie. It was the most affection I'd had in days, and I didn't even know the dog's name. I asked if it was hungry. The collie looked up at me, and then continued its licking. I put out some food and fresh water just in case.

Just before noon, I retraced the straggly path up to the village that Lili had shown me. Today was even hotter than yesterday's pre-storm humidity, and by the time I reached the road my clothes were damp with sweat. This time, the village was deserted. The men seemed not to have made much progress on the chapiteau, and the square was quiet enough that I could hear the water burbling from the fountain. I pressed on to the main street, past the track to the castle ruins, past the road leading to the mairie, where several tables and chairs were scattered beneath red and white parasols that shaded their elderly occupants.

The church bell began to peal over the courtyard. Noon. The sun hit the parasols flatly while customers of the small café sipped beer in the shade. I thought about sitting down and ordering a coke, but the only free table had no parasol. I sat anyway and took out a book from Artur and Valerie's shelf, *MYSTICISME & ECOLOGIE*. After only a minute or two I felt my skin begin to slip against the plastic. The page was white hot and the words were swimming; I couldn't read a thing and left without ordering.

Away from the courtyard, I was plunged back into the empty quiet of the main street. I was about to head back to the farm when I noticed a crudely painted wooden sign next to a set of stone steps: *CÉRAMIQUES PAR MIRACLE*. 'Ceramics by miracle'. What did it mean? The letters were a bright sky blue, with lilac squiggles and polka dots filling the space around them. As I got closer, I realised I'd misread the word. It wasn't 'Miracle' but 'Mireille'. Ceramics by Mireille. Underneath, in a smaller font, I read: *24 RUE DE COLINE, MALMOT. OUVERT MARDI–DIMANCHE 11–6.*

The door was slightly ajar, and inside I could see a wall of shelves filled with jugs, plates and cups in dull blues and browns. I climbed up and pushed the door. The room was surprisingly light and high ceilinged, and seemed to be both a studio and shop display, filled with ceramics at various stages of production. The floor was busy with sacks of clay, and the shelves running all round the room were lined with finished pieces, their glazes glinting in the light.

In the centre of the room, a young woman was sitting at a potter's wheel with her back to me. She hummed as she worked, keeping time with the whir of the wheel and the light smacking sound of the wet clay in her hands. Her thick brown hair was braided into a single fishtail plait that snaked down over her spine; its frizzed end dangled just above her coccyx.

She turned round when I knocked, and I saw that she wasn't young at all. She had a girlish face but must have been in her fifties. She smiled and turned off the wheel, standing up to greet me.

'Bienvenue,' she purred, gripping my shoulders and kissing me roughly on both cheeks. She was a good head taller than me, and her accent was thick and strong. I couldn't place it. Her skin was glowing, the skin of a pale woman who has slowly acclimatised to the sun, the freckles joined up to give the illusion of a tan. She stepped back and wiped her hands on her apron.

'Are you a visitor?' she asked, with an inflection on 'visitor' that made it sound like an endangered species.

I nodded and looked around. 'You have a lovely studio.'

'Thank you,' she said, following my eyes as if she was also seeing the room for the first time. 'Yes,' she said, 'it's my life!' Her eyes were warm and dry. 'How long are you here for?'

'Just a week, volunteering.'

'With Valerie and Artur?'

It seemed everyone knew about Artur and Valerie's volunteers.

'So what are you escaping from?' she continued, then laughed. 'Sorry, I meant, what do you do otherwise? Are you a student?'

'Yes.' I nodded. 'Or I was. I finished before the summer.'

She brushed some plaster dust off a wooden stool and gestured for me to sit down. Would I like some fresh mint tea? I nodded, and she disappeared into another room. When she came back she looked slightly flustered, but apparently pleased to have company. She poured from a blue teapot and handed me a matching cup with no handle. I took a sip, immediately scalding my tongue. The tea was almost painfully sweet.

She asked me how I came to be in Malmot and I told her about working in the archives after graduating. She said she didn't care much for Paris, didn't like the people, and seemed pleased that I'd left the capital to come south. The manuscript seemed to pique her interest, and she told me to talk to Artur about it, as he had an interest in that sort of thing. I told her I hadn't spoken to Artur long enough to get any sense of him as a person and, in any case, he, Valerie and Lili had gone away for a few days.

'Gone away where?' she asked.

'I'm not sure. Somewhere near Nice, for a family wedding or something. They haven't left me any work to do.' I felt like I was babbling.

She raised her eyebrows. 'Oh! So what are you going to do?'

I shrugged. 'I thought I'd start with exploring the village, but – I think I've already seen most of it. This afternoon I was going to try and find a way into the mountains, go on a walk or something.'

'Well there are lots of beautiful walks nearby.' She paused. 'But you have to know where to start; the mountains are so wild and dry up here.'

She began to tell me about a young couple on a walking holiday who had gone missing two summers ago.

'They were fit, and experienced, but just one step off the right path is all it takes—' She sighed and tucked a strand of hair behind her ear.

She seemed lost in remembrance for a few moments, and then offered to show me where the paths were.

'We could walk together, if you like, as long as you don't mind waiting until it's cooler and I've closed up the studio.'

I replied that I'd love to, and that it was kind of her to offer.

'I have to walk, otherwise I become a pudding, you see?' She slapped her apron-covered thighs with a laugh. I smiled. She looked down at my flip-flops. 'Do you have proper shoes?'

'I have sandals.'

She sighed. 'You need walking boots. Proper ones. What size are you?'

'Five . . . thirty-eight, I think.'

'Great. You will wear Anaïs's shoes.' She didn't make it sound like a choice. 'See you at six?'

I loitered for a few seconds but she started humming again and turned her back to me, hunting for something on a shelf. 'See you, then,' I called. The sound of humming followed me out. It was only halfway down the street, when the tune faded from earshot, that it occurred to me I hadn't asked her name.

When I returned that evening it was not yet six, but the woman I presumed was Mireille was already stood outside the shop waiting. She smiled on seeing me approach and held up a pair of hiking shoes. Her long plait had disappeared, and instead her hair was braided to her head like a laurel wreath.

'Here.' She pressed the shoes into my hands. I sat on the step and wrestled my hot feet into them. They seemed to fit fine. 'You can leave those here and pick them up later,' she said, pointing to the sandals in my hands. I thanked her and she locked them in the studio. My attention snagged for a moment; no one had locked anything in Lazeaux.

We introduced ourselves properly. She was indeed Mireille, and smiled when I told her my name.

'Like the saint!'

'Different spelling.'

We walked up the main street, past the empty square and half-built chapiteau. We took a road uphill to the mairie that looked like a dead end. Mireille pressed on. The road curved behind the building and thinned to a dirt track. We were soon surrounded by trees on either side, trekking through a forest I hadn't known was close by. The land fell away on either side of us, and every now and then the white valley glimmered through the trees. The air was mild and fragrant. Mireille was right; evenings were better for walking. We kept a steady pace. The only sounds were our footsteps rustling the undergrowth, and the rhythmic slosh of Mireille's water bottle.

'So are you all right at Valerie and Artur's by yourself?'

'Yes, fine.' I blinked.

She gave me a sidelong look.

'I think I'd be a bit pissed off,' she said. 'That they'd left me alone up here.'

Her directness caught me off-guard.

'Well – I did wonder why they didn't tell me sooner,' I said carefully, as if Valerie and Artur could somehow hear me. 'But they have their own lives to live, and I'm the one who's imposing on them.'

She raised her eyebrows. I noticed a crucifix dangling from her neck. 'Are you always this docile?' she asked.

It sounded like an accusation. I felt heat rising to my face. 'What do you mean?'

'Nothing, really. I'm just over-cautious, I suppose, about young women travelling alone. I started late, myself. When I was too old to attract any danger. Now I mostly travel with my girlfriend, Anaïs. You'll notice her shoes are well worn.'

I waited for her to continue, but she seemed to have finished on the topic. We walked on. The sun was lowering behind us, lighting the larch a dim orange. The white stones beneath our feet turned lilac.

'It's nice to have someone to walk with,' she said after a while. 'Anaïs doesn't like this path, and no one from the village comes here.'

'Why not?'

'Not interested. Some of them graze their goats a bit on the next mountain, but other than that . . .'

She made a popping sound through her lips. It was akin to a shrug. There was a definite lilt to her accent that I couldn't place – German? Austrian?

I asked how long she'd lived in Malmot.

She thought for a moment. 'Well – it will be almost ten years. Ten years!' It seemed to be news to her too. 'But I'm from Alsace, originally. Do you know it?'

I shook my head.

'It's a very different place. I think that's why they don't like me much here.'

'Who?'

Mireille looked at me with a playful smile on her face. 'The villagers. They tend not to like outsiders in general. Like Artur and Valerie.'

'But they're from Nice, aren't they? Or nearby, at least. Lili told me.'

We'd reached a clearing. The grass stretched out like the lawn of a grand estate. Mireille reached down to shake a stone from her shoe.

'When you live somewhere this isolated, even the next village is foreign to you,' she said. 'Although half of them aren't from here, anyway.'

'Where are they from?'

'Mafia families who stayed on. That's the only business up here in the mountains now. No industry left. I think I'd go mad if I was here all the time. I go down to visit the sisters in Nice every month. They keep me sane.'

'So why do you stay?'

'You're very inquisitive.'

'Sorry.'

She laughed. 'No, it's good. Why wouldn't you want to know? Who wouldn't want to know everything if they could?'

I didn't know how to answer. The sky seemed suddenly very big, and I had the feeling that our conversation could go anywhere.

At one point we began to descend; the trees thickened and then suddenly gave way to ankle-high scrub. I picked wild thyme and crushed it between my fingers. We stopped on a plateau that had views on either side. To the right, our route had curved enough that Malmot was back in view. Its buildings dotted the tip of the mountain, and reminded me a little of Bouéry, the hilltop town I'd cycled to with Paul on that awful bike. But Malmot's mountain seemed colossal in comparison. The drop was sheer to our left and the valley stretched at least a mile across, with dry striations of blue and brown. Mountains rose up opposite, rocky and tree-topped like our own.

'Are you tired?' Mireille asked.

I shook my head.

'Well, I've never been further than this, and we still have to walk back.'

I noticed her cheeks were flushed, and that several hairs had come away from her braid, frizzed by the heat.

On the way back, Mireille told me how she'd ended up in Malmot. It was a sad story, and I had a hard time reconciling what she told me with her cheerful disposition. She'd grown up poor in Alsace, and had drifted between low-paid secretarial and sales jobs. There'd been a husband. He ran a garage and drank. Sometimes he beat her, but it was never anything to write to the papers about, she said. They were childless. She was relieved when he ran off, though everyone else seemed to think her life was over. Then, at forty, she was diagnosed with cancer. The doctor informed her it was terminal, and advised her to take up a hobby.

She'd never had a hobby in her life, she said, unless you counted housework. She moved to Strasbourg, into a small apartment with a balcony. A hobby was supposed to help weather the inevitable storm of treatment, she told me, with a snort of derision. She tried knitting, painting, collage and jewellery-making. She hated it all. Then in a last-ditch attempt she signed up for a ceramics class, and it was as if her hands had been craving the material her whole life. She stayed for the full course, and it was during one of these classes she met Anaïs. Anaïs from a village close to Nice, who happened to be holidaying in Strasbourg.

I was hanging on her every word. 'And then what?'

Mireille shrugged, a small smile on her lips. 'It was very simple. We fell in love. She knew I was sick. We came here anyway. Anaïs heard from a friend there was a house for sale in the village, with a shop on the ground floor. She said it could be my studio. The whole thing was ridiculous, but we just did it. Had nothing to lose. We've been here since.'

I was burning with questions. 'But—'

She cut me off with a laugh, anticipating my question. 'Yes, I got better. It was a miracle. I was healed.'

'Healed?'

'Yes, by Mary. She is my namesake, after all.'

I faltered, looked again at the crucifix. 'You're religious?'

'Of course!' She looked at me as if I'd just grown another head. 'Baby Jesus is my daddy; sweet Mary is my mother. They take care of me . . .' She tailed off with a faraway expression on her face. At least the remark about seeing her 'sisters' made sense now; she must have been referring to a convent.

'And do your sisters know about Anaïs?'

She nodded brightly.

'And they don't mind?'

She rolled her eyes. 'Don't be so old fashioned! They live with dozens of women. It's like ancient Lesbos.' Her eyes were teasing.

'Sorry. My mother's Catholic too. But a different kind. Very strict ...' Suddenly, a word from a few days ago came back to me. The autoroute stop, the host, buns glowing in the dark ... 'Mireille, do you take the Eucharist?'

She nodded. 'Although not much. The wafer has gluten in it.'

'Why do they call the sacramental bread "the host"? What does it mean?'

'Didn't you have a Catholic upbringing?'

I shrugged.

'*Hostia*,' she said. 'It's Latin. It means "sacrificial animal".'

We spoke about religion for a little while, and then I got the feeling she wanted to change the subject. She began asking me about Lazeaux. It wasn't long before she realised I was skirting around the main event.

'Alors, this Paul,' she said, 'what's he like?'

I paused, reflected on what I'd already told her: mid-forties, single, amateur anthropologist and travel photographer. I didn't know what else to say.

'It just sounds very romantic,' she said. 'The way you tell it, I think I'd have fallen for him too.'

I felt myself blush.

'You love him?'

I didn't know what to say. Mireille grinned.

'It's nothing to be ashamed of.'

I combed my thoughts for evidence of strong feelings, but I couldn't find anything distinct. Everything in Lazeaux had seemed to happen in quick succession, with no deliberation on my part.

'It's not that I'm ashamed,' I said. 'But I don't know how I feel. It just happened.'

'Did you sleep with him?'

'Yes.'

'And he was a good lover?'

At that moment we were interrupted by the sound of bells. A herd of goats was crossing the path a little way ahead. Mireille was distracted and pointed into the trees.

'The troughs collect rain for them to drink,' she said. 'But obviously not when it's as dry as this. The farmers are useless.'

She turned off into the trees to inspect the trough. I followed, and heard her swear under her breath. I peered over her shoulder; the container was empty. She poured the remaining contents of her water bottle into the trough. It sputtered onto the metal and pooled pitifully.

Mireille had a grim expression. 'They belong to a farmer just outside the village. I've told him a thousand times the goats are thirsty, but he doesn't seem to care.'

We picked our way back to the path. The evening was beginning to cool now, the first ribbons of violet streaking the sky. The goats scattered as we approached.

'Tomorrow we'll bring water,' she said. 'If you come by the studio at the same time.'

Not long after, we emerged at the road above the mairie; we'd been closer to the village than I'd realised. My stomach was rumbling with hunger, but my limbs felt deliciously heavy.

We walked down to the main street in a comfortable silence. At her door, I began unlacing Anaïs's shoes. Mireille noticed and shoed my hands away, telling me to bring them tomorrow. We kissed goodbye and I left for the farm. About halfway down the street I turned back and saw she was still sitting on the step outside the shop, massaging her feet.

It was dark when I got back to the farm. The dogs didn't hear me until I was nearly at the bungalow, which I tried not to take as their lack of vigilance; maybe they'd just got used to my scent. I started down the path to the cottage and then remembered Paul's email, still unanswered. I crept into the bungalow. It smelt stale inside – I'd forgotten to open the windows earlier. I started up the computer. The white screen gleamed in the dark. Paul had sent another message since the first, this time with no text. It was an image attachment, bad quality, clearly taken on someone's phone. I rotated it to see Paul sitting on a donkey. He was smiling goofily at whoever was taking the picture; their hand holding the reins was also in shot. The donkey itself looked morose, but it was hard to tell whether this was its natural expression or because Paul was sitting on it. Either way, he was far too big for the donkey, his feet planted firmly on the grass on either side. I closed the image and began drafting a reply.

Dear Paul,

It's ~~great~~ good to hear from you. I've arrived safe and sound. ~~I miss you too!~~ Malmot is beautiful but very different to Lazeaux. My host family keep to themselves and don't mix much with the village. They've left me here for a few days as they have a family wedding in Nice. ~~It's strange to be alone again. I keep wondering if I made the right decision coming here.~~ The farm is impressive. You'd like it – they really live off the land.

The slow travel festival sounds ~~wonderful~~ great. Is the picture of you on the donkey the same one the couple took to Jerusalem? I'm glad you're having a good time. Glad the photos are popular.

And yes ... I did find the present. ~~Who is Tehura?~~ Thank you so much. I wish I had thought to give you something too. ~~Maybe I could come back to Lazeaux after my week here?~~ Thinking of you.

Bisous, Frances

(P.S. don't worry about me being alone; I've

met an Alsatian ceramicist called Mireille who is showing me all the mountain paths. She is religious but very kind.)

vendredi

The next day was long and restless. I set up a workspace on the picnic table to go over my notes from the archives, as I'd been hoping to put together a proposal for a Master's degree. I leafed back through the pages, but couldn't concentrate for more than a few seconds at a time, reading and re-reading my words without comprehension. It was like they had been written by someone else. Then I realised the only person I could ask to write a reference was A.B. I gathered up my pages and resisted the urge to tear them. The notion of academic work seemed suddenly futile, absurd.

Instead I sent a few emails to friends, and a cursory one to my mother. I pretended I was still in Paris and told her when I was likely to be back. With friends I went into more detail about Lazeaux and Paul, but when I read the messages back I was baffled. They seemed gushing and saccharine: the Tour passing beneath my window; the festival; Léa, Laure and Ève; Patrice and the cathedral. Not to mention Paul, who I'd depicted as some kind of Zeus-like figure who'd shown me favour.

In the middle of this an email flashed up from A.B.

Hi, Frances. Sorry for the radio silence. Hope you're having a good break. Let me know you're doing okay. A.B.

I stared at the email until the words blurred, willing there to be more to it. I wanted pages – whole missives – from him. But the message was thin, insubstantial – it had come too late. I felt no urgency, or even ability, to reply. It seemed to belong to a past life, directed at someone who no longer existed. I opened another tab and checked the news, scanning the articles quickly, but felt the same sense of unreality. Everything seemed so far away. I shut down the computer and spent the rest of the afternoon daydreaming about never going home.

That evening I walked up to the village to meet Mireille. I was looking forward to speaking with her again, eager to hear more of her story, although I worried about exhausting her generosity.

In the square, men were grouped around the chapiteau. It still didn't look like they'd made any progress. I spied Francis, his belly bulging beneath a bright yellow shirt. He clocked me and nodded; I waved and hurried on without stopping.

This time Mireille wasn't waiting outside the shop. I peered in and saw her sitting at the wheel in an apron, finger marks of wet clay smeared over her skin and clothes. She jumped when I knocked on the door.

'Is it time already?'

'Yes,' I said, faltering, 'but I don't want to disturb you—'

She waved a hand at me, coated in dried clay that was beginning to crack. 'Just give me a minute to clean up.'

I lingered in the studio as she got changed in the next room. I drifted to the ceramic objects lining the walls and ran my fingers over their edges. They were cool to the touch. Their colours seemed to come directly from the valleys around Malmot, streaked in murky blues and brown. I heard a murmur of distinctly female voices from the next room. Mireille was speaking under her breath with another woman. Their conversation was too soft for me to hear; and when Mireille reappeared, I tried to convey an expression of not having heard a thing.

'Do you like them?' She gestured to the set of dappled bowls I'd stopped in front of.

I nodded, and told her they made me want to learn how to make them.

Mireille smiled. 'Yes, they have that effect. I think you can tell when the person who's made something has loved doing so. When I hear Sister Magda playing her mandolin, I always think, I wish I knew how to play. But I wouldn't if she hated it.'

She reached to a shelf just over her head and took down a squat brown jug with a blue fluted lip.

'Passion is infectious,' she went on. 'This one has your name on it.'

I accepted the jug and thanked her.

'And what's yours?' she asked.

'My what?'

'Your passion, of course!'

I turned the jug around in my hands, hoping that something would come to mind.

'I don't know,' I said finally, feeling like a failure.

'Never mind,' she said brightly. 'You're young. God knows, I didn't figure it out until I'd almost hit the menopause.'

She took the jug from my hands and began to wrap it absently in a sheet of tissue paper.

'Did you know,' she went on, 'in France, in the nineteenth century, they used to treat women for the menopause as if it were a disease?'

I shook my head.

'They did. They must have seen all these middle-aged women having epiphanies and thought *we have to put a stop to this somehow!*'

We set off on the same route as before. Past the chapiteau and the road to the mairie, into the spruce forest. Mireille asked how it was being alone at the farm, and I explained I'd been scared because the cottage was separated from the main house, that it didn't have a lock. She threw up her hands in exasperation. Why hadn't I slept in the house? she wanted to know. Valerie and Artur were away, and would have no way of finding out. I didn't know, I said. The idea had never occurred to me.

Every so often a particular tree or view of the valley brought back fragments of yesterday's conversation, mosaicking the fresh one laid down as we walked. There was a shift to our talk this evening that I couldn't put my finger on. Mireille seemed detached, less gregarious than the day before. I asked after Anaïs but she answered evasively.

We drifted into silence. The rhythm of our walking was reassuring, and I began to pay more attention to our surroundings. Small birds dipped in and out of the trees, and at one point one landed on the ground a little way in front of us. It was smaller than a fist, grey-bodied with a black bonnet. A band of red circled each of its eyes, making them appear large and fierce. Mireille gestured for us to stop a few paces away, but it flew off between the trees, where something was glinting strangely.

'What?' Mireille asked as I started off the path towards it.

Sun turned to shade as the canopy thickened overhead. A clearing was coming up, partially obscured by large rocks. Mireille's footsteps crunched the undergrowth behind me. Then we both stopped to stare: the clearing was more or less a junkyard, strewn with old washing machines, microwaves, corded telephones and fax machines, nestled together in various stages of rust and decay. The forest had begun to grow up through them, grasses and saplings sprouting between surfaces. The glass of an old television had been smashed in, and flowers bloomed in place of its screen.

Mireille took a loud intake of breath.

'It's like some ancient civilisation,' she said.

We stood quietly for a few moments. The junk-garden was eerily beautiful.

'Do you think it's all from Malmot?' I asked.

Mireille shrugged. 'I'm more curious about how it got here. There's not a road – that I know of – anywhere nearby.'

We crept into the clearing, treading reverently between machines. I took photos on my phone. On my screen they looked like a mass of bones and cartilage.

'This is why I have to go and see the sisters,' Mireille said after a while. 'People around here, they become like animals, shitting where they eat.'

Back on the main path, Mireille seemed to be in better spirits. She wanted to know where and how I'd learned French.

I felt instantly ashamed – A.B. always told me my accent could be better. I began to apologise, and told her I'd learned a bit in school and then supplemented it with bits of Middle French from translating the manuscript. If my French seemed slow or wooden, that was why.

'That's not what I mean.' Mireille shook her head. 'Sometimes – no offence – I can tell you haven't fully understood. But your eyes light up; you listen like a child. Which is the right way to do it, of course. Adults are terrible at learning languages.'

I smiled, puzzling over what she'd said. I had noticed that every so often I would reach saturation point, where it was a struggle to pick out individual words. Instead I'd settle into the rhythm of speech, feel its familiar sounds and cadences. It gave me the impression of having understood, but maybe that was just delusion on my part. I tried to explain as much to Mireille.

'Like a baby, then,' she said. 'The way they listen before they understand.'

I nodded, though I'd never been interested in babies. Then I remembered something I hadn't thought of for a long time.

'I used to, though. Apparently I started to speak French when I was really little.'

'How?'

'My dad was French. I don't remember him, but we lived in France, with my mum. She's from Cornwall. They broke up when I was three, or something, and Mum and I moved back to the UK.'

'And you spoke French?'

'I guess – or as much as you do when you're that age. Baby talk. But I don't ever remember speaking French. I learned it later on in school, like everyone. And foreign language education in the UK isn't exactly great. I had more of a problem with English.'

Mireille asked why, and I repeated what I'd been told by my mother, that when we moved back I'd been so slow to pick up English that for a long time they thought I had learning difficulties. But that one day, when I was six or seven, I just started speaking normally.

Mireille was quiet. I was worried I'd said too much. We had reached the point where we'd turned back yesterday.

'Let's sit,' she said, gesturing to a flat lump of stone.

She sat down heavily and I took a seat next to her. To my surprise, she took a small bag of tobacco from her pocket and began to roll. She smiled and raised her eyebrows guiltily.

'You know, it took me forty years,' she paused to lick the paper, 'to realise that men are overrated.'

I laughed as she patted down her pockets, presumably looking for a lighter.

'Your father, for example – the Frenchman. What happened to him?'

I looked out over the dry valley. Its colours merged with my memory of Mireille's ceramics and my misreading the sign two days before. *CÉRAMIQUES PAR MIRACLE.*

'I don't know. There's an unspoken rule that we don't speak about him. She won't even tell me his name.'

Mireille nodded, inhaled.

I stared ahead, trying to find the dividing line in the fissures between blue and brown, brown and blue . . .

'That must be difficult,' she said gently.

I blinked without looking away from the view. 'No, not really. It's never upset me.'

Mireille tilted her head back and blew a plume of smoke above us. I suddenly recognised its smell.

'That's . . .'

She registered my confused expression and erupted into giggles. I began to laugh too.

'I got into it when I was sick,' she said. 'It's good for you . . .'

She passed me the joint. I took a long pull and breathed

deeply. I half felt, half imagined it coursing down my neck, spine, over my shoulder blades and down my arms. I relaxed into my body as if it was finally my own, as if I'd been wearing someone else's for weeks.

samedi

The next day, Mireille invited me to come early to her studio. The afternoon began slowly enough. She wanted to teach me to throw, and so we spent an hour or so going through the basics. There was only one wheel so we took turns sitting. I watched her attentively, but each time I sat down I felt lost. The clay – wet and unruly – seemed only to work against me.

At one point a customer came in and Mireille made a great show of pretending I was her assistant. The customer was a wiry, glamorous-looking woman in her sixties, with dark sunglasses on her forehead and a green silk scarf around her neck. The woman watched me at the wheel as Mireille chattered on. At that moment, the wet column of clay began to sway and swerve precariously out of shape. I slowed the wheel down to a halt, revealing the collapsed clay and, for lack of knowing what else to do, grinned. The woman left not long after, buying only a small unglazed ashtray – the cheapest thing in the shop, Mireille told me deploringly.

My ineptitude seemed hilarious to her. 'I was so sure you'd be a natural,' she said, laughing.

But I still worried that somehow I'd disappointed her. I must have looked tense, as she asked if I wanted to smoke. She disappeared through a door and came back a few minutes later, flopping down on a threadbare sofa to light up.

'The clay will soak up the smell,' she said, winking.

Soon I was feeling lighter. I was still at the pottery wheel, pushing my fingers through the clay in front of me. The studio was warm, almost too warm, and the clay was soothing to touch.

Mireille started telling me the things she'd hated about her husband. He seemed like a classic villain: he drank, he gambled, he'd lose some money and come home and take it out on her. One time he said he wished he'd married her sister instead. 'I bet she'd be better in bed,' he'd told her. But the worst thing, Mireille went on, the worst thing was remembering that she hadn't stood up for herself.

I don't know what it was that made me blurt it out; maybe it was smoking or feeling comfortable with Mireille, feeling united with her against the monstrous figure of her ex-husband. It occurred to me, as I began to tell her, that it was the first time I'd ever said it all out loud. I knew in reality these things had only happened a few weeks ago, but the silence following them made them seem older, arcane some-how. As if I was telling the story of another girl altogether.

A girl who was told she'd had a 'breakdown' in her last year of university, although all she remembers from that time is the thinness of the light on winter mornings, how blue it was against the cold walls of her bedroom. The bedroom was in the basement of a shared flat and must have been the maid's room, at some point, as it had a large enamel bath in one corner, with taps that never ran hot. Sometimes the girl would take her duvet into the empty bath and curl up in it, maybe with a book, otherwise staring at the ceiling for hours on end.

By the time the first glimmers of spring came around she knew she couldn't stay in the bath all day, and so she threw herself into academic work instead. The names of dead scholars became like friends; they were so much easier to be around than people. She went to all her lectures. She went to extra lectures, anything that would keep her out of the bath and the mesh of unstructured hours. The time came to plan her dissertation. She was unsure what to write about. One of her lecturers encouraged her to develop an essay she'd written for his class on a manuscript from the mid-fifteenth century. He had a theory that the manuscript served a pedagogic function, to teach children how to read. He was going to spend the summer studying it in Paris, but in the meantime he would be happy to supervise her dissertation.

The lecturer was very encouraging. For her, it was like feeling the warmth of the sun after only ever knowing its absence – the sense of something lost being restored, a homecoming she couldn't explain but felt, deep in her body.

She struggles to recall his features. Balding, greying; he had stone-coloured eyes and wore only dark shirts. Dissertation meetings ran over their allotted time, in which she told him about what she'd read in the bath – although she didn't tell him *about* the bath. He smiled, told her he'd never met anyone like her. She went home and stayed awake through the night, frantically replaying their conversations, trying to decode their meanings. What did he really think? He liked her, but just in the way a teacher likes a student, she concluded. She didn't want to get ahead of herself. But the thoughts were uncontrollable. She wanted to know more: who did he go home to? What did he lie awake thinking about at night?

The days she didn't see him, she imagined him. She felt his eyes on her at all times. During long hours in the library she could almost feel his presence. She wanted his approval, but it was more than that: she wanted to belong to him. Studying became an act of devotion. How else can a student honour a teacher? He began to email her later and later at night. She walked through the days full of adrenaline for their next contact. The day she handed in her dissertation he asked her out for a coffee, off-campus. There was nothing clandestine about it; it wasn't far from the university and anyone might have seen. She imagined seeing herself with him in third person, and wondered what they looked like to onlookers. The café had tall glass-plated walls; the reflection of the two of them thrilled her more than anything.

Just after exams finished he asked her to join him in Paris

over the summer. He had a temporary office in the archives there and needed an assistant. She said yes before his words had even registered; she had no plans for after graduating, other than increased hours in the restaurant where she worked at weekends. Should she have had plans? Her friends seemed to: some were going home or on holiday; the ones with family connections had internships and grad schemes lined up; the others were frantically applying for any jobs they could find. But the bath days had troubled her ability to think clearly about the future. Her tenancy was due to expire, but the contents of one day alone – filled to bursting with uncontrollable variables – was enough to overwhelm her and reduce her to listless inertia; coping with tomorrow had seemed a far off, mammoth task, let alone the arbitrary markers of weeks, months.

A friend agreed to store her boxes over summer, and soon she was in Paris. A.B. had found them neighbouring rooms in the Marais, a short walk from the archives. She didn't use her room at all other than for storing her luggage and getting dressed. There was a full-length mirror there, framed with moulded ceramic roses. Some mornings she'd stand in front of it, pinching herself – how far she had come since whole days spent staring at the ceiling! Despite the novelty of it all, he kept a scrupulous schedule; they arrived at the archives at 9 a.m. each morning, and worked ceaselessly until 5.30 p.m. As a result, the little she saw of the city was on their short morning walk through the Marais, or wherever they might drink or dine out in the evenings.

To begin with, he was as doting as he had been when they used to meet for coffee. There were impromptu flowers, evening walks along the Seine, a fish-shaped pendant from an antique shop, loosely articulated to make the fish appear to swim as she moved. But he soon became impatient with her for little things – always needing to be told what to do, her quiet pliability around his colleagues, making the occasional mistake due to daydreaming. They never argued seriously, and even though she tried to fight against it by telling herself how lucky she was – how she had everything she had fantasised about – she began to feel the same dull tug that had first led her into the bath. The hot days bristled with oblique hostility; crowds left her dazed and disorientated. She began to dread leaving the archives at the end of each day. She liked it inside, where the light and temperature were regulated to preserve the manuscripts, where no one could see her. She began to wish she could sleep there overnight, where it was always cool, and not too bright. When they did meet his colleagues for drinks after work she sat silent, lethargic, until he couldn't put up with it any longer and pressed their room key into her hand beneath the table, murmuring she should leave before she embarrassed him any further.

That much wasn't too difficult to remember. I could recall each stage of events and their attendant feelings as I told them – though it was strange to relate, out loud, how much had changed from winter to summer. As if I was describing the yearly life cycle of a strange, symbiotic organism, comprised of a young girl and an older man – who might be any young girl and any older man – and how their behaviour responded to a series of environmental fluctuations: hormones, obsessions, boredom, fear – I realised too that I felt no animosity towards A.B.; I missed him, but he had been right to send me away. I would have done the same thing in his position.

Mireille had a strange expression on her face. She looked dissatisfied. 'But how did you leave?' she wanted to know.

That was the difficult part. I told her I didn't really know; I knew A.B.'s version of events, which he'd told me afterwards, when he didn't believe my ignorance about the whole thing. Mireille said she'd rather hear A.B.'s version than nothing at all.

I thought back to my last day in Paris. That was the week that I'd stopped working on the manuscript. I should have been sightseeing, but I mostly hung out in the Airbnb room A.B. had booked for me on the other side of town. That was kind of him, at least; he knew I didn't have any money. When he finally agreed to talk, I went to meet him in his office at the archives, avoiding the wary looks the security guards gave me on the way in. I assumed everyone knew about what had happened. My heart was unnervingly slow as I knocked on the door and his voice called me in. He was leaning back in his chair with a cold expression on his face. He told me he'd written an official statement and needed me to sign it. He gestured at a piece of paper on the table. I took it, then looked at him. He seemed to have aged since I saw him last. How had this man ever been the sun?

I spent a few minutes reading and re-reading the statement. It might have been true. I really couldn't remember. I couldn't see any trace of myself in the portrait of the girl he'd described. He informed me, in an affectless tone, that if I signed now the archives wouldn't press charges. His eyes were dull as dead stars. I leaned the paper on the desk and signed with a shaking hand.

Archives Nationales du Moyen Âge

Déclaration de témoignage

Date: vendredi 23 juillet
Nom: Prof. A— B—

Yesterday afternoon, at approximately 4.15 p.m., I temporarily left archive reading room A.3 to use the restroom. Apart from my assistant, Miss Frances Hawthorne, the reading room – to my knowledge – was empty. I did not consider it necessary to arrange supervision for my assistant as we have been working in room A.3 on the same manuscript (MS 7601) for the past four weeks, and throughout this time Miss Hawthorne has shown herself to be a highly competent and diligent assistant.

This latter point explicates my utter horror at what I found on returning to A.3, at approximately 4.20 p.m. My assistant had moved the manuscript from its display pillow and set it on the floor, and was lying on her

*stomach in front of it. A series of coloured pencils (which
I had never seen before and assume she must have secreted
on her person and passed through security) were scattered
next to her, in addition to the one in her hand, which
she was beginning to use on the unprotected page of the
manuscript. I immediately called out and rushed over to
her, pulling her back from the manuscript. She appeared
confused at my distress and informed me she was 'just
colouring' the manuscript. After that I carefully replaced
the manuscript on its reading support and informed
security.*

*On reflection, having become acquainted with
Miss Hawthorne over the past few weeks, I put it to
management that this incident was entirely out of
character, and suggested it was a temporary psychosis,
with no malicious intent. I ask you to consider that only
very minor damage was done to the manuscript (see
the bottom left corner of r104, where green pencil has
been used to 'colour in' a network of vines enclosing the
margin), and that Miss Hawthorne did not remove her
gloves, ensuring no skin contact with the manuscript. As
her superior, I take full responsibility for her wellbeing
and will ensure she has the necessary support and recovery
from this incident.*

Signature de témoin . . . .

Signature de témoin . . . .

dimanche

Late next morning I was in the kitchen when the phone rang. Artur, Valerie and Lili were due back around noon, and I had almost finished preparing lunch for their arrival. I hesitated, and then let the phone ring out. It was silent for a few seconds then began ringing again. I panicked and picked it up.

'Frances? It's Mireille. Valerie and Artur have been trying to get through to you. Something has happened in Nice – they won't be back until this evening.'

'What's happened?'

'I don't know. They called Anaïs. She was going to come down and tell you in person but I thought I'd just call. They didn't want you to worry.'

Mireille made a muffled voice at the other end of the phone. I looked at the salad; it was struggling under the too-thick dressing.

'Do you want to walk again, this evening?' I asked.

More muffling. 'I can't. I'm not in the studio today. Anaïs wants us to go out en bas. But tomorrow I'm free.'

I didn't say anything. A fat fly buzzed over the salad.

'Frances? I've got to go now. But I'll see you tomorrow. Take care.'

She hung up. I stood with the phone for a few seconds, gazing through the kitchen window. My research files and notes were still stacked on the bench outside. Even the sight of them made my thoughts feel slow and fuzzy. I abandoned the salad and put on the walking boots I'd left by the door. The heat was thick, but there was a light breeze. Mireille didn't like to walk in the daytime, but I didn't mind. I locked up and set off for the village.

It was twilight by the time I got back. For dinner I forced down the salad and helped myself to a glass of wine. I was showering when the dogs began to bark, and the sound of tyres crunching on gravel came into earshot. I quickly hopped out and dried off. A car door slammed, and then a few minutes later there was a knock on the door.

'Frances?' Valerie's voice sounded cracked.

I opened the door with a towel around my body, feeling awkward. Valerie stood on the step outside, swaying a little; her crossed arms looked like an attempt to hold herself together. Her face was screwed up, and the skin around her eyes patched with red.

'Sorry we're later than planned,' she mumbled.

'Is everything all right?'

She sniffed, and drew the back of her sleeve beneath her nose.

'I just came . . . I just came to tell you that at the wedding – Artur's mother died.'

'What?'

'We knew it was coming soon. She's been very sick, but—'

I thought about reaching out and touching her on the shoulder. It seemed wrong somehow, almost perverse. I held back and said I was sorry.

She shook her head. 'Please,' she said, sounding shaky. 'It's unfortunate that this has happened while you're here. You'll understand that you can't stay on as planned. We need space, time to focus on funeral arrangements . . .'

My head was spinning. I told her I understood and would make plans to leave as soon as I could.

Valerie nodded. 'There's only one bus a day. Francis leaves around 5 a.m. Maybe it's too short notice for the one tomorrow. But the day after – if you could make plans to leave then, that would be good.'

I nodded. Valerie's eyes were brimming again and she looked at the ceiling, as if to hold back the tears.

'It would help if you tried to keep out of the way until then. We'll do some work in the morning, as usual. I think the routine will be good for Artur—'

She nodded one last time then turned to walk back up the path. I watched her disappear from view, feeling guilty for being there. The dogs' barking quietened. I stood on the step for a while, still wrapped in my towel, watching a bat swoop in the violet light.

I still had a few weeks until my flight home. I ran through my lack of options – I couldn't afford to stay in a hotel, and BénéBio hosts required more notice. I would have to go back to Lazeaux. What else could I do?

I got into bed. My thoughts passed seamlessly into dreams where Paul appeared and spoke to me. I woke in the dark, still hearing his voice. *It was fate*, he was saying. *Fate brought you back to me.* Would fate kill a man's mother just to have its way? *Yes*, Paul was saying calmly, rubbing the backs of my calves. I was lying on my front unable to move. His voice chirruped in my ear like a cicada. *Yes, coquine. Yes, yes, yes.*

lundi

In the morning Artur wasn't at breakfast. Valerie and I sat in our usual silence, although its nature seemed to have changed overnight. Before, the quietness had been filled with murky hostility; now its origin was clear. I needed to email Paul as soon as possible, but it didn't seem appropriate to go into the house; it was quarantined for grieving. Just after 8 a.m. Lili dashed out, grabbing a hunk of baguette from the table and hurriedly kissing her mother goodbye. I watched her scramble quickly up the path to the village, school bag bouncing on her back.

Valerie and I set to work in the courgette bed. A hot, flat heat hung low and heavy over the hillside, making it difficult to focus. I was crouching with my knees bent, and at one point almost lost balance when my calves slipped on the sweat pooling beneath my thighs. My hands moved mechanically, soon covered in a gluey starch leaking from the courgettes.

Valerie frowned as she worked, her movements quick and dexterous.

'Valerie? T'ES OU?'

Artur's voice rang out from the top of the garden. Valerie stood up and waved. Within a few seconds Artur was standing by the courgette bed, catching his breath. In spite of his stature he looked small, like a lost boy. I had a sudden, absurd urge to comfort him. He nodded vaguely in my direction and began to speak with Valerie in their rapid idiolect.

'She's leaving tomorrow,' I heard Valerie say at one point. I glanced up. She had a courgette in hand, gesticulating with it as she spoke. I looked from Valerie, to Artur, to the trug of gleaming courgettes. I felt dizzy. I became aware of the gentle curve of the vegetable in my hand. Then, for a fraction of a second, I felt it throb. Was that possible? The way a body can twitch or convulse some minutes after death – could a vegetable do the same? I rummaged through the courgettes in the trug at my side, examining and squeezing each in turn.

'Ça va, Frances?'

Valerie and Artur were looking at me questioningly. I dropped the courgette like a hot coal. I was fine, I told them, trying to sound calm. 'It's hot, isn't it?'

After lunch, with Valerie's indifferent blessing, I used the ancient desktop to email Paul. My uneasiness at being in Artur and Valerie's private space made me type faster than I usually would. I tried not to think about what I'd do if he said no. I settled on a tone that was somewhere between matter of fact and affectionate, telling him the series of events leading to my imminent departure, asking if it would be possible to spend the remainder of my trip in Lazeaux. In exchange for work, of course. I fretted over the sentences to Paul, worrying about the grammar, then the sentiment, until a cough from Artur brought me back to the room. The house's midday shade felt raw and oppressive; I quickly hit send and scurried outside.

On my way up to the village I found one of Lili's hair beads. Its bright pink plastic caught my eye, half-trodden into the dirt on the path. Maybe she'd already noticed its absence, and the braid had begun to fray. I put it in my pocket and carried on.

The door to Mireille's studio was open, and I was surprised to find it empty. I knocked and then called out. A shuffle sounded from the next room and then Mireille appeared in the doorway.

'Come on in,' she said. 'I'm just finishing lunch.'

I followed her into a bright kitchen. We sat at the table and she offered me cheese and gluten-free crackers. Had Anaïs told her the news, I asked? She nodded, and slowly cut a sliver from a half-moon of cheese.

'I knew when I called yesterday. But I thought it was best if Valerie and Artur told you themselves.'

I watched her smear blue cheese onto the cracker. It looked uncannily like the back of my mother's knee, varicose blue.

'What will you do?' she asked with her mouth full.

I looked around the room. It was not that different to the

studio; almost every surface was cluttered with misshapen ceramics and dried flowers strung up or arranged in vases, seashells and pine cones dotted in between. There was a gold icon over the mantelpiece, of an effeminate Christ with almond-shaped eyes. Something like lavender hung in the air.

I told Mireille that I was planning to go back to Lazeaux, that I'd just emailed Paul and was waiting to hear back.

'Is that what you want to do?'

'I don't know.' I picked at a stain on the small dish in front of me. 'I don't *not* want to.'

'But you don't want to.'

I told her I didn't think I had a choice.

Mireille sighed. 'You could stay here.'

'What?'

'Sure.' She shrugged. 'You could help out in the studio; it would only be, what, a couple of weeks?'

'But – what about Anaïs?'

'I've already asked her. She said it'd be fine.'

I felt light-headed. I put down the dish and heard it thud, far away. 'That's really kind of you, but . . .'

'Look, I didn't want to say anything before,' she said, hesitating, 'but after everything you told me last night – are you sure going back to Paul is the best idea?'

'What do you mean?'

'Well, maybe you just need to be somewhere calm for a while, and safe. You haven't known him that long.'

'Longer than I've known you.'

The words surprised me and I regretted them as soon as

they were out of my mouth. Mireille raised her eyebrows and nodded as if in admission.

'True,' she said softly. 'True.'

'I'm sorry, I didn't mean—'

'It's fine, Frances. I understand. Emotions are very powerful things. I'm not the one to say what you should or shouldn't do.'

'I'm sorry, it's just ...' I paused, struggling to articulate the murky thoughts that had attained an aura of certainty overnight. 'Paul isn't like him – like my supervisor. He's different.'

Mireille bit into her cracker.

'And I know it sounds stupid,' I went on, 'but I was already thinking about going back to Lazeaux at some point. Then this all happened, and ... I don't know. Part of me thinks maybe I was always meant to go back.'

Mireille seemed to be mulling it over as she chewed. After a few moments she began to speak with slow deliberation. 'To some people that would sound "stupid", yes. But you're speaking to someone who believes in coincidence. Not that I always did; I had to be converted to it.'

We were quiet for what felt like a long time. I didn't feel that I even had a choice; everything seemed more like a relentless, inevitable stream. All I could do was flow downhill from the mountains, buoyed by the current running straight back to Lazeaux. What use would it be to swim upstream?

Mireille pulled a scrap of paper towards her and began scribbling on it.

'This is my address and my phone number,' she said, handing it to me.

'Email address?'

She shook her head. 'No. But look, if you change your mind, there's room for you here, okay? Even if you turn up in the middle of the night.'

I smiled weakly. I thought about flinging my arms around her and agreeing to stay, imagining whole weeks of us walking in the woods or laughing as I disfigured lump after lump of clay. But instead I said thank you, watched the moment pass.

'Don't worry about it,' she said, waving her hand. 'The good news is you've made Anaïs want to come walking with me again.'

We laughed a little, and then she stood up and clapped her hands, the brightness bouncing back into her eyes. 'Alors, I should get back to work.'

I stood up, aware of a sinking feeling, as if I had wanted her to persuade me to stay. She seemed removed as she followed me through to the studio and out onto the steps leading down to the street. We kissed. Lavender again. I turned and walked away from *CÉRAMIQUES PAR MIRACLE,* or *MIREILLE,* whichever it was, back down to the farm for the last time.

PART THREE

mardi

The next morning, I get up while it's still dark and struggle with my suitcase up to the square. Francis is already there, smoking outside his minivan as a queue of people shuffle to keep the chill from their feet. He nods at me gruffly and stubs out his cigarette. He opens the door and people begin filing in. Mostly women, in off-white shirts and trousers, with dark rings beneath their eyes, which close as soon as they sit down. On their way to work in Nice, I presume. Francis takes my case and loads it into the back. I'm the last to take my seat. He slams the door behind me, and he doesn't call me 'Frances with an e'.

The day is an eternity of waiting, punctuated by various buses and car shares, by trams and connecting coaches. I spend most of the journey staring out of windows. Thoughts crawl through my mind, slow and furry as caterpillars. During changes of transport I try to keep alert, consulting Paul's directions to the slow travel festival so I don't miss anything. But the task seems to exhaust most of my concentration, and by the time each leg of the journey ends I feel drained, unable to face the next.

As I watch the countryside slide past I feel blankness settling, like snow, over the blurry view. Blankness – I can't think of another word for it. Articulation drips away from me like ice thawing. I don't fight it; I let the words melt and leave. We pass bright fields, where yellow on the hills tells me it's evening. The coach judders to a halt. My whole body is humming. Soon, it's time to get off.

Paul is sitting on a wall on the other side of the car park. He calls to me across the tarmac. A few of the other passengers look up then look away. I detach myself from them and trundle towards him with my suitcase.

Then his arms are around me. He holds my face and kisses it. 'Coquine. You've come back to me.'

He steps back and I take in his face. His eyes are wet, and his skin more leathery than I'd remembered. His smell, dry and familiar.

'Was the journey okay?'

I nod. His head eclipses the sun.

He regards me, slightly puzzled. 'Ça va?'

Another nod.

'You don't feel like talking?'

His words pour over me like warm oil. I bow my head and look down at the ground. It seems crystalline, sparkling with mica.

'You must be tired.'

I do something halfway between a nod and a shrug. When Paul grins back at me I realise I must be smiling.

'Okay then, sleepy. We'll take your case to the tent. And then I'll show you around. I can't wait for you to meet everyone!'

He takes my suitcase and we walk hand in hand out of the car park. The village is a few minutes down the road and Paul chatters as we go. He tells me there's a 'farewell dance' in the square this evening, that tomorrow everyone here for the festival will go home. As we near the village Paul points to the skyline. An enormous outcrop of rock towers over the village, which sits more or less in its shadow. On top is a large neon crucifix, glaring electric blue over the town. I think of Mireille, then push her from my mind.

'Don't pay it any attention,' he says, with a grin. 'We've been dancing like pagans!'

Later, tired of dancing, Paul and I sit on plastic chairs pushed to the side of the village square. The small crowd writhes in front of us, the thin music of the brass band snaking into the night. It's a cool, clear evening. The burble of conversations and laughter rises above the square. Nearby there's a man grilling vegan hot dogs, infusing the air with a herblike aroma. Every so often someone in the crowd raises a plastic cup of beer to Paul, smiling as they whirl past us. I've already been introduced to more people than I can remember, Paul parroting the same line each time with his hand on the small of my back. Je vous présente Frances, ma copine, he says, to which they reply Enchanté, and kiss my cheeks. When I do nothing but smile in return, Paul explains that I am very tired from travelling. Oh! they say, and make a little joke about getting used to slow travel, before moving on to greet someone else.

When the band announces their last song, Paul pulls me to my feet and leads me past the crowd. We dip out of the square and onto an unlit street. The houses are quiet in the dark, and the sounds of the music and the crowd grow fainter as Paul leads me on, peering into stoops and doorways. Soon he seems to find what he's looking for: a passageway between two houses ending in stone steps that curve out of sight. We follow them up through an archway and emerge onto a path under the stars, next to a tiny old church and its graveyard. The humpbacked grass with its gravestones looks like a cat with its hackles raised. 'This way,' says Paul, leading me further up. We climb with our hands and feet when the path becomes rocky. Paul clambers up then holds out his hand, heaving me onto his level.

The plateau looks out over the town, and the fields and villages beyond. Next to us is the blue cross I'd seen earlier, glowing into the night. It's disappointingly small close up, and its tubing looks cheap and tacky, more Las Vegas than Golgotha.

'Impressive, isn't it?' Paul looks out at the view, hands on his hips. The square is lit up beneath us. The band play their last notes, and the crowd erupts in a cheer. Beyond the rooftops of the town, a few lights glimmer in the distance.

'We're not far from Montpellier,' Paul says. 'A few hours at most.

'My brother lives there,' he goes on. 'Titi. I was thinking of dropping in to see him on the way back to Lazeaux. If that's okay with you?' He turns to look at me, peering into my eyes like an optician checking for irregularities. I follow his pupils back and forth, the whites illumined by the cross's neon glare.

'What happened, coquine?' he asks tenderly.

When I fail to answer he drops my hands in frustration, anger creeping into his voice. 'Was it the other host? Are you in love with him?'

I shake my head.

'Was he handsome?' Paul rounds on me.

I shake my head again, reach for his hand.

I feel Paul's fingers curl around mine. He sighs deeply.

'Sorry, coquine. I've missed you, that's all. If you don't want to talk – it's fine.' His finger traces a line from my ear to my lips. 'Je t'aime. You know that, don't you?'

mercredi

Next morning, I wake up to an empty tent. There are sounds of activity outside, with birdsong in between. I poke my head out into the fresh air. People are moving around methodically, packing away their tents, leaving patches of limp, pale grass in their wake. Everyone has been staying in a field next to the garden that belongs to Eric, the organiser of the festival. I spot Paul and Eric sitting on the balcony of his house drinking coffee.

I had been introduced to Eric last night. He's a somewhat squat, jovial man in his sixties, with a lit-up expression and booming voice. I remember his hands were clammy when they grasped mine. Afterwards, Paul whispered in my ear that he thinks of Eric like a father, that Eric used to be a tour guide in the Himalayas and is solely responsible for setting up the festival. He assured me reverently that Eric was a wise and generous man.

I pull on some clothes and wander over. Already I know

that nothing has changed overnight. I won't be able to speak; my mouth is too full of its own meat.

Eventually last night Paul had become exasperated by my inability to talk with his friends, when the music had finished but people were still up, buzzing and drinking around the fire. He didn't appear to mind my quietness when we were alone, as he could seek out the reassurance or reception he needed from my face. But with others it was too out of the ordinary. At one point he took me to the tent and shook me, asking if I knew how this was making him look. A familiar ocean of guilt rolled inside me and I knew he was right. I nodded apologetically, and searched in my bag for a small notebook A.B. had bought for me from the Musée d'Orsay, printed with Gauguin's *Jacob Wrestling with the Angel*.

I opened up the first page and wrote, by the dim firelight: *I'm sorry – I'll be better tomorrow.*

He squinted to make it out. 'This has happened before?'

I didn't know what to say. The glow from the fire was making the tents dance like some contorted mountain range, and Paul had become a fuzzy, indeterminate shape in front of me. Next thing I knew I was inside the tent, and Paul was folding my limbs lovingly into my sleeping bag.

'Get some sleep, coquine,' I heard him call as he walked back to join the others.

'Bon matin,' Eric calls brightly. He holds a boiled egg in one hand and a teaspoon in the other. A runny strand of yolk clings to his beard.

Paul is wearing an orange bandana, the same colour as the stray yolk, and his dark hair curls beneath it like tentacles. I feel a little sick.

Over his shoulder is a calendar, pinned open on the wrong month, with an image of a rust-coloured mountain reflected in a lake. For some reason I can't take my eyes off it.

'You like it?' Eric says.

I don't want to look at him in case the yolk is still in his beard.

Paul appears at my shoulder. 'Lac du Salagou. It's not far from here. We can go on the way to Montpellier, if you like?'

I see now that the mountain is more of a hill, an island in the middle of the lake, peppered with garrigue and veins of dark sediment.

'It's artificial,' Eric is saying. 'I remember them making it when I was a boy, in the '60s. For irrigation purposes. See the different rock colours? The black soil is volcanic, and the red soil, la ruffe, is very rich in iron . . .'

His voice fizzles out like a radio losing frequency. I don't try to tune in.

We're only a few hours' drive away when the distinctive red soil begins to appear on either side of the road.

It had been almost noon by the time Paul took down his exhibition from Eric's caravan and said goodbye to everyone that was left. He's been sulking: not as many of his photos sold as he anticipated, and Eric surprised him by taking a forty per cent cut on those that had. It was in the contract,

Eric insisted, and pointed out the small print when Paul looked on the verge of an outburst.

Now, driving south, the late afternoon sun strokes the soil into red-hot dunes around us. It looks scalding to touch. When the lake streaks into sight, sparkling blue, Paul is still frowning.

I keep the small notebook on my lap. I haven't written anything else in it yet, and don't want to. The blankness reminds me of the first day of term at school: new books, blank pages. I'd rather not write anything, and instead fill them with colours. Today would be the red soil of Salagou, red for Paul's anger.

We take a turning off the main road and begin to trace the shore, where families are picnicking and playing. The lake is smaller than it had looked in the picture, and beyond the blackish blue water I make out clusters of settlements on the far side.

The sun has disappeared behind clouds that darken in its absence, looming over the lake. Paul nods to the rocky shoreline and says we'll camp by the water tonight. I follow his gaze to the shore, strewn with shingle and scrub; it doesn't look flat enough for a tent.

Paul suggests we have dinner in a restaurant he visited with a friend some years ago. We spend over an hour passing through several villages, small and dusty, with peeling shutters and dried-up shrubs. Each of them seems to have at least one restaurant, but Paul insists on finding the right one. Overhead, the sky lets out a low cracking sound.

I unclip the biro from my notebook and hesitate before writing: *Maybe we should set up the tent before dinner? It looks like it's going to rain.* Paul glances at the note and smiles. He tells me not to worry, that we have plenty of time.

After dinner, we barely make it back to the car before the storm is in full flow. We'd spent far too long at the restaurant, the last diners to leave. Paul was animated, excitedly recounting the times he'd visited the lake valley as a teenager and camped under the stars. The wine seemed to induce sentimentality; he had stroked my face absently and told me I made him feel like a teenager all over again.

Closing the car door, I dry my hands on my shorts before reaching for the notebook: *Maybe we should stay somewhere else tonight?*

'Where!?' Paul laughs.

I think about writing *Anywhere*, but instead write: *Your brother's in Montpellier?*

'We'll be fine,' he says, turning on the engine. 'It's too late now. We'll find somewhere sheltered and get set up in no time. I've camped in worse than this.'

We drive back roughly the way we came. No part of the landscape suggests shelter and the black water is roiling with waves. 'This will do,' Paul says, pulling over at a seemingly arbitrary stretch by the shore. 'Let there be light!' he says, turning the headlights to full beam. White light bounces out, exposing the wet ground. 'Come on,' Paul says. I close my eyes and try to think of somewhere warm and dry: Lazeaux, gathering flowers with Béthanie, cycling along lanes in the fragrant afternoon air.

We pull the tent out of the boot and spread it out on the ground. It's a tangle of strings, fabric and poles. Kneeling half on fabric and half in the dirt, I hunch over against the rain. Paul calls out some kind of instruction; I see his mouth move but the words are carried furiously downwind. He hands me a pole and rummages around in the tent bag, withdrawing a roll of duct tape. He gestures frantically, winding his hands around each other. I look down and see the pole is snapped, and then, that the purple tent fabric is covered in a patchwork of duct-tape plasters.

My T-shirt is wet through, and Paul's hair is stuck to his head, his fringe divided into two black leeches.

'She isn't bad for a twenty-three-year-old,' he says.

She? I momentarily think he is talking about me and has misremembered my age, before realising he's referring to the tent. It is two years older than me.

We work as methodically as we can. I stop noticing the rain. The tent begins to take a lopsided, semi-erect shape.

'There!' shouts Paul, which is swiftly followed by a thin cracking sound. The main pole has snapped in half, making the tent look like two kites propped against each other.

I think of all the questions I could write in the notebook: *Why is the tent so old, why didn't you buy a new one, why didn't we set it up before the storm, why didn't we stay somewhere else once it had begun?* I let them all die in the wind. Paul is trying to wipe his hands dry on his shorts, which are completely wet through.

'It will be dry inside,' he calls. 'We might as well get in.'

He hunts around for the door and finds it flat against the ground. He unzips it and gestures for me to crawl in. I realise then we forgot the groundsheet.

Paul notices too but tells me it's too late, that we'll be fine without.

I wriggle inside. It *is* dry, but I can feel every grain and contour of rock beneath us, and the fabric that should have been a metre or so above hangs a few millimetres over my face. Paul gets in after me and we lie side by side, arms pressed to our bodies.

'Perfect,' Paul says.

I breathe in the stale air and marvel at the tent's age. *Her* age. She's a grande dame. Rain ricochets off the fabric. I feel strangely calm, as if I am not really here at all. Paul's hands begin to move over me in the darkness. His breath is as loud as the downpour. I roll over, thinking of soft rocks weathered by rain, how the water invisibly sculpts them, grain by grain, until they take on another form entirely.

jeudi

By morning, the storm seems to have passed. I grope around to find my phone – 5 a.m. – it's too early, but Paul is already stirring beside me. My head is thick with a bad night's sleep, though I'm amazed we managed to get any at all.

We search for an opening and crawl outside. After a night of stale, damp air, the freshness outside is delicious. The lake is totally calm, glasslike, and the sky is beginning to brighten. I close my eyes, savouring the light breeze over my skin. The tent looks even more pathetic in the light; she's more or less totally deflated, a pile of dirty, torn sheets on the ground. No one walking past would suspect that we had spent the night inside her. Paul squats down and begins to pack up, putting the snapped poles to one side and rolling the fabric into a cylinder.

*

In the village we buy pastries, coffee and a baguette from the boulangerie. We sit in the car to eat, the pastries so hot they burn the sides of my mouth. I gulp down a mouthful of coffee and take another bite. It's the best thing I've tasted for months, like sugared air. I can hear a stream trickling somewhere nearby, and see the first signs of the village waking up: a woman opens her shutters and leans out to water the geraniums; a dog wanders onto the street, yawning and stretching in the early sun.

Paul swears suddenly, loudly.

His eyes are screwed up as he cups his mouth with his hand. I think he's about to be sick, and look around frantically for some kind of receptacle.

'No!' Paul bats his hand at me. 'It's my – fuck! – it's my tooth. My bad tooth.'

I didn't know he had a bad tooth. I touch his shoulder and offer him a tissue. He takes it, dabs at his mouth and pulls it away covered with blood. He puts a finger in his mouth, wiggling something out of sight. Then, with another cry of pain, he jerks his head forward and the tooth falls out onto his lap. It looks like a tiny clothes peg, yellowing and blood-streaked. Paul wraps the tooth in the blood-soaked tissue and puts it in his pocket, swears once more, and spits a mouthful of blood into his coffee cup.

He throws the remainder of his coffee out of the window and starts up the engine. I gulp mine down to stop it spilling. Soon we're out of the village, Paul swerving recklessly along the winding lanes.

'That fucking dentist,' Paul says. 'This is the second time, you know? The second time!'

We speed round a corner and brush against a hedgerow; last night's rainwater sprays into my face. I put my hand on his leg, hoping to calm him. He turns and smiles. 'Sorry, coquine. My teeth have been bad since travelling. In Tahiti I used to try and chew kava with the girls! But they've been doing it all their lives; their teeth are strong.'

Kava ... the meaning evades me until I remember Paul's notebooks: *human mastication of kava root ... customary to select virgin boys or girls of tribe ... believed sexual purity essential to quality of kava. Also desirable: clean mouth, strong teeth and jaws.*

I take out my notebook. *What does it taste like?*

Paul looks over and grins. 'Kava? Like nectar, coquine. Pure nectar.'

Once we rejoin the main road leading to Montpellier, Paul begins to tell me about his brother, Thierry, who goes by Titi. Titi is only a few years older, but they were never close while growing up.

'We went like this,' Paul says, and takes his hand off the wheel to cross one arm over the other, forming an X. 'Titi was a very rebellious child – always drinking, partying, staying out late. My mother couldn't stand it. I was the total opposite – very devout, religious. She loved that – although I outgrew it eventually.'

He pauses to let a large lorry overtake us. 'And then, we

223

completely swapped. I was the one that ran off to go travelling; I didn't get my Bac, didn't go to university – at least not until I was much older. They had no idea where I was other than a postcard every couple of months. There was no emailing back then.'

'But Titi,' he sighs, 'Titi had one disaster after another. He enrolled in uni then flunked it, had to stay home for months on end. He's a very ... depressive type. The same thing happened with jobs. He'd start enthusiastically then end up sacking it off, staying home to smoke. Not much luck with women, mostly went with prostitutes, until Sandrine – ah!' Paul smacks himself lightly on the forehead. 'Fuck. I should have asked before ...' He trails off.

'Sandrine is his ex,' he explains. 'They were together until very recently. She's a shaman too. That's how they met, I think. Anyway, she's very talented, very beautiful – to be honest we all wondered what she was doing with Titi – but it turns out she's crazy. They fought all the time, and once he caught her trying to set fire to his stuff after cursing it ... I don't know.'

I scribble in the notebook: *Titi's a shaman?*

Paul nods. 'Yeah he's into all that stuff: stars, séances, fortune telling. It all started as an attempt to deal with his moods. He tried drugs, counselling ... This was the next logical step. But it's been good for him – he has a lot of friends in it; they take courses together, go on retreats.'

Are you close now?

Paul shrugs. 'Closer than before, I guess. But, like I said,

Sandrine has just left, only a few weeks ago, and I think Titi's not in a good way.'

Will he mind us visiting?

'Not at all!' he says excitedly. 'I've told him all about you.'

I lean back and stare out of the window, wondering what there could be to tell. I feel perfectly blank. Formless except for the shape I can make by curling around others.

The approach to Titi's apartment is anything but idyllic. Paul tells me his brother lives on the outskirts because rent prices have been hiked in the centre. At one time they shared a large flat in the old town, overlooking the botanic gardens, when Paul was a mature student at the university. But Titi's had money troubles since then, and their parents refuse to help him. He's still bitter that they helped Paul buy Noa Noa, which he wouldn't have been able to afford otherwise. That's why Titi won't visit Lazeaux, Paul says.

We wind through streets of dilapidated industrial ware-houses before arriving at a gated estate. It's nearly 10 a.m. but it takes Paul four attempts at buzzing before Titi's voice, in a deep monotone, crackles over the intercom.

The gate swings open. We park up then I follow Paul to a door on the ground floor, where a man, as large as Paul is skinny, is already waiting. They kiss each other, then embrace, Titi's fleshy hand patting Paul on the back.

'Je m'excuse,' Titi says. 'I was still asleep when you called.'

Paul steers me towards him. 'Titi, voilà, Frances.'

We kiss. He smells of cigarettes and not much else, and

when I step back I notice the dark hollows of his eye sockets, the stain on his greying T-shirt. He looks kind, but worn out. We follow him into an open-plan living room and kitchen with a small patio out back. The space is so bare it looks uninhabited.

Titi wanders over to the only chair and flops down. 'She took most of our things, as you can see.'

I notice flies buzzing around a fruit bowl on the counter, filled with rotting satsumas and bananas.

'Alors,' Paul clears his throat. 'We camped by Salagou last night.'

'Oh?'

'But there was a storm, and – anyway we didn't sleep much. Do you mind if we catch up later? I think we both need a nap.'

Titi shrugs again. 'Sure. I mean, there's the spare room, but it's filled with boxes Sandrine hasn't taken yet.'

'That's fine. Go on up,' Paul says to me, pointing to the staircase. 'Upstairs on the right. I'll just be a moment.'

Once out of sight I loiter on the landing for a few moments, straining to hear their conversation. Paul is speaking quickly, and Titi responds in low, indecipherable syllables.

The spare room is filled floor to ceiling with brown cardboard boxes. There's a dusty carpet and a window at the far end overlooking the patio, but not much else. Soon, Paul bounds up the stairs after me.

'Ghosts of Sandrine,' Paul says grimly, nodding to the boxes. He retrieves a pile of spare bedding from a cupboard and we make up a bed on the floor. He tells me that I should get some sleep while he goes to the dentist; last time he tried to make an appointment in advance the dentist ghosted him. 'He's a real criminal,' he says.

I sit down on the sheets, boxes towering around me. Paul looks for his car keys, swearing under his breath. He eventually finds them in the cupboard he took the bedding from. When he kisses me goodbye there is a crazed look in his eye.

When I wake up it is still light outside and a woman is singing in another language, her song drifting in through the window. I stare out of it, trying to recollect: had I opened it before falling asleep?

Dream fragments are still lodged in my mind. I was standing at the back of a cave, looking out to the opening, where a large, pearlescent shell was glowing and quaking. The ground beneath my feet was damp and squirming, and I realised two things at once: that the cave was in fact a mouth, Paul's mouth, and the shell was his bad tooth. Then everything began to shake violently, I saw the mouth begin closing ahead. I tried to run towards the opening but I couldn't move; my legs were tendons attached to the tongue. The last thing I saw before waking up was the bad tooth, bright in the fleshy dark.

I try to sketch out the cave and the bad tooth in my notebook, scratching with the biro for some minutes. But my attempt is so lifeless, and fails so miserably to capture the dream, that I feel disgusted with myself, and toss the notebook aside. I think absently about stabbing the biro into my thigh.

I dress slowly, looking in the boxes that are open. Inside are books, mostly, with titles like *LE DESTIN DE SOI-MEME* and *L'ASTROLOGIE ET L'ÉCONOMIE: VOTRE CHEMIN*.

Downstairs, the living room is empty; the woman is still singing somewhere outside. I peer round the patio door and see Titi sitting on a plastic chair, staring into space. On the table next to him is an unopened book, an empty packet of cigarettes and an ashtray, almost full. The little garden is a sad affair; halfway down the path, a hammock is tied to a tree at one end, the other falling impotently to the ground. The few plants are dried and wilted, save for an enormous cheese plant in the corner that makes a canopy over Titi, his face daubed with the sunlight leaking through its holes. A parakeet squawks from the next garden.

I knock on the glass so as not to surprise him. 'Salut.'

Titi looks round. 'Oh – salut.' He pushes back on his arms and tries to sit up a little, runs a hand through his hair.

I pull up a chair next to him and we both sit looking at the garden, watching the sun crawl down the roof of the flats opposite. Titi reaches under his seat and withdraws two cans of beer from the shade. He hands one to me; it's warm and bitter but not unpleasant.

'So how long have you known my brother?' he asks.

'Didn't he tell you?'

'He told me he's in love with you. That you're a student,

from England. That you're quiet because your French isn't very good and you're embarrassed about it.'

Something constricts in my chest.

'But it sounds fine to me,' Titi adds. 'And Paul's always been a perfectionist.'

'We met a few weeks ago,' I explain, surprising myself in saying it; a few weeks – is that really all?

'He's never had much luck with women,' Titi goes on. 'He's much too flighty, you know? But he seems happy. And I've never thought age difference is as big an issue as people make it out to be.'

I take a long, evasive drink of warm beer, searching my mind for a way to change the subject.

'Paul told me you're a shaman?'

He nods and stifles a burp. 'Yes. Well around my work hours anyway. I work abroad for half the year, and when I come back here there's not much to do except admin. I started shaman school a few years back but I'm still learning. It keeps me out of trouble.'

'Where do you work abroad?'

'Wherever the job is. I've been going to the Congo the last few years, overseeing a mining operation. It's basically a desk job. It's all run from France but they need someone to sit there in person, making sure everything's working smoothly.'

'What are they mining for?'

'A few diamonds, but mostly cobalt.' He taps the screen of my phone resting on the table. 'Where do you think they get the stuff to make these?'

I stare at my phone and try to imagine how the mineral components fit into its angular compactness; in my mind the device morphs into some strange, calcified hybrid, part artificial, part organic.

'The DRC has a reputation for being dangerous,' Titi says. 'But half of Paris is just as bad. And the trips are good for my practice; I've made loads of contacts and worked with some local practitioners. People there are already open to the spirit world. Makes my job easier – getting clients onside is half the job.'

He speaks about the occult like an entrepreneur, with business savvy and a matter-of-factness that reminds me, bizarrely, of Mireille.

'I've been trying to persuade Paul to let me read his stars,' Titi says. 'Maybe you can help convince him.'

'Why won't he?'

'I gave him a reading with some bad prospects when I was just starting out. He was furious. I've tried to tell him I'm better at seeing nuances, now, but he refuses.' He lets out a sigh and downs the last of his beer. 'Wait here, will you?'

He pushes himself to standing and pads off indoors. Somewhere nearby a window opens, and a conversation eddies into the air. At some point, without my noticing, the singing has stopped. On the block opposite, a woman appears on the first-floor balcony to hang up her washing. She has one peg in her mouth and the others clipped to her shirt sleeves as she works, keeping her hands free.

Titi reappears with a small black laptop and sets it down on the table. He tells me he's going to do my birth chart. A friend copied him some advanced astrological software, he says, so he'll be able to give me a much more sophisticated reading than I'd find online.

He asks me a series of questions, only some of which I can answer with certainty.

'I had you down as a Virgo sun,' he says, frowning in concentration at the screen. 'But you're Libra. Interesting.'

I smile, although I don't know what the difference is. After a few minutes of staring at the screen and muttering under his breath, Titi swivels it round so I can see. It shows a large circle divided into segments, dotted with symbols and lines drawn between them. I can't make any sense of it.

Titi stands over my shoulder. 'If I was doing this for a client I'd have a week or so to sit with it, flesh out the interpretation. But I can try and give you a crude impression now ... Let's see. At first glance it seems good: no real obstacles, everything's okay with your career, travel, money ... Oh, wait,' he points to one of the squiggly symbols. 'Venus in twelfth. Hmm.'

'What? Is it bad?'

'Not bad. Just a little difficult. And combined with a dominant moon ... It means you trust easily, may have a tendency to put others' needs before your own.'

'That's good isn't it?'

'Not if no one's looking out for yours. But that's what people don't understand. There's no "good" or "bad"; any sign can manifest in a variety of ways, or sometimes not at all. It depends on the situation, the person.'

'So the good way would be . . .'

Titi returns the cursor to hover over the Venus symbol. 'The positive manifestation would be a warm-hearted and compassionate outlook; you might be loyal and devoted in love. I think in English you say "wearing your heart on your sleeve"?'

I nod. 'And the bad?'

Titi types something in and begins to read from a list. 'Alors, immobilising passivity; tendency to idealise others and swallow down feelings to please them, to play dumb or shut down completely to avoid conflict; difficulty in making decisions and/or identifying own needs—'

'Really, Titi, what are you poisoning her ears with?' The sudden appearance of Paul in the doorway makes us both jump. He laughs and pulls off his T-shirt, balling it in his fist.

'How's your rogue dentist?' asks Titi, looking away from Paul's skinny torso back to the laptop.

'Vanished!' Paul says with a grin. 'Fled to Saint-Tropez or the Costa del Sol or somewhere.'

'Then why do you look so happy?'

'Because enough people have complained that I'll get free representation from the courts! I spoke to a lawyer just now and he said there's no way I won't come out of this richer.'

'Great,' Titi says without enthusiasm. 'Maybe you should lose teeth more often.'

In a mood of celebration, Paul has bought a kilo of fresh oysters and two bottles of wine on his way back from the dentist's. He upends a bag of oysters, which scatter over the kitchen counter, enormous compared to the ones I'm used to seeing at home.

'Fresh from Sète this morning,' he announces. 'Have you ever seen anything more beautiful?' We spend a few minutes arranging them on a dish, then take them outside.

We clink our oysters together like wine glasses and say santé. Paul drowns his in vinegar; Titi and I take ours plain. I try to forget that the creature is still alive as I swallow it down.

'This would be perfect with mignonette,' Paul says, 'but vinegar will have to do.'

He splashes one liberally and offers it to Titi, who refuses.

'Titi has never cared much for food,' Paul says to me. 'Although you'd never guess it, looking at the two of us!'

He laughs at his own joke and reaches for another oyster. 'So, what's the latest with Sandrine?'

Titi shrugs, avoiding eye contact.

'Come on, Ti, it'll be good for you to talk about it. You can't wallow forever.'

Titi plays with a frond of parsley. 'I'm not wallowing.'

'Ah bon?' Paul says with mock surprise. 'Of course you're wallowing. When was the last time you left the flat?'

'None of your business,' Titi answers coolly.

I put down my wine glass and hold my breath, wondering if an argument is about to break out. Titi looks like he might snap at any moment, of which Paul seems completely unaware.

'Look,' he changes tack, 'I'm only asking because I care. I want to help. I hate seeing you – like this.'

'I'm not "like" anything. I'm fine – work is slow right now, and I've been packing up Sandrine's stuff all week. What do you expect, for me to start doing cartwheels around the place?'

'Mon cher frère,' Paul says with his mouth full of bread, 'there's no need to be facetious. It's just *hard* for me, when I'm so happy, to see you struggling.'

Titi closes his eyes and inhales deeply. He appears to be counting under his breath. Paul smiles apologetically at me, as if embarrassed by Titi's behaviour.

A few minutes pass in which the only sounds are the brisk, wet bursts of each oyster being prised open, and the dull thud of glasses on the wooden table.

'I don't know what your plans are,' Titi says eventually, 'but you won't be able to stay here past tomorrow morning. I'm hosting a séance and we need the entire apartment.'

Paul shrugs without looking up. 'That's fine. I was thinking we'd drop in and see Vanessa and Fabian anyway.'

I look at Paul, confused. The names are unfamiliar to me – has he mentioned them before?

'Vanessa your friend from university?' asks Titi.

'Yup. She's shacked up now. Three kids. They live not too far away. I've been meaning to visit for years, but it's not often I'm this far east.'

'I thought you were going back to Lazeaux?' Titi asks.

I remember Paul saying that Titi had never been to visit Noa Noa, and I wondered how much he'd told him about it. What was it that Titi imagined – a fully functioning farm, overflowing with crops and animals?

'We are!' Paul takes a large gulp of wine. 'But Frances and I thought we might as well make a trip of it.'

Titi glances at me and I try to smile convincingly. Paul raises his wine glass to his mouth, and mis-aims, clinking it against his teeth.

He swears loudly and stands up, holding a hand over his mouth.

'I have some herbs that might help—' Titi begins.

'Fuck your herbs,' says Paul, his voice slightly muffled by his hand.

'He'll be fine,' Titi says once Paul has gone inside. 'Stubborn as a bull.'

Paul's swearing from inside the flat echoes out over the garden.

'Taurus,' Titi whispers conspiratorially, 'if you hadn't already guessed.'

vendredi

The following day, we leave before noon. Titi begins preparing for the séance as we pack up, lighting incense and arranging cushions on the floor. He looks nervous in a way someone might before a date, and seems distracted when we kiss goodbye.

Back in the car, Paul calls his friend Vanessa. She says she'd love to have us, as long as we don't arrive until the evening. So we have the whole day to explore, he says. He reels off a list of things he'd like to show me: the old town, the botanic gardens, flats where he used to live, bars he used to drink in. Montpellier was his university town, after all.

We get lunch from an organic produce shop he insists on visiting. We buy bread, some fruit and snacks, a few basics like soap and toothpaste. The bill comes to twenty-eight euros, and Paul starts to pick an argument about the price with the pale girl at the counter, who can only repeat the total with a worried stammer. I smile apologetically at her and hand over a twenty euro note. Paul shrugs, finds the remainder in change and stalks out after snatching our paper bags off the counter.

'Can you believe it?' He explodes as soon as we're out of the door.

We picnic in the shade of an enormous sand-coloured aqueduct that towers over the nearby buildings and trees. Paul tells me it's Roman, that the city has a long and varied history with a patchwork of architecture from different periods. I struggle to summon any interest.

Before we finish eating, Paul takes out a knife and cuts all the rinds and skins from our fruit into tiny pieces. He makes a rough gouge in the grass and tips the pieces in.

'Compost,' he says. 'It won't decompose otherwise.'

We climb steps to a tree-lined esplanade. It's enormous, and bustling with people strolling along the wide paths. On all sides there's a clear panorama over the city, and a large arch at one end that reminds me of the Arc de Triomphe. I wander over to a placard declaring Montpellier 'The Paris of the South'. I read on a little, about the eighteenth-century aqueduct installed to solve the city's water crisis. I point it out to Paul, who shrugs.

'I meant the *style* is Roman, not the actual thing.'

From the esplanade we take a winding street into the old town. It's lined with souvenir shops, delis and fancy boutiques, altogether less expensive-looking than Nice. Paul tugs me over to an ice-cream vendor and buys us both a cone of lemon sorbet. It's so sweet it makes my teeth hurt. I wonder how he can stand it.

He tells me he wants to take me to his favourite spot. Holding his cone above his head he leads me through the tangle of tourists down to the bottom of the hill, where trees from the Jardin des Plantes spill over high stone walls. He tells me it's the oldest botanical garden in France, that as a student he used to come here most days and read on the grass.

On the way in, an elderly security guard checks our bags. Paul smiles at him throughout but the guard's expression doesn't change. He points to a sign propped in his office window. *GRANDES SERRES FERMÉES AUJOURD'HUI.* Paul asks him why the glasshouses are closed, but the guard ignores him and moves on to inspect the bags of the people behind us.

Once inside, we drift through a parterre and emerge by a large pond hugging one of the glasshouses. There's a shimmering haze over the water, gold and green, as insects skim its filmy surface and settle on giant lily pads. On the other side of the lawn, a family with a buggy share a picnic.

'I used to sit here,' Paul points to a patch of grass in front of the water, 'and watch out for pretty girls.' He looks at me and winks. 'But now I don't need to, of course.' I squint at him in the sun. He puts his hand on the small of my back and pulls me to him. Sweat pools between my dress and my skin.

'Gardens make me amorous,' he murmurs.

We wander through the arboretum, passing a few people,

and step up onto a shady pine grove with staggered terraces. Herbs overflow from large urns and infuse the air with their scent. In the distance I can hear children laughing, though here in the coolness of the pines it feels more or less deserted. I feel calm, and pause for a few moments with my eyes closed, taking in all the sounds and smells. When I open them again, Paul is standing in front of me.

I can't read his expression; is he hurt, bewildered?

'Coquine.' He takes my upper arm and leads me over to an alcove, pushing me up against the tree. The rough bark digs into my back. His hands are inside my dress and then one of them slides down into my knickers. Suddenly he's unzipped and pushed himself in. I almost gag on the overwhelming scent of rosemary. I'm skewered between him and the bark, and for a fleeting moment my feet leave the floor and I feel weightless, bodiless.

Soon he groans and slumps over me. We stay like that for a moment before he pulls away, breathing heavily. My pulse is thumping in my ears.

'Sorry,' he says, panting. 'There wasn't time for a condom.' He zips up and looks around. 'Ça va?' He caresses my face with one hand.

In the dappled sunlight he looks beautiful again, a Byzantine icon.

'We can get a pill in the morning or something.'

I nod, and begin to button up my dress. An elderly couple saunter past, crunching on the gravel. Paul smirks at me as if to say *just in time*.

We carry on along the path. I feel a bead of liquid trickle down my inner thigh. Paul is feeling sleepy and wants to nap. We wander back to the lawn and he settles on his back with his bag beneath his head. He says he can get to sleep anywhere like this – it was one of the things he learned while travelling. 'And if anyone tries to move this,' he gestures to the bag, 'I wake up instantly.' He snaps his fingers for effect.

I don't feel tired at all. I leave him a note saying I'll meet him back there in an hour. I walk across the lawn. The family with the buggy have since moved on.

Once I hit the treeline I start running.

Leaving the gardens, three things occur to me. First, that I have no idea, really, where I am; second, that I don't have to go back to Paul at the time I said I would, or even at all. This thought leads to the third, in which I realise the second works both ways: if Paul doesn't stay put, I'll be left with nothing – my passport, money and clothes are all stowed in the back of his car.

I dismiss the thoughts and begin down a street I hadn't taken with Paul. It's more or less a replica of the street with the sorbet seller, filled with ambling tourists, and I duck onto a quieter side street. The buildings lean wonkily into each other, all of the same dun-coloured stone. Cats perch on balconies, eyeing me as I walk. At the end of the street two figures disappear into a doorway. As I approach it, I hear the faint sound of an organ playing, and follow them in.

The inside of the church is dimly lit. I linger on the fringe of a tour group for a few minutes, letting incomprehensible waves of German wash over me. The organ is mounted high overhead, making it impossible to see who's playing. I entertain the thought that it's not being played at all, that ersatz organ music is being fed in through unseen speakers.

At the back of the church are three alcoves, each for a different saint. In the first I recognise a man studded with arrows as Saint Sebastian, soft gold hair curling over his shoulders. Two men from the German tour group pose in front of the painting, arms entwined, one kissing the other's cheek while their friend takes the photo. Her phone makes a fake shutter sound and they rush over to inspect. The second alcove is blocked up for repairs. In the third, the portrait is so bizarre it takes me a few moments to recognise it as Saint Margaret the Virgin. She's usually depicted slaying the dragon that swallows her, but here she is still half caught in its jaws, her torso rising out of the gaping scaly mouth that dominates the lower third of the scene. The hellmouth.

Leaflets are scattered on a table nearby, available in five different languages. I pick up the one marked *ANGLAIS*, and read:

Saint Margaret lived in Antioch, the daughter of Theodosius, born around the year A.D. 291. Her father was a Pagan priest, though Margaret disappointed him by being baptized as a Christian at a young age.

Margaret was as beautiful as she was humble, as pleasing to look at as she was chaste. She is remembered, even today, as a white gem, a rare and virtuous virgin saint. Unfortunately, her pleasant countenance and her beauty, at the age of fifteen, attracted a local governor. He ordered his servants to bring the maiden before him, that he might claim her either as his wife or concubine, if she be free or slave.

When asked, Margaret proudly declared her faith and refused to denounce it. When she continued in this way, the governor ordered she be sent to prison and threatened that her fair flesh would be torn asunder. Still she refused to reject Christ, and was placed inside a torture instrument and beaten with iron rods that tore her flesh to the bone, causing her blood to run, as if water from a spring. Still, the weary and beaten Margaret refused to pay homage to any other gods.

There, Margaret the Virgin prayed. She asked the Lord to reveal the fiend that fought with her, and then appeared a terrible dragon that attacked her. In some stories, the dragon swallows the maiden whole and, inside the belly of the beast, she makes the sign of the cross, which causes the dragon to explode, expelling her. In other versions, the dragon seeks to devour her, but before he can swallow her, he is slain by the sign of the cross. In either case, Margaret bests the dragon with a symbol that frees her body . . .

The story carries on for another page and a half, but I stop reading because I feel queasy. Before leaving I take one last look at the painting, and notice a date engraved in the peeling gold frame: my mother's birthday. Does she know, I wonder, that her birthday shares its date with Saint Margaret's feast?

Outside, a man is selling watermelon. He carries the slices in a box strung around his neck, entreating passers-by to sample a cube of fruit from an outstretched plastic cup. The street isn't busy, and what few pedestrians there are walk straight past him. There's something reassuring about his lack of business savvy, so I end up buying two large slices but only take one of them. I wander back down the quiet street, juice running over my chin. I take another turn and climb stone steps leading up to a small plaza. On the topmost step I sit with my knees apart, letting the juice drip onto the stone between them as I eat.

When I've finished, I hurry down the steps and back onto the main street, the melon skin still in my hand. By the time I get to the gates of the Jardin des Plantes, the edges of the rind seem to curl inwards, like a scroll.

It's almost evening when we get back to the car. Paul tells me it's about an hour's drive to Vanessa's small village, where she moved after getting married. The last time he saw her was at the wedding, when he'd met her husband Fabian for the first time. He's been meaning to visit for ages, he says, but she keeps having kids.

As we drive, the sky begins to darken with clouds, throwing the fields either side of the autoroute into blue shade. Along the edges of the road, in lay-bys, I notice small groups of women stood together, and a few standing alone. I make eye contact with one of them as we pass; when I look in the rear-view mirror she has already turned back to face the oncoming traffic.

'Do you have this, in England?' Paul gestures to the two young women we pass at that moment.

I nod.

Paul looks straight ahead. 'I am ashamed, but ... there were times I used to stop here. When I was a student.'

He clears his throat.

'I didn't *want* to. But I had to – you know?' He glances at me as if trying to gauge my reaction. 'Do you judge me, coquine?'

I shake my head calmly, although my chest feels like it's about to explode. I want to be anywhere but here in Paul's car. I don't know how I feel about what he is telling me. I know what I *should* feel, or what my mother would think of the women by the road, but I've never been able to cleave right from wrong as easily as her.

Paul reaches for my hand and caresses my fingers. 'Incredible,' he says, shaking his head slightly. 'You are an angel.' I say nothing, and stare out at the fields. 'All the French women I've told that to,' he goes on, 'they shouted at me, called me names. But you would never do that, coquine. You are too wise. Sometimes, I feel like no one knows me like you do.'

He gives me a watery smile and I try my best to return it.

For the rest of the journey, Paul tells me about his friendship with Vanessa at university. They were in different anthropology classes, but quickly became friends after attending the same Arabic language course. Vanessa was in her early twenties, just a little older than most of the students, but old enough to nudge her closer to Paul, who, then in his mid-thirties, definitely qualified as a mature student. She was still living at her parents' outside Montpellier at the time, to save money, so if there was a party she'd crash at Paul's apartment in the old town.

'But it was never romantic,' he clarifies. 'En fait, I was about the only guy on our course she didn't sleep with.'

He tells me that Vanessa was very troubled, that she'd gone off the rails after her cousin, who was also her best friend, was killed in a car crash.

'It's weird,' Paul says, 'because his name was Paul too. Anyway, the way Vanessa coped with it was drinking, smoking, sex – you get the idea. Everyone thought she was just a party girl. I thought so too – the first time she stayed at mine – I'd heard the rumours going round, you know – so I tried to get into bed with her. But she pushed me away, told me she just needed a friend. I was a bit pissed off but I could see that she meant it. From then on she'd crash on my sofa at weekends, if she didn't stay with one of her guys.'

I nod along. It begins to rain, and Paul rolls up his window. For some reason Vanessa's story unnerves me, as if her history with Paul invalidates my own.

Paul says he's pleased that Vanessa has settled down, that he hopes to find her, finally, happy.

*

The rain is heavy by the time we reach Vanessa's sleepy village. The car crawls along the wet streets, Paul peering through streaked windows as he tries to locate the house. When we find it – a tall, once grand, now dilapidated town house – he scurries out of the car and runs round to the boot. He returns, rain-dappled, but sheltered beneath an enormous black umbrella, which he holds over me as I step out into the damp air.

I squint up at the house and try to count its floors. Orange windows and balconies flicker in and out of focus. We pound repeatedly on the large wooden doors on street level, and a few minutes later they swing inwards and a man's voice tells us to quickly come inside. A dim light flickers on as we step into a large garage. There are several vehicles covered with cloths, and a messy array of tools, furniture and plastic toys.

'Paul.' The man who let us in claps him on the shoulder and kisses him briskly.

'Fabian.' Paul's voice sounds deeper than usual. He gestures to introduce me: 'Frances, my girlfriend. From England.'

'Oh!' Fabian exclaims. Did he think Paul would be alone? I lean down slightly to kiss him; he's short, with the physique of an upside-down triangle. He wears faded grey tracksuit bottoms and a white vest, showing his upper body bulk. His head is closely shaved, and bluish tattoos snake over his neck, chest, arms and shoulders.

He motions for us to follow him up a curved flight of stairs and asks Paul how the journey was. They exchange a few banalities back and forth, and then there is only the sound of our wet sandals squeaking on the stairs.

'It's great you've found a moment to visit. Vanessa speaks so fondly of you. I know we probably met at the reception, but . . .'

'If you could remember everyone you met at your wedding reception you couldn't have been having enough fun,' Paul quips.

Fabian laughs and agrees.

At the next landing he pushes open the door and we file out into a hallway. It has a grand, arched ceiling, and is littered with toys and clothes that Fabian kicks aside to lead us into the kitchen. It's as high-ceilinged as the hallway, with a large table in the centre and an enormous cast iron range cooker. At the far end, a woman is leaning on the balcony, smoking and gazing out at the rain. She turns round and breaks into a smile.

'Salut, Paul!' She slips her sandals on and wanders over. Holding her cigarette over her shoulder she reaches up to kiss him.

'Vanessa.'

They hold each other's gaze before she approaches me. 'Et vous, bienvenue.' Her eyes are as dark as a wet road. We kiss.

'Forgive me,' she addresses Paul. 'I wanted to have dinner ready when you got here. But,' she sighs, 'it's been one of those days.'

She speaks slowly, tiredly, without seeming to open her mouth much at all. Her dark, cropped hair is scruffy around her shoulders, and she wears a dress that looks more like a slip. Her mascara is clumped and flaked a little over her eyelids; I get the impression she's just got out of bed.

Paul wanders over to take her place on the balcony. 'It's like an old palace in here,' he says, whistling.

He takes the beer offered to him by Fabian, who then holds up a couple of bottles of white and rosé from the fridge. Vanessa shakes her head. 'We'll have those with dinner. There's already red on the table.' Paul and Fabian open their beers, and she takes another drag on her cigarette.

'Come,' she says, beckoning us to the table. As she speaks, I notice her full figure straining against the fabric, the raised tips of her nipples.

In front of her are two glass ashtrays, and a cluster of bright plastic cups and beakers. Where I sit there's a half-eaten piece of toast smeared with jam. She scoots it out of my way and wipes off the crumbs. 'The kids get everywhere,' she says. I try to communicate with a smile that I don't mind.

'Une vraie maman!' Paul teases.

Vanessa rolls her eyes. 'Stop.'

'It's been too long, Vanessa. How many do you have now?'

'Three.' Fabian takes a swig of beer. 'But it feels like more, even with this much space. Roban is nine, from my first marriage . . .'

'Then Rosalie is five, and Léon is two.'

'And Vanessa's sister is staying for the school holidays. Her Cyril is six months.'

'Jesus,' Paul mutters.

Fabian laughs and Vanessa raises her eyebrows.

'And they all get on?'

Vanessa glances at Fabian. 'More or less.'

There's silence for a moment or two, verging on uncomfortable. Fabian clears his throat. 'Et toi, Frances, what brings you to France?'

I start to answer when Paul cuts over me. 'Her French isn't all that good yet. She's shy about it.'

I feel my cheeks turn scarlet.

'Ah bon?' Vanessa addresses Paul. 'So how do you talk to each other? Have you finally mastered English?' Her smile seems coy.

'We get by.' Paul deflects the question. 'Non, it was a miracle. I didn't have to do a thing. You know that volunteering scheme I told you about on the phone – BénéBio?'

Vanessa nods.

'I got this email from an English girl in Paris and then, voilà, a few days later, Frances arrived! The gods were smiling on me.'

Fabian's eyes flicker between Paul and me. 'Very romantic,' he says. 'Love at first sight, and all that. Like us, baby.' He rubs Vanessa's shoulder, slurring his words a little. He holds out his bottle to toast with Paul's.

'Exacte.' Paul raises his bottle and drinks. His other hand finds my leg beneath the table. The muscles in my face have locked into a permanent smile.

Fabian asks Paul about his work. I zone out as Paul begins talking about the 'farm' at Noa Noa, about the various exhibitions of his photography. I stare at the wipe-down tablecloth. It's the colour of the Rastafarian flag, with a tessellating portrait of Bob Marley.

Vanessa reaches across the table and touches my arm. 'Would you mind giving me a hand with dinner? It's almost done.' She speaks slowly, sounding out each syllable.

She leads me over to the counter and brings a handful of fat, ripe tomatoes from the fridge. 'Could you cut these for a salad?' She passes me a knife. 'I just need to season the chicken.'

We set about working, though it's clearly not a job for two people, and I get the impression that Vanessa just wanted an excuse to speak to me. Paul and Fabian are talking loudly and enthusiastically, already on their second bottles. There's no risk of us being overheard.

'So Paul tells me you're a student?'

'Yes.'

'And what do you study?'

'Medieval history.'

Vanessa removes a selection of rings and silver charm bracelets before rubbing a spice mix onto the raw chicken breasts.

'Go on.' She nods.

'It's not that interesting.'

'Indulge me, please. It's been too long since I got to think about anything but nappies.'

I look down at the tomatoes. 'I was studying a manuscript from the fifteenth century. It's French – well, Middle French. That's why I'm in France – I came to see it in the archives in Paris.'

'A religious text?'

'Not really, it was more educational. We think someone used it to teach children to read, but we don't know who. That's what I was looking at – provenance, methods of early education.'

'Jesus, and Paul thinks your French is no good? Well,' she carries on, 'it sounds fascinating.'

'I don't know.' I move onto a bunch of parsley. 'It feels very far away now.'

Just then there's a high-pitched shriek from outside the kitchen door, and a small girl with white-blonde curls peers around the door frame.

Vanessa wipes her hands on a tea towel and beckons her in. 'Rosalie, come and meet our guests.' Rosalie disappears then peeps into the room again. 'This is my friend Paul, and this is Frances, une Anglaise.'

'Une Anglaise?' Rosalie echoes, and reappears to stare at me. She tiptoes in, kisses Paul on the cheek, takes a long look at me and then runs, screaming, from the room. I hear her thud up the stairs calling 'Roban! Roban! Il y a une Anglaise dans la cuisine!'

'BE QUIET!' Fabian shouts after her. 'You'll wake your baby brother.'

Vanessa hisses at him and turns back to the chicken. 'Sorry about that. She'll probably be infatuated with you the whole weekend.'

My mind jogs: the whole weekend? I glance over at Paul, joking with Fabian. I thought we were staying for the night, and heading back to Lazeaux tomorrow. But I can't ask him about it now; I try to concentrate on Vanessa instead. She is telling me how she and Paul met.

'We were in the same Arabic class. But we didn't hang out properly until the trip to Algeria. He must have told you all the stories?'

'No,' I lie quickly, wondering if she'd feel betrayed or embarrassed by what he had told me. 'I think he didn't want to say too much, before we met.'

'That makes sense.' She nods. 'To be honest, I think we became friends because we were the worst in the class! There was Paul, already a seasoned traveller, and me, a hopeless trainee diplomat, and we couldn't even string a sentence together!'

'But I thought – Paul's really good at languages, isn't he?'

Memories flash up of looking through his notebooks, being overawed by the pages filled with complex grammar and vocabularies.

'Not unless he's become so in the five years since I saw him.' She lights another cigarette, and takes a long drag. 'I'd forgotten how pissed off it made him though. I thought it was kind of funny to be bad at languages – I was never a serious student, as you can probably tell – but Paul couldn't stand it. He thought it shouldn't be hard. He would collect all these words, and then be angry when they just sat there, and didn't form sentences by themselves.'

I can't think of anything to say. I ask for a cigarette, and Vanessa lights one for me off hers.

'Paul is very charming,' she says under her breath, 'but very proud.' She hands me the cigarette. 'But then, I'm sure you know more about that than me!'

For dinner we're joined by Vanessa's sister, Tiffanie, who's been upstairs taking a nap. Roban, Fabian's son, is summoned to the table too. He plods into the kitchen with no shirt on and sullenly takes a seat next to his father. He has pale blond hair, and abundant puppy fat.

Tiffanie greets me with a lopsided smile. Her hair straggles out of an unmaintained pixie cut, and she wears a loose T-shirt and cargo trousers. She moves like a dancer, tucking her legs to sit in a lotus position at the table.

Vanessa tops up everyone's glasses while Fabian carries the tray of sizzling chicken to the table and tells everyone to help themselves. Roban's pink hand shoots out to grab the largest piece, and Fabian scolds him, slapping his wrist. Fabian takes the piece for himself and forks a smaller leg onto Roban's plate. To my left, Paul takes a breast and tears into it hungrily. I notice he doesn't ask, as he usually does, if the meat is organic.

'A toast,' Fabian announces, 'to our guests: Paul and Frances!' We clink glasses. Everyone smiles at me, their gazes corrosive.

'Like the saints, non?' Vanessa says. 'St. Paul, St. Francis—'

'So what's next?' Fabian asks Paul with a mouthful of chicken. 'Long-term, I mean. I don't care about what you two do upstairs once we're asleep!' He laughs and Vanessa hits him lightly around the head.

Paul puts his arm around me and begins to trace a circle on my shoulder. 'Well, Frances has graduated, so she's going to help me translate my book. And there's a room at Lazeaux if she wants it.' He turns to smile at me.

'Makes sense,' Fabian mutters. 'I don't think I could do long distance. Not between countries, anyway.'

'Well I can always go and visit her in Durham, bien sûr.'

Durham! I wince at Paul's mistake, but internally excuse him; English geography *is* confusing. I'm relieved when Fabian drops the topic and the conversation splits us into pairs; Vanessa and Paul become engrossed in discussing their former classmates, while Roban attempts to interest Fabian in the online game he's obsessed with.

Tiffanie and I observe the others for a while before she says she would have guessed I was Dutch.

'Close enough,' I say, although I have no idea why.

It's not long since Tiffanie graduated so we speak a little about university. She studied languages in Paris, but now lives in Marseille, where she's a speech therapist in a primary school.

'It's tough,' she says. 'It's a very diverse place, Marseille, which is great in some ways, but there's a lot of conflict too. We get all these kids who don't speak French, but still somehow have to get through the same curriculum as everyone else.'

She pauses to heap more salad onto her plate. 'I put on classes after school and there'll be twenty, thirty of the non-French-speakers in the room. I speak some of these kids' languages – enough to help them anyway. But I'm forbidden from doing so.'

'Why?'

She shrugs. 'That's the system. It's fucked up.'

I ask if she got some time off to have Cyril, and she smiles at the mention of her son's name. Not enough, she says, but she's lucky because he sleeps like an angel.

I begin to lose my grip on the conversation with Tiffanie, and feel myself being lulled into Paul's voice speaking next to me, addressing Vanessa: *And after that, he took a forty-per-cent cut, can you believe it? He said it was on the form I'd signed, and I said at no point was that indicated on the form, and even if it was, it's a matter of principle . . .*

I manage to haul my attention back to Tiffanie and ask if Cyril will have any brothers or sisters. It's a clumsy question, but I feel relieved to have remembered something relevant to the conversation. Maybe she hadn't noticed my absence, after all.

'Not likely,' she says flatly. 'His father ran off five months in.'

It's past midnight by the time the wine bottles are empty and the tray is filled with chicken bones. The giddy phase of the alcohol has worn off and my eyelids are drooping. Across from me, Roban looks half asleep already. I hang around, waiting for everyone to say goodnight. Instead, Vanessa suggests moving to the front room. The others get up and I start clearing plates until Vanessa shoos my hands away, tells me it can wait until morning.

The front room is lined with wide sofas on every side, presided over by a giant flat-screen TV that soaks the room in a blue glare. I'm surprised to see Rosalie sitting on the sofa with a small boy I assume is her brother, Léon. Both are staring at the screen and barely look up as we enter.

'Move,' Vanessa orders Rosalie, who wriggles aside without taking her eyes from the screen.

Fabian flops down with a sigh and picks up the remote. 'What crap is this?'

Rosalie gives a shriek when he changes the talent show to a sports channel.

'Je déteste le foot,' she moans.

'Shut up,' Roban tells her, for which he receives a light slap from Fabian. He settles grumpily next to his father and tries to pay attention to the game. Tiffanie curls up on the next sofa, absorbed in an iPad, while Vanessa scrolls through something on her phone.

Paul pulls out an ancient-looking laptop from a bag I didn't even know he had with him. He asks for the Wi-Fi password, and without looking up Vanessa throws a card at him across the coffee table. Soon, he too is engrossed. Everyone around me is glued to screens, apart from Rosalie and Léon who now seem tetchy and restive. I watch as Rosalie begins playing with her brother's face, pulling on his lips and earlobes as if to test their elasticity. At first Léon seems only slightly annoyed, jerking his head away as if she is a bothersome fly. But then a few seconds later, he lets out a loud wail.

'What now?' Vanessa demands angrily, looking up from her phone. She grabs Rosalie's arm. 'What have you done?'

Rosalie begins to whimper. Vanessa sighs and withdraws several pots of play dough from a box beneath the coffee table. 'There,' she says, placing them in front of the children. 'See if you can play nicely.'

Léon and his sister recover quickly and set about pulling the play dough from the pots. Rosalie chatters away, either to herself or Léon, until her mother's foot nudges her into silence. At one point she looks up and notices me watching. The discovery of an audience transforms her; she breaks into a wide grin, and grabs a pile of play dough to bring to me.

'See?' she says, holding out the blob.

'Very nice.' I take it from her. 'What is it?'

She smiles in response. I try to give the blob back to her but she tugs on my hand.

I let myself be pulled down to the table. Léon seems entirely preoccupied with the strange shape he's making, but Rosalie is alert to my every move. She soon gives up on her own designs and demands that I make her, in turn, a snail, a cat, a star, a hedgehog. When I don't make them quickly enough she begins to boss me about, telling me to go faster.

After twenty minutes or so I feel my patience wearing thin, and it's a struggle to keep my eyes open. I finish the fluorescent turtle I'm making and set it on the table. 'Finished,' I say, yawning. I sit back on the sofa with Paul, hoping to send him a signal about going to bed. But as soon as I sit down

Rosalie pouts, and says in a small, whingeing voice that we haven't finished playing. It's gone 1 a.m.

Vanessa glances up at me from her phone. 'Rosalie still wants to play with you,' she says. I hold her gaze. It feels like a command.

Reluctantly, I kneel back down at the table. Léon is dozing on the floor. Rosalie presents me with a blob of every colour. Her small eyes fix onto mine.

'So,' I say with resignation. 'What shape shall I make this time?'

samedi

I wake up with a furry mouth and a throbbing head. The room we slept in looks more or less like a teenage boy's bedroom, albeit one from another decade; the sloping loft walls are lurid green and covered with peeling posters of Tupac and Linkin Park. Light spills in from a window, onto what looks like a locker unit stolen from a boys' changing room, scrawled over with graffiti in fading marker pen. A few dusty guitar cases lean against the back wall. But at least, I think, wriggling a little in the sheets, there's a proper bed. I haven't slept in one since leaving Malmot.

My eyes flicker to the large wardrobe with a mirror-plated door, and I remember watching our reflections in it last night. Paul had wanted me, though I was tired, and we did it drunkenly, messily. At one point I was on my front, facing the mirror, while Paul worked into me from behind, watching my reflection, or his own – it was hard to tell. He'd looked so thin that for a second it had looked like I was being fucked by a skeleton. But mostly I was elsewhere, still thinking about Rosalie, her demanding that I make shapes for her over and over again.

'The beast awakens.' Vanessa grins at Paul as we step into the kitchen. 'I'd forgotten what you look like when you're hungover.'

Rosalie sits alone at the table, surrounded by toys. Vanessa gestures for us to sit down opposite. On the wall above her daughter there's a painting I hadn't noticed last night, depicting the word *PAUL* in large capitals, with each letter picked out in lurid blocks of colour. The letters are assembled from fragments of Gauguin paintings, their shape taken from his signature. I remember the story Paul had told me about Vanessa's cousin, that his name was Paul too. She must have bought the painting in memory of him.

'You've just missed the boys,' Vanessa says. 'They've gone to pick up lunch from the market.'

'So it's just us girls,' Rosalie says, patting her hands on the table. 'And Paul. Maman, what's for breakfast?'

Vanessa sits down next to Rosalie and begins to butter her a slice of brioche. 'Paul never eats when he's hungover,' she explains to me. 'That's how he stays so thin!'

I fix myself a bowl of cereal. The phone rings, and Vanessa gets up to answer it.

'Make sure she eats that, will you?' She points me to Rosalie's breakfast.

*

If we get into town before noon, Paul says, we might be able to spend an hour or so in the market, before getting a lift back with Fabian. I'm quickly on board with the plan, as the alternative seems to be a morning spent pacifying Rosalie.

Once outside, he suggests we should hitchhike to save petrol; it's how he got everywhere when he was young, he says. The market is in the next town, famous for the play-wrights who lived there in the seventeenth-century, and the theatre troupes who performed outdoors on the winding streets of the old town. Paul tells me it's a twenty-minute drive, and if all else fails should only take us an hour or so to walk. We're sure to find a path near the road, he adds.

At the bottom of the village we turn onto the main road, flanked by fields of crops. Walking along it feels dangerous; the cars barely leave inches to overtake us. There's no pave-ment and a sharp drop to a ditch on our left. The sun blazes overhead, with no trees or clouds for shade. My feet feel heavy, and begin slipping about in my sandals.

'Turn around,' Paul says. 'It'll be easier this way.'

He begins to walk backwards in the direction of the traffic, holding his thumb out into the road, his smile gormless. He struggles to walk in a straight line, and has to turn every few seconds to make sure he doesn't fall into the ditch.

'Try it,' he urges me. 'It'll work better if they see you first.'

Walking backwards is even harder than Paul made it look, and I trip on every other step. The cars speed past with no signs of slowing. I worry that we'll have to walk backwards the whole way to town; does anyone even stop for hitchhikers any more?

After twenty minutes or so, a car finally slows down.

'See!' Paul shouts excitedly. The grin is still on his face as we get into the back of an old four-by-four. The lone driver is a middle-aged woman with long, silvery hair and woven jewellery. I notice an Om symbol dangling around her neck. 'Where are you headed?' she asks.

'To the market,' Paul says.

The woman nods. 'I'm passing by. I can drop you outside the town; it won't take long to walk from there.'

'Merci, you're very kind.'

'How long have you been out here for?' she asks. 'You could get sunstroke.'

I catch her eye in the mirror. Paul laughs and shrugs it off.

The woman asks our names and what we do, and Paul immediately launches into a monologue about his travels, his photography and the farm at Lazeaux. I'm amazed at the speed and enthusiasm with which he bounces from one thing to the next, and notice the woman is nodding along, smiling and laughing. Before long he's pulled some postcards of his work out of his bag and hands them to her.

'My email address and phone number are on the back,' he points out.

I look at Paul's small duffel bag. Did he always carry copies of the postcards around with him?

'And you?' The woman meets my eyes again in the mirror.

This time, I don't even try to talk. I hear Paul's voice cut in, explaining my studies, how we came to meet in Lazeaux. I turn to stare out of the window. In some ways it's a relief to have him speak for me, to no longer have to account for myself. He tells it so much better than I can.

Despite Paul's predictions, we miss Fabian and Roban at the market, and end up having to hitchhike on the return journey too. When we get back, the garage door is open, and we walk through the house, calling for them. We find everyone out back, sitting around a table on the veranda. Baby Cyril is dozing in his buggy in the shade. There are empty plates in front of them, streaked with an oily residue.

Fabian stifles a burp, and apologises that they've already eaten, as they didn't know what time we'd be back. Vanessa tells me there's some leftover paella in the fridge. I retrieve a plateful each for Paul and myself, then join them at the table. The cold paella tastes good, but Paul forks out the seafood and inspects it suspiciously before putting it to the side of his plate.

I tell Vanessa it's delicious, trying to express gratitude on behalf of Paul as well as myself. He looks elsewhere, at something Fabian has just pulled up on his phone.

The afternoon heat makes everything feel sluggish. Rosalie and Roban play in a freestanding pool that takes up half the garden, while Vanessa and Tiffanie sunbathe. I sit with Fabian and Paul while Fabian explains the intricacies of his income. He used to work as a mechanic in a garage but found the percentage of his salary going on taxes was extortionate.

'It wasn't so bad when I was an apprentice,' he says, 'and

I didn't have a big family, you know? But then Rosalie was born, and Vanessa got pregnant with Léon not long after.'

Paul takes a swig of beer. 'Right. There are no tax breaks for kids,' he says, with surprising authority on the subject.

'Vanessa was always the main earner anyway. But she hasn't been back to work since having Rosalie.'

Paul glances over to where Vanessa is sunbathing. 'Do you think she will?'

Fabian shrugs. 'I don't know. We make enough to get by, for now.'

Paul explains that Fabian buys in motorbikes, does them up and sells them on illegally. He tells me very slowly, as if I might have trouble following his words.

'Sometimes cars, too,' Fabian adds.

'So basically tax avoidance,' I say.

They both flinch. 'If you have to put it like that,' Fabian says, looking offended.

Paul stares at me angrily, as if I've just slapped them both across the face.

Later, Roban and Paul are playing in the pool, which is filled with brightly coloured inflatables. I don't feel like changing into my swimming costume so I join Vanessa and Tiffanie who are lying beneath parasols, taking pictures of Rosalie in a smaller paddling pool.

'Jump!' Vanessa commands, watching her daughter come into focus on her phone screen. Rosalie jumps but the camera misses her moment in mid-air. 'Encore, Rosalie,' her mother says. 'Sautes, sautes!' Rosalie jumps a few more times but Vanessa keeps missing the take.

'Let me see!' Rosalie cries. She is wearing a miniature pink bikini, trimmed with orange netting on the shoulders and hips. She clambers over to Vanessa and they crowd around the phone. Léon is playing in the sandpit, unaware of the photo shoot around him.

'It would be better if it looked like she'd just come out of the pool,' Tiffanie observes. 'She's dry now.'

'Yes, I'm all dry,' Rosalie agrees.

'Well, coquine, we'll have to correct that!' Tiffanie says as she splashes Rosalie with water. My heart skips. Rosalie shrieks with glee.

I try to keep my voice calm and detached as I ask, 'Coquine – what is that, a nickname?'

Tiffanie carries on splashing Rosalie. 'Coquine? No, it's like ... it's something you'd say to a little girl. If she's being cheeky, like this one!' Rosalie's cries are shrill and piercing.

'Unless you're a grown woman,' Vanessa says, flicking through photos on her phone. 'A man would call you "coquine" if you were teasing him.'

'I think in English you say "'tart'"?' Tiffanie offers.

'Oh,' I say, my head reeling. Paul's voice is pounding in my ears, drowning out everything else: *It's a kind of shell. A seashell . . .*

Just then, we are hit with a wave of water. Rosalie, Vanessa and Tiffanie all scream. Roban's large, pink face appears over the side of the pool, grinning victoriously.

'ROBAN!' Vanessa yells angrily. 'That went all over my phone!' She looks around for something to wipe it on. 'I swear, Roban, if it's broken, it will be coming straight out of your savings . . .'

Roban's smile flickers. 'But it was an accident,' he says.

'What do you think I am, an idiot? Fuck, it's not working.' She jabs the screen aggressively with her fingers. 'Fuck. Well I hope you're pleased, Roban. You'll be buying me a new phone.'

Roban begins to whimper. 'But it . . . it was an accident!' he says between sobs. 'Ask . . . ask Paul. He'll tell you!'

Paul appears at the lip of the pool. His face is entirely straight, expressionless.

'Tell her!' Roban commands.

Paul begins to hoist himself out.

'Don't leave,' Roban whines. Paul jumps down onto the grass and rubs his face on a towel. After a few moments he starts off in the direction of the house. 'But who will play with me?' Roban calls after him. 'Paul? Paul!'

Paul disappears into the house without looking back, leaving the chaotic family scene behind him.

I find him upstairs throwing our clothes into a bag.

'Let's get the hell out of here,' he says.

I nod in relief. There's something about Vanessa and Fabian, the children, the house, that makes me feel suffocated.

'I've got another friend who lives not far from here. I'll give him a call.'

I watch him pace the room, still in his swimming trunks. The hairs slicked to his legs look dark and venous. I search through his bag for my notebook, and he glowers at me as I begin to write.

'What?' he whispers irritably. 'Can't you see I'm on the phone?'

I hold the notebook out to him. *When are we going back to Lazeaux?* But he just takes the book and tosses it on the bed. His frown snaps into a smile as the line connects.

'Salut – Salut, Mathieu? Ouais, c'est Paul . . .'

I stare past him, out of the window. Only one more night until Lazeaux.

'I feel a little bad for Vanessa,' says Paul once we drive onto the main road, 'but I couldn't have stayed any longer. Families are awful, don't you think?'

He puts an arm over the back of my seat. 'I have been waiting to be alone with you all day,' he says.

I think about wriggling out of his grasp. The thought is so vivid that for a moment I almost believe I've done it.

Mathieu, the friend he'd called, is staying in a town just a few hours' drive along the coast. It's on the way home so we may as well stop off and say hello, Paul says. But there's somewhere he wants to take me first, somewhere he knows I'll love.

The land flattens as we head towards the coast; lines of poplars dance in the ditches between fields, and silhouettes of swooping birds punctuate the green. Clouds drift flatly on the blue horizon, softly clawed by the treetops. Paul is unusually quiet. I glance at him a couple of times but he avoids my gaze, nonchalantly checking the wing and rear-view mirrors, something he never bothers to do.

It's late afternoon by the time we park up. People around us straggle up from the beach to the car park, carrying towels and parasols, leaning against cars to brush sand from their feet. Paul tells me we're here to visit an ancient monastery. It's situated on an island that can only be accessed on foot by an isthmus running parallel to the sea. It's about a half-hour walk, Paul says as we set off.

To our left, the sea is obscured by high sand dunes, peppered with scrubby plants. I can hear waves breaking on the other side, though it's impossible to tell how far away they are. To our right are vast bodies of water cut off from the sea that have long gone stagnant. Earlier, I'd seen the pools from the car and pointed, not knowing what they were. L'étang, Paul had said, le marécage. Marsh, fen, salt lake; I don't know which exactly. There's a strange dissonance between the silence of the static green water and the sound of waves, crashing out of sight. In the distance, the narrow strip of land widens to a dense cluster of trees.

'The monastery is in there,' Paul says, pointing. A flock of birds rises from the trees and flies out over the fens. Their bodies seem too large to fly; I think it's a trick of perspective until they land at the swamp's edge, pink against grey, and I realise, excitedly, what they are.

'Flamingos,' Paul says, without interest.

I had no idea there were flamingos in France. I spend the rest of the walk wondering if they are wild or somehow looked after by the monastery.

Soon, we reach the end of the path and the forest of tall, full-skirted fir trees. Between the sand dunes and the trees, lush vineyards curve round to the other side of the island, out of sight.

'That's where the monks used to work,' Paul says, gesturing to the vines. 'They would make an income from vendange to finance the monastery. It's some sort of social initiative now, though. The people working here are mostly disabled.'

I squint back along the narrow path, so exposed to the sun. It seemed anything but accessible, if it was, as Paul said, the only way to reach the monastery.

A shaded path leads us from the dune into the woods, where the air is cooler. Insects click calmly out of sight, and the soft peal of a bell sounds further down the path. Paul takes my hand as a middle-aged couple appear round a bend. They seem somehow not to see us, and follow the path leading behind us to the dunes. The peal of the bell becomes louder. When I turn round, the couple have disappeared, and I can see only tall, dark trees. The sea seems suddenly very far away.

Paul tells me in hushed tones what he can remember of the monastery: its foundations date to the rule of Charlemagne and are somehow tied up with the Knights Templar. Its shape is half-cloaked in rhododendrons, and even at its tallest point it is overshadowed by the treeline. The side facing us is an uneven colour, mottled lilac where flowers cast their shadows over the stone. A shallow campanile extends from one end, its bell no longer ringing.

I suddenly realise that he's brought me here as a gesture, thinking the medieval monastery might interest me. *This is kind of him*, I reason, pushing down my confusion about us not returning to Lazeaux straight away. I should be grateful.

The path takes us to the main entrance, where an elderly man sits on a camping stool in the shade of another, slightly squatter tower. A melody eddies out from the interior, distinctly medieval.

Paul gives two euros to the man at the door, one for each of us. The man offers us an information sheet with the floorplan and history, and asks which language we would like.

'I don't need one,' says Paul, 'but she's English.'

I take the sheet the man gives me, feeling too tired to protest. Paul promptly steps inside and the shadows engulf his back.

I hesitate. The doorway is topped with a thick tympanum, engraved with roundels of leaves and vines. A semi-circular arch runs above it – Gothic, I think, although the bell tower is definitely Romanesque. Pasts folded into other pasts. The Romans called it 'spolia', the ransacking of the whole to build anew from its parts. Churches stacked on foundations of temples; turn the inscribed stone the other way round and a new religion is born. Even buildings have roots, if you know how to look.

I follow the curve of Christ's robe to where it sags over his knee. There are four animals around the throne representing the evangelists. *Matthew, Mark, Luke, John; angel, lion, ox, eagle.* I don't realise I have listed these out loud until the elderly man cries bravo! which makes me jump. He remarks that my father must be proud to have such a clever daughter. I'm momentarily confused until I realise he's referring to Paul.

Inside, a low, barrel-vaulted ceiling arcs overhead, rising further down the aisle to a height I can't yet see. The air is warm with the scent of oil and hot wax. The walls are bare save for racks of votive candles, whose flames seem to flicker in time with the echoing music.

The tune slows as I walk, its notes melancholic and sparse. When it suddenly stops I hear a low murmur of people talking, one of them Paul. In a deep alcove on the left are three musicians: two men and a woman dressed in medieval costume, each of them cradling an instrument. Paul addresses them, praising their music and telling them that he first came here many years ago, that he has spent time in a host of other countries but there is something about the mystique of Catholicism that always brings him home. The men, both older than Paul, respond politely, looking down at their instruments. The woman, slightly younger, flushes with the attention, as he reaches out to touch the large stringed instrument on her lap.

A few minutes later, once we've moved on, I realise I am still carrying the information sheet. At some point I have gripped it so tightly that it's screwed up into a ball. I try to flatten and uncrease it, but it's torn through at the fold-lines, making most of the text unreadable.

'I think I could have been a monk,' says Paul as I join him on the stone balcony overlooking the forest. It feels good to be back out in the open air, close to the lush density of the trees. The sun has expended the last of its light, and the sky is a pale blue. A chill in the air signals the onset of twilight.

I pull on my cardigan and lean over the stone wall. Paul stares off to a point in the distance, hands together with his fingers interlocked like the vertebrae of some strange, impossible animal.

'It suits me, this kind of life. Nature, meditation, solitude . . .' he trails off. 'Have I told you how religious I was as a child? When Titi and I were small, our mother always made us go to Mass with her. But around eleven or twelve I became very fervent, on my own account. Really zealous.

'My father hated it,' Paul carries on. 'He couldn't ever abide her religiosity, and held it against the both of us. Of course, that made me all the keener to pursue it.' He pauses. 'I realised when I was very young that there was nothing I could do to make him proud of me.'

He gazes out at the trees, seemingly lost in communion with them. 'It's so peaceful here.'

Small birds chatter in the canopy above, and the fading light makes the rhododendrons take on a mass that is almost sinister. It is undeniably peaceful, but claustrophobic too.

'But wouldn't you feel cooped up, cut off from the world?' I wonder aloud.

Paul snaps around with a sharp look on his face. I'm surprised too, barely aware of having opened my mouth.

'It's nice to know you can talk when you want to,' he says.

I feel my throat tighten and close up again. The air seems to become thick, as it does before a storm. Paul reaches out and pulls me over. He stands behind me, holding the balcony on either side. I feel safe and swaddled, like a baby. We stand like this, listening.

'*Their throats are open graves; their tongues practise deceit,*' he murmurs after a while. 'That verse has always stayed with me.' His voice purrs somewhere near my ear, his breath on my neck. 'It's referring to the guilt of sin that covers all mankind. But it can be interpreted as an outcome of defying human nature, I think.' He begins stroking my hair.

'This is how we were designed to exist, Frances. To be close to nature, living off the land. In small groups where everyone is known to each other. If I've learned anything from all my travelling, it's this. Catholic monks, the Arioi, whatever names we give ourselves – it's all the same dynamic, you see? It's what we all crave: to belong. La nature humaine.'

His voice echoes out over the woods. I strain to hear the rustle of birds, movement, anything; but nothing stirs. It's as if Paul's voice has muted the entire world.

'But the most central, the *essential* part of belonging, is the polarity between a man and a woman. There can be no true harmony without it. Every ancient civilisation knew this. For all the places I have been, all my experiences – it's been worth-less, in a way. Because I was lacking this fundamental thing. That's why you're so precious, Frances. The right woman is like a pearl. Once you've found it, you should never lose it.'

Paul is quiet and thoughtful as we walk back along the dark-ened forest path. I fall into step behind him. Before reaching the sand dunes we pass by a small gift shop we'd somehow missed on our way in. They are just closing up, and I linger at the back of the shop while Paul selects a bottle of wine to buy for his friend Mathieu. I browse the souvenirs with disinterest until a small display catches my eye. A wooden bowl filled with flat, grey stones, each about the size of a credit card. I pick one up and turn it over in my fingers. Its irregularities have been buffed smooth, and a card propped up next to the display explains that the stones are unique to the island; they are taken from a river that runs in from the sea, where the currents give shape to the stones. The card declares the stones' felicitous and healing properties. Paul calls to me from the front of the shop, and without deliberating I slide the stone up my sleeve.

Outside, I shake it out into my palm. Paul asks me where I got it and I say nothing, skipping ahead to where the path rises up to the sand dune. I kick off my shoes, relishing the cool, damp grit between my toes. I want to walk on the other side of the dune, where the sand meets the water. I clamber to the top and finally get a view of the sea. The tide is out, further than it must have been when we walked along the isthmus earlier and heard waves crashing out of sight.

A few groups of people are clustered along the shore, and several boats dot the horizon. On the other side, sea spurge and marram grass crest the dunes and rustle in the breeze, while the far edges of the salt lakes are daubed with flamingo pink.

Paul joins me at the top and nods to the figures further down the beach. He complains that it's too busy, like all beaches in the South.

We walk back the rest of the way in silence, Paul on the dry sand while I tread through the parts still waterlogged. At one point we reach what must be some kind of meeting place; where men of all ages are lying in groups of two or three or sometimes alone. They are all naked, or near naked, and fall quiet as we pass. It's too dark to make out their faces, but their penises, pale and docile, seem to peep out at us, like the soft bodies of molluscs emerging from their shells.

'Dégoûtant,' Paul says once we get back to the car. 'It's not that I'm homophobic.' He holds his hands up in mock submission. 'I just ... I just don't want to *see* it. They can do whatever they want in private.'

I lean down to brush the sand from my feet. We settle into our seats and Paul starts up the engine. A few cars trundle into the car park as we exit.

'They're so obvious,' Paul says, eyeing the cars warily. 'You know I have had a couple of run-ins? Once or twice, hitchhiking when I was younger. Some men don't take no for an answer. It's the only time I've felt scared. I think it was then that I began to understand what it's like for women; you know? Trying to fight off unwanted attention … even if you're not dressed like a prostitute. Some men just don't understand the difference. Not even in Lazeaux …'

I ask what he means, although I think I already know the answer.

'Patrice, when I first moved there.'

'What happened?'

Paul screws up his face. 'What do you think?' he says bluntly. 'He propositioned me; I said no.'

I think back to when I've seen them together. The first time – in Noa Noa with the Tour de France crowd cheering outside – I thought I'd imagined Paul's hostility, but it made sense now. He didn't want to be wanted in *that way*; it made him afraid. And he resented Patrice for it.

The road hugs the coast, keeping the sea in view. Paul tells me about his friend who he teasingly calls 'Frère Mathieu' on account of his fanaticism for a strict, environmentally sustainable lifestyle. They met a few years ago picking grapes in an organic vineyard, but haven't seen each other since. Mathieu doesn't have a fixed home, or any kind of vehicle. He moves around from town to town, picking up small renovation and decorating jobs.

'He just sleeps on the floor of wherever he's working,' Paul says. Mathieu used to be a high-flying businessman in Paris, with a wife, Paul explains, but he gave that all up before he met him. Now he can fit everything he owns into a small box.

'He eats only organic, seasonal, and locally produced food,' Paul says admiringly. 'And he never uses power to cook. It's very impressive.'

At one point Paul glances over and interrupts himself. 'Where's the bracelet?'

I look down at my bare wrist, where a faint tan line marks the days I'd worn it in Malmot. In truth, the bracelet had got soaked the night we spent camping by Lake Salagou; I'd left it out to dry at Titi's and hadn't put it back on since.

'Didn't you like it?' He looks at me with a hurt expression.

I nod vigorously and make a show of rooting around in my bag, even though I know it's in the boot, in my suitcase.

'Good,' Paul says, returning his gaze to the road. 'It's actually quite valuable.'

Suddenly, I remember what the other Francis had said to me: that Tehura was a girl's name. But why would Paul have lied? I spend a few moments deliberating over what to do before asking, 'Who is "Tehura"?'

For a second Paul says nothing, then blurts: 'What are you talking about? I've already *told* you what it means.'

When I don't reply, his lips thin into a grimace.

'I can't believe this,' he says. 'It's always the same. You know, I thought I'd finally found someone who really cared, someone I could *respect*. How could I be so stupid as to give my heart to you? To believe that you'd take care of it?'

I shrink into my seat, racked with guilt as he continues without looking at me.

'I've given you everything I have,' he says matter-of-factly.

'I've offered you my home, introduced you to my friends, driven you around on your holiday. And you thank me like this.'

We slow down to approach a tollbooth. The driver of the car next to us glances over. As I avoid the woman's gaze I feel as if my face is on fire.

Paul's right, of course. He gave me a gift and I threw it back in his face. What reason would he have to lie?

I begin writing an apology in the notebook and hold it up for him to see. His eyes flicker over it but his expression doesn't change. I put my hand on his knee. After a few seconds he sighs and puts his hand over mine.

'It's okay, coquine. I know you're sorry and that you didn't mean it. You know as well as I do that I would never throw you out by the side of the road, or even entertain the thought, like some men would. You know that, don't you?'

I nod and squeeze his leg.

'I'm a good man,' he says.

We sit in silence for a few moments, and my pulse slows back to its regular beat. Soon the headlights flash over a sign declaring our arrival in the town. Paul follows the road through the deserted town centre, then on to the residential area Mathieu had described. We park up outside a cluster of pale, dilapidated tower blocks that loom against the dark sky.

Paul holds a hand out to stop me opening the door. 'Just one more thing, Frances,' he says. The interior light switches off. 'I couldn't help but notice last night at Vanessa's, when we went to bed, you were dry.'

I hold my breath.

'It didn't feel good for me,' he says simply. He pats my thigh and opens his door. 'Just try to make sure it doesn't happen again, okay?'

dimanche

When I wake up, I forget where I am. The ground is hard and the air so close over my face that for a few moments I think I'm back in the tent at Salagou. Is the storm over? I feel around for the shape of soil and rocks but feel instead cool lino against my palm. The smell is distinctly surgical, and I remember where we are: the disused doctor's surgery that Mathieu is renovating into private flats. The stained peach walls of the room we slept in are lit up in the morning sun. It must have been some kind of consulting room, now gutted apart from a single shelf stacked with peeling medical journals. I remember staring at their spines before eventually falling asleep on the blow-up mattress we'd never managed to inflate.

I pull on a few clothes and stumble out into the hallway, looking for a bathroom. The long corridor still looks more or less like a surgery, off-white and nondescript, with numbered rooms on either side. I eventually find an en-suite in a treatment room, but the taps don't work and there's no flush. I find my way back to the corridor and hear voices coming from the other end. I walk slowly, softly, as if the surgery is still a place of work, as if doctors and nurses are still going about their business behind the closed doors. At the far end, the corridor opens out into what must have been the waiting room, where Paul and Mathieu sit at a white plastic garden table.

'About time!' Paul exclaims with a grin.

I smile and sit opposite Mathieu, remembering too late that I should have kissed them both good morning. It was late when we arrived last night, and Mathieu had done little more than greet us and show us to the room with the deflated mattress. In daylight, he's nothing like the bohemian type I'd imagined from Paul's description, which I realise now was more or less an extreme version of Paul himself. But where Paul's hair is long and straggly, his fingernails dirty and unkept, Mathieu is a vision of order and cleanliness. His dark hair is cropped close to his head, his black T-shirt spotless and crease-free, his hands oddly smooth for his trade. He looks out over a pair of thin, elegant glasses and seems to speak without moving his lips, a considered economy of movement that makes him harder for me to follow. Paul was right, I think, as Mathieu tells me quietly to help myself to bread, cereal and coffee; Mathieu is exactly like a monk.

'Everything's organic, of course!' Paul declares and claps his friend on the back. 'Look,' he points to a small wooden box on the table. 'This is how he cooks without electricity.' He lifts the lid to show what looks like a polystyrene interior. 'You can cook rice, beans, vegetables – isn't that right?'

Mathieu nods and smiles thinly. He apologises for the uncomfortable surroundings; he's used to camping in the places he works, but this is the first time he's had guests and the call from Paul had caught him a little off guard.

'Don't apologise,' Paul says jovially. 'It'd already been too long. What is it, two, three years?'

'Four,' Mathieu corrects him.

'Ah! You know, I haven't worked in a vineyard since. I used to go most summers, but I've been busy setting the farm up at Noa Noa.'

'And how is farming life?'

Paul's smile flickers for a moment before he launches into a speech about jam from the fruit yield, about the vegetable patch and the goats.

'It's still early days, of course,' Paul says, 'but I've got great ideas. I think in a year or two we'll be totally self-sufficient. N'est-ce pas, Frances?'

Both men turn to look at me and I feel my head bobbing up and down in agreement, like a cork being swept downstream.

We spend the morning walking around the town centre, past countless crumbling churches, ornate, graffitied fountains and dusty streets. It's simultaneously grand and dilapidated, and there's an alluring dissonance between its former luxury and now dishevelled state. Mathieu tells us it used to be the centre of winemaking in the South, and a popular holiday destination. But investment stopped decades ago, and it's now crippled with poverty, overrun with drug lords and far-right extremists.

'It's not uncommon.' Mathieu shrugs. 'You take a once prosperous place, watch it decline through de-industrialisation and lack of investment, then find someone to blame. Here it's immigrants people target: Romanians, Muslims. The town is full of hate.'

Paul nods knowingly. Mathieu has a habit of talking in aphorisms, and throughout the walk maintains the distance of a tour guide, rather than the familiarity of a friend. Paul is lively and keeps joking with him, but Mathieu shows no sign of yielding. The less receptive Mathieu is to the joking, the lewder Paul seems to become. Mostly, Mathieu and I walk quietly while this goes on, and into our joint silence I project some kind of imagined solidarity; I have a fleeting, strange impression that we are Paul's parents, that Paul is our excitable child.

Sometime past noon, Paul sulkily complains of hunger, and Mathieu suggests stopping for lunch. He tells us he doesn't often eat out, but an acquaintance of his from Turkey runs a pizzeria, and has been struggling to make ends meet.

'It would help him out,' Mathieu says, 'if we all bought lunch there.'

'And I take it all the ingredients are organic,' Paul comments with sarcasm.

Mathieu seems not to notice and leads us down a quiet

residential street on which the pizzeria seems to be the only establishment. Inside it's lusciously decorated, if a little confusing; a mirror-plated wall on one side reflects the sepia panoramas of Paris, Venice and London on the other, and the booths are lined with a geometric, carpet-like fabric that would look more at home in a hookah lounge. Paul cheers up on scanning the menu, listing the ingredients aloud like the sacred words of a homily: mozzarella, tomates, champignons . . .

We seem to be the only customers, and it's a few minutes before a large man emerges from a beaded curtain at the back of the restaurant. He makes a cry of recognition on seeing Mathieu, who embraces him, then introduces Paul and me to his friend, Sami.

Sami smiles and welcomes us in Italian. His teeth are noticeably yellow, and a tattoo of the Italian flag is visible under the straps of his white vest.

Mathieu asks how business is, and Sami's smile fades.

'Not so good. The same guys keep dealing outside the front window. I've told them to move on, that it's scaring away customers. But they won't listen.'

Mathieu nods, frowning. 'It will take a little time. But things will get going.'

'Inshallah.'

On Sami's recommendation, Mathieu and I each order a vegetable special, while Paul chooses quattro formaggi. When Sami disappears, Mathieu tells us how they came to meet. It was not long after Mathieu arrived in the town, having accepted the job in the surgery. He'd taken a walk in the evening to get his bearings. The central strip of kebab shops and noisy bars had driven him off to the side streets, where he heard shouts the next street over. He hurried down an alley and found a man pressing Sami up against a wall. The man started hitting Sami, but he fled when he saw Mathieu – presumably he felt outnumbered, Mathieu said. Sami was shaken but overcome with gratitude, and insisted Mathieu come in for a free dinner. Soon, Sami had told him his life story: as a young man he'd moved from Turkey to Italy, based on a childhood obsession with the place. In the course of ten years he'd set up a popular restaurant, married an Italian woman, and had a daughter with her. But Italy was not what Sami had imagined it to be; he was subject to a constant low-level discrimination that slowly chipped away at him, and in the end he discovered his wife had been unfaithful since the start of their marriage.

'So he came here for a fresh start,' Mathieu explains. 'A friend of his used to live here and told him he'd be able to make a living, that there were plenty of tourists. But that was the town thirty years ago. He didn't realise he'd bought premises in a backstreet with no footfall, more or less reserved for dealers and prostitutes. To be honest, I just feel sorry for him. So I try to come and bring custom when I can.'

Paul is picking at the label on his beer bottle.

'What about his family?' I ask.

'I think he sends them money,' Mathieu says.

We fall silent as Sami reappears from the back, expertly carrying all three pizzas. Mathieu and I thank him, and on the first mouthful of olive and artichoke I'm convinced it's the best pizza I've ever tasted.

Paul breaks the silence. 'I feel sorry for Sami too,' he says, pulling a strand of mozzarella from his pizza with his teeth. 'It's not good for any man to be alone.'

Mathieu glances at him; I see him notice the string of mozzarella. 'Better to be alone than with someone you can't trust.'

'No,' Paul says, swallowing his mouthful. 'I think people forget you have to *earn* a woman's respect. Once you've done that, there's no obstacle.'

Mathieu raises his eyebrows. 'Perhaps.'

Paul looks at me, then at Mathieu. 'So have you spoken to – what was her name? Marsha?'

At this, Mathieu seems to momentarily lose his composure. 'Arshi,' he says, clearing his throat. 'Arshi. And no, I haven't spoken to her since I last saw you.'

He looks down at his food as if it's turned into a mound of ashes.

'It's a shame,' Paul goes on. 'She seemed like a great woman.'

'Yes.'

'So are you seeing anyone else?'

Mathieu shakes his head.

'Why not?' Paul exclaims. 'You're still handsome. And young—'

'And I live in a different place every month of the year,' Mathieu interjects. 'I'm unlikely to find someone compatible with the things I care about. And that's what's important to me now.'

'But there are so many types of women. You just have to look—'

'I don't want to look,' Mathieu cuts in sharply. It's the first time I've heard him raise his voice, and even Paul looks a little taken aback.

'Okay, ça va, Mathieu,' he says as if addressing an over-sensitive child. 'Ça va. I just don't want you to be lonely—'

'I'm not lonely, Paul. I enjoy my own company and my work, and I'm very happy with it being that way.'

When Sami arrives a few minutes later, full of good cheer, no one rises to meet his enthusiasm. Mathieu tells him in a dispirited monotone that the meal was superb, as usual. I reach into my bag to get some cash but Mathieu refuses and pays the whole bill.

'Je vous invite,' he says without meeting our eyes.

Just as we're about to leave, an elderly man staggers into the restaurant. His clothes are in tatters, and his long grey hair matted into lank ropes. He curses and sits down in a booth

Sami sighs and excuses himself. He takes Mathieu's money and returns with half a pizza, which he sets down in front of the man.

'He comes in here most weeks,' Sami mutters as he hands Mathieu his change. 'He's more or less my only customer, and he's never paid for a crumb.'

Paul eyes the old man warily. 'Maybe *he's* the reason you don't have any business.'

The four of us turn to look at Sami's customer, who is pulling at the pizza sluggishly, with his head bowed over the plate. I notice the boniness of his hands and fingers; his thinness must be hidden in the layers of clothes.

'I can't turn him away,' Sami says with a sigh. 'And sharing a pizza between us costs nothing at all.'

Mathieu nods and stands up. 'You're a good man, Sami.'

Sami grips Mathieu's shoulders and they kiss goodbye. 'See you soon, friend.'

Paul uncharacteristically holds out a hand, and wishes him luck with the pizzeria. If all else fails, Paul says, he could always start up a homeless shelter.

We leave town not long after. Whatever has soured over lunch remains so, and, after leaving the pizzeria, Mathieu politely tells us he'll need to get back to work this afternoon. We're welcome to stay with him as long as we like, of course, but it would be better if we weren't in the surgery during his work hours. Paul thanks him, and says we need to get going to reach a friend's before dark.

I glance up at him, barely surprised. I don't feel able to summon enough energy to ask when we are going back to Lazeaux.

'Sanctimonious jerk,' Paul mutters the second we get into the car.

Mathieu is well out of earshot, standing on the steps

outside the surgery to see us off. He holds up his right arm in a robotic wave. I keep waving as we pull onto the road, until he fades from view.

'Don't you think he was unbearable?' Paul explodes. 'God, he was nowhere near this bad last time I saw him. You know, I'm probably the only person that's called him in four years. It's a miracle he still keeps a phone.'

I stare out of the window, at the stones changing colour as the sun withdraws behind a cloud.

'Don't you think he was irritating?' Paul says. 'So self-righteous.'

I hadn't thought so at all, but it feels safer to shrug than to say so.

'Oh, I see,' Paul sneers. 'You fancy him.'

I look at Paul to see if he's joking, but there is a deep frown set into his forehead, and his pupils are narrowed threateningly.

'Yes, he was a bit annoying,' I hear myself say.

Paul's hand moves to my leg, and his voice changes as he murmurs, 'You know, coquine, we didn't make love last night. I've been waiting all day.'

'Who's Arshi?' I ask, clutching at a change of subject.

Paul moves his hand back to the steering wheel, seemingly distracted.

'Mathieu's ex-wife. Or girlfriend – I can never remember which. They had broken up when I met him but he was still crazy about her. I think he still is.'

'What happened?'

'He went nuts, I think. He had an "ecological awakening" and cut ties with everything. Before that he had the right degrees, a high-powered job in Paris, a beautiful woman who was a successful lawyer. They had a penthouse flat in some fancy arrondissement. But he gave it all up.' Paul sighs. 'I met him not long after – it was like he'd had some religious experience, but for sustainability. He went from one extreme to the other: quit his job, sold everything he owned, left Paris. He cut everything out of his life, Arshi included.'

The buildings give way to scrubland and a chain of run-down garages.

'I used to really admire him,' Paul says. 'I had a lot of respect for his way of life. It's extreme, but it's *pure*, you know? But now I'm not so sure. I think it's just selfish. There's no room for anyone else.'

As we drive, I realise that at no point had Mathieu asked how Paul and I met. I'd been presented as Paul's girlfriend; for all Mathieu knew we'd been together for years, or at least since he and Paul last saw each other. I realise that anyone who's happened to see us in the last week – other drivers, passers-by at Salagou, the monastery or the market – might think the same. That Paul and I are in love; that we've been together long-term; that we met – how? Through work? Mutual friends?

I look out of the window and feel a heavy pressure behind my eyes. More stretches of garrigue, more mountains in the distance. I feel like I've been staring out of windows for weeks on end; I am losing track of how I got here.

I thought we'd be back in Lazeaux by now, tending to the garden, making jam at the long table, exploring the hills and woodland where, Patrice had told me, bears still roamed. Maybe he and I would visit another church, or Marcel would take his daughters to Tagire and I'd tag along. We could picnic at the top and on the way back down have a water fight in the streams that twist down from the peaks.

I shake the images from my head, realising how little they contain of Paul. I knew he would be there in Lazeaux, of course, but I thought it would be different. Different to these days spent drifting between his friends. The days and faces blur into one inchoate mass, like an unformed planet on which Paul is the only horizon, the limit of everything.

Soon Paul brightens and starts talking excitedly about his anthropology book. He's had lots of ideas over the past few weeks, he says. There'll be chapters organised by chronological periods – childhood, coming of age, adulthood and so on – with plenty of room for regional variations. He'll invent two characters, a girl and a boy, and take the reader through two speculative versions of their lives, parallel narratives of growing up in France and the South Pacific. Maybe Tahiti, or Vanuatu – he hasn't decided yet. But he has thought of a title: *GRANDIR AVEC LA DIFFÉRENCE*. Growing Up With Difference.

He says he's been trying to make sense of his notebooks

for years, but he suffered a massive lack of confidence after commencing his studies at Montpellier.

When I ask why, he glances at me as if he can't decide what to say.

'Well, I never actually got my degree. I was planning to use my notebooks as material for my dissertation. I had years' worth of research and experience, more than any other student they'd had. But when I showed them to my supervisor she said they were inappropriate.'

'In what way?'

Paul shrugs. 'I don't know. A list of reasons I didn't understand. I consider myself a feminist, but she's one of those staunch, unforgiving types. I don't even know why she was in the anthropology department in the first place; she seemed to hate everything about the subject. It was all appropriation this, neo-colonialist that.'

I shift uncomfortably, remembering the suspicions I'd had about the photographs in his exhibition.

'But I left on my own account,' Paul goes on. 'Even though one of the other professors was begging me to stay. He was from the old school, does a lot of work with the Société des Océanistes, was close with Lévi-Strauss at the end of his life – anyway, he read the notebooks too and was very encouraging.'

'And he wanted you to stay?'

'The opposite! He said the discipline had become too institutionalised; that what I'd done, as an outsider, was closer to the original spirit of anthropology. More attuned to its essence. He encouraged me to work on the book and get it published outside of the academy, said he'd be happy to look over any drafts, offer advice.'

I gaze out of the window, wondering why Paul hadn't told me this before.

'Don't worry, my love,' he teases, misreading my silence. 'You can still do the English translation, I promise.'

I respond with a taut smile; it's all I can manage. 'Are we going back to Lazeaux, now?'

'Soon. There's just one friend I promised to see on the way; it won't take long. His village isn't far from Carcassonne.'

Carcassonne? The medieval city's yellow turrets rise up in my mind. I've never visited, though it made frequent appearances in my architectural history lectures.

'We can visit the citadel if you like,' Paul says with distaste. 'But it's worse than Disneyland. Crawling with tourists.'

'I'd like to see it.'

He sighs and pats my knee. 'D'accord, coquine. Anything for you.'

Not long after, the fairytale grandeur of Carcassonne looms on the skyline. We park in the town at the foot of the hill, a twenty-minute walk from the entrance. Though the streets are more or less quiet, we soon join up with the crowd flowing over a narrow bridge and through the city walls. Paul was right: it *does* look like Disneyland, albeit a squat, less spindly version. Turrets of different heights press up against the crenelated walls, jostling for a place in the foreground, while the bridge over a wide, grassy moat provides the only entrance. I think of the walled town around Saint Pascal, which seems a quaint facsimile.

The crowd swells around us in a deluge of languages and ages. Children are everywhere, chattering loudly and eating ice cream. I'd expected Paul to be irritated but he seems surprisingly cheerful as we cross the bridge, extolling the sweeping views of fields and towns, of the Pyrénées rising up in the distance.

Inside the city walls, narrow streets curve upwards in a labyrinth of postcard stands and candyfloss vendors. It's so dense with people I can barely make out what the place looks like. I reach for Paul's hand and find it, let him pull me through the crowd. The air smells of sugar and frying oil.

'It's like the end of the world!' Paul calls back to me.

He leads me onto one street, then another; they all blend into one. After a few minutes we arrive back at the spot where we started.

'This is it,' he says. 'A whole town of overpriced churros.'

'Is there a museum?'

'One that costs a fortune to visit, yes. Although I do remember there being a cathedral, if we can find it . . .'

We set off again, the cobbled streets a blur of crêperies, restaurants and souvenir shops selling replica weapons and suits of armour. Paul gives a running commentary about the town; apparently not a single person can afford to live inside the city walls; there's no supermarket or doctor's surgery any more. Everyone lives outside and commutes in to work.

'It's a theme park,' he says. 'This would never happen in England. You have your national heritage boards, your restoration trusts ...'

Soon we arrive at the cathedral, an enormous gothic structure that looms over a small, dusty square. I gaze up, squinting at the spires against the sun. Slender gargoyles veer out at right angles, a mixture of animals and wailing saints, all of their mouths open in silent screams. I think about telling Paul the etymology: 'gargoyle' from 'gargoule' the Old French for 'throat', that before modern plumbing existed the gargoyles' throats served to divert rainwater from eroding the mortar below. Drainage as a spiritual symbol: siphoning out sin and impurities.

A man in robes outside the cathedral beckons us over. He tells us vespers will soon begin; would we like to join? Paul says we'd love to. But for once, I don't want to go in. I hang back and tell Paul I'll meet him after the service instead.

He shrugs with indifference, and then the man in robes opens the heavy wooden door for him to enter, closing it behind him. The organ starts up, slow and heavy. I close my eyes and concentrate on the feeling of the sun on my face. For the next hour, I can do anything I please.

It passes too quickly. I find a path that traces the ramparts, and follow it as far as I can without having to pay for the full guided tour. I'm asked to take pictures of three separate couples. I buy a postcard of the city set against a sunset, and aimlessly follow a Dutch family from the shop into a nearby café. The mother looks tired and the father bored; they order three large sundaes, one for each of their blonde daughters. A waitress comes up to take my order. She has a lip piercing and bright green hair. I ask for a Diet Coke, and watch the Dutch couple follow her to the bar with their eyes, the woman disapproving, the man curious.

On the postcard I write:

Dear A.B.,
I thought you might like this postcard of the cité.
Not exactly your specialism, but an overlapping period
nonetheless. I assume you've been? Paul hates how busy it
is, but I don't mind. Maybe it's not so far away from its
thirteenth-century heyday; there's something carnivalesque
about the crowd milling around, the garish window
displays ... I saw the Tour de France a few weeks ago,
which was similar. So much pomp and spectacle, etc.
I've seen more of France than I thought I would –
there's been a lot of moving around, a lot of different
names and faces. But we're nearly going home. I've met
an anthropologist (that's Paul) who I'm going to live with
here in the Pyrénées. I'm going to translate the book he's
writing ...

I read back, then score through everything furiously. I wasn't committed to sending the postcard, but even writing it makes me feel sick – the writing of a little girl, a stupid, naïve girl ...

I glance at my phone and realise an hour has long since passed. I'm the last customer left in the café; the waitress has already begun stacking chairs around me. I stuff the postcard into my bag and throw down a few coins.

It takes longer than I expected to make it back to the cathedral; somehow I take a wrong turn and arrive at the other side of the square. I spot Paul, leaning against the cathedral in the shade. He doesn't see me. Instead, he's staring straight ahead at the tables outside a restaurant. I recognise one of the couples I'd taken a photo for earlier, and the Dutch family from the café. The three daughters are playing in the forecourt while they wait for their food to arrive, some kind of game that involves leapfrogging over each other's backs.

I look back at Paul. There's an expression on his face as he gazes at the girls. A few seconds go by before I recognise it. Part lust, part fascination; it was there in his kitchen at Noa Noa, in the gardens at Montpellier. I feel dizzy, as though the world has turned upside down; but I'm the one that's been standing on my head, mistaking the sky for ground. Not wanting to believe what my body, exhausted, already knows.

A long second elapses before Paul looks around, as if having sensed someone watching. He clocks me and comes over, looking calm and serene.

'Salut, coquine.' He reaches down to kiss me.

I jerk away from him. 'Don't call me that.'

Paul's smile drops into an expression of innocent bewilderment.

'I know what it means.'

'What?' he says softly. 'It means seashell. What did you—?'

'Don't lie,' I say. 'Vanessa told me!'

A waitress from the restaurant looks over as I raise my voice. Paul smiles and gestures for her attention.

'Don't,' I hiss. 'What are you doing?'

Paul ignores me for the few moments it takes the waitress to reach us.

'Can I help you?' she says. 'We have a table free in an hour—'

'Thank you, we haven't decided on dinner yet – but I wondered if you could help us clear up a small translation issue.' His smile is unwavering. 'Do you happen to speak English?'

The waitress looks confused. 'A little,' she says tentatively. 'But I'm quite busy—'

'It will only take a moment,' Paul interrupts her. 'Would you mind telling my friend here, the meaning of the word "coquille"?'

'Coquille?' she repeats.

Paul nods.

'It means "shell",' she says simply. 'Like a seashell.'

No! I want to scream at Paul. You said *coquine* –

'Merci, mademoiselle!' Paul exclaims triumphantly.

The waitress looks from me to Paul in bafflement. 'Anything else?'

'No, that's all. Thank you for your time!'

At that Paul grips my shoulders and steers me into a side

street. It's quieter now, the shops and food stalls closed or closing.

'Happy?' he asks.

I squirm out of his grip.

'Look, Frances, I'm sorry if you misheard me—'

'You never called me "coquille". I'm not deaf.'

'Just mute,' he mutters, so faintly it's almost inaudible.

'What?'

'Coquine, coquille . . . what does it matter? Je t'aime—'

I shake my head and think of all the words I could say. They pile up like dead leaves around a drain.

It's a short drive to Paul's friend, Félix, but it feels like hours. Paul talks on and off about how Félix and he met, but without the same unselfconscious flow as before; it's as if he's suddenly aware of being the only one speaking. It turns out they met at the slow travel festival a few years ago, although Félix hasn't been back since. Paul tells me that when he'd called earlier, Félix said there'd be plenty of room as his wife, Hannah, and their young daughter are away until autumn. Paul suspects they are having some marital problems, but doesn't elaborate on what they might be.

The village turns out to be half abandoned. Derelict barns and boarded-up farmhouses pepper the densely forested valley, and every now and then I catch glimpses of old machinery through the trees, rusting in yards and garages. The road drops down to the river, crosses a precarious-looking bridge and then rises sharply on the other side. Halfway up the hill we turn into the driveway of a house that looks only marginally less shabby than the boarded-up ones in the valley. A black Labrador bounds down the drive to greet us, and leaps up to the window when Paul turns off the engine, panting excitedly in his face.

'Get off!' Paul mutters, pushing the dog by its throat. It whimpers and falls back to the ground.

The front door of the house swings open and a man steps out, beckoning the dog.

'Ciao, Félix,' Paul calls.

I follow him to the porch, where Félix is fussing over the Labrador.

'Nice of you to stop by,' he says.

He has the sun-drenched complexion I've become accustomed to among Paul's friends, but is younger than I'd expected, although the weariness in his smile ages him. He straightens up to greet us, and when we brush cheeks I notice a warm, sweet smell, somewhere between cinnamon and freshly cut grass.

'Ça va, toi?' Paul asks.

Félix shrugs. 'Fine, pretty quiet. It's just me and the hives. And Elsa.' He nudges the Labrador with his foot. 'You?'

'Better than ever.' Paul grins. 'Me and Frances have been on a road trip. But this is our last stop. We're going back to Lazeaux tomorrow.'

Félix nods, looks at me. 'And you live in Lazeaux too, Frances?'

'I—'

'She came to work for me, through BénéBio.' Paul turns to me. 'You know, it was Félix and Hannah who told me about BénéBio in the first place? They did it in – where did you go again? Latvia?'

'Croatia,' Félix says.

'Anyway,' Paul shrugs, 'it's a great thing. It reminds me of travelling when I was your age. Although, of course, the spontaneity's been lost. I used to hitchhike everywhere, but Frances is scared to. Now it's all car-sharing and taxi apps. Sure it's organised, but it lacks the adventure of just holding your hand out, not knowing who you're going to end up sat next to.'

In a fraction of a second I catch Félix's eye, and it suddenly becomes very difficult not to laugh out loud.

But Félix keeps a completely straight face, nodding along to Paul's observations. Maybe I'd imagined the look altogether, because when he asks us in for dinner, all trace of his amusement at Paul is gone, and he doesn't meet my eye.

The wood-panelled walls of the large kitchen are covered with postcards and children's drawings. Stacks of books teeter precariously around the furniture, and the table is strewn with well-thumbed copies of *Le Monde*. Félix offers us beer and says dinner won't be long. He sets about cooking while Paul leans over the kitchen bar to talk to him. I take a seat at the table and watch them, half listening. Paul's T-shirt has ridden up at the back to show a strip of skin, garishly yellow in the overhead light. He's speaking in that rapid tongue again, the one that takes all of my effort to comprehend. The rhythm is so familiar I half convince myself I can understand it: the low babbling stream of Paul's talk, the occasional murmur from Félix like a fallen leaf punctuating its flow. Behind them, the shelves are filled with dozens of jars of honey, each a slightly different hue. The lightest is barely yellower than water, while the darkest is as brown as mud.

Félix sets a large bowl of pasta on the table and sits down next to Paul, across from me. The set-up reminds me fleetingly of an interview panel; they are asking me why I'd be suited to the position—

'So much is changing these days,' Félix says, serving portions, 'that in some ways it's a relief to see you haven't changed at all.'

Paul's grin flickers slightly. 'What do you mean?'

'You could still talk your way out of murder, if you wanted.'

'Ah!' Paul laughs. 'C'est vrai.'

'Or romance my wife.'

Paul reaches for the cheese grater. 'Yes, where is lovely Hannah?'

Félix sighs and slumps in his chair. All of a sudden he looks older again; his age seems to shift moment to moment.

'At her parents' in Germany, with Anya. My daughter,' he adds to me.

'How old is she?' I ask.

'Eight this year.'

I make a quick estimate in my head – then he must be around thirty, late twenties at least ...

'Eighteen,' Félix says.

'What?' I feel heat rising to my cheeks.

'We were eighteen. Hannah got pregnant – we didn't know what to do. Thought we'd make a go of it.' His tone is abrupt, but not unkind.

'Oh,' I say, feeling unprepared for his honesty.

'He's a true gentleman,' Paul says with his mouth full. 'Very old-fashioned.'

Félix raises his eyebrows. 'I don't know about that.'

'It's true,' Paul goes on. 'You could be half my age, and look at you: you have a wife, a child, a home ...'

Félix laughs. It sounds tired, haggard. 'But imagine, Paul. I could have been a great adventurer like you.'

Paul considers for a moment, then nods. 'Yes, you could have.'

Félix looks at me across the table and pretends to whisper. 'Stay young while you can, Frances.'

'Surely it's not that bad?' Paul says. 'Last time you and Hannah came to stay – what was that? Two years ago? – Anyway, last time you seemed happy. Both of you.'

Félix shrugs. 'I thought so too. But things always start coming to light after a while, don't they?'

'Like what?' Paul asks.

'Like – Hannah always wanted to live in the city. I knew that – she's very urban, at heart, loves the rush and everything going on – but I think she buried that for a long time because she knows I hate it. But now Anya's older, less dependent on Hannah – I think Hannah just resents being here, to be honest.'

Paul gestures at him with a fork. 'But you're not going to separate?'

Félix shakes his head. 'No, no. We've said we can't do that, not while Anya's so young. But the arguing isn't good for her either. We just need to arrange our lives so we each get a break.'

'And that's why she's away now?'

'Exactly. Except I was meant to use this alone time to get started on some projects, and all I've done is mope around.'

'That's not true,' Paul says, nodding to the shelves in the kitchen. 'You've made all that honey.'

Félix smiles and then looks suddenly remorseful. 'Jesus. Sorry for venting. You can probably tell I haven't had much company recently.'

'It's what friends are for,' Paul says lightly. 'So, are you going to offer us some of the goods or not?'

Félix gets up and ponders a while in front of the shelves, returning with five jars and a handful of teaspoons. He got into apiculture not long after they moved to the village, he tells us. It gives him a good routine.

'The difference in colour comes from the type of plant the bees collect nectar from. This one here,' he picks up a jar so pale it's almost translucent, 'is alfalfa. Then clover, buckwheat, sage.'

Paul and I try each of them in turn. The flavours are

extraordinary, not too sweet – apart from the clover – which turns out to be Paul's favourite.

'I love sweet things,' he says.

I feel his leg brush against mine beneath the table. He looks at me, pointedly, and I become conscious of the spoon in my mouth, the curved head of metal on my tongue, my lips closing around its neck. All of a sudden its metallic tang is all I can taste. He is looking at me with that look, his eyes saying 'coquine' loud and clear; he doesn't have to open his mouth.

I pull the spoon out quickly, hoping to cut off his gaze.

'Which is your favourite?' Félix asks.

I stare down at the jars. As I look they turn into urine samples, or vinegars for pickling specimens, body parts.

'I don't know – they're all good.'

'It means she has to try them again,' Paul says.

Félix shrugs.

'Are there more flavours?' Paul asks.

Félix twists to look at the shelves. 'There's acacia, lavender, almond – but I'm almost out—'

'I think Frances wants to try all of them.' Paul's eyes are boring into me; his thin smile is mask-like, painted into place.

Félix looks at Paul, then me. Some kind of understanding passes between us, and in that moment I realise he'd picked up on it from the beginning, feigning ignorance to keep the atmosphere light.

He clears his throat and says in a mock-serious voice, 'I'm not so sure. As a professional apiculturist I wouldn't advise any more honey in one sitting.'

'She can handle it,' Paul says. 'Frances has a sweet tooth, don't you?'

I look at Félix, willing him to intervene.

'Maybe we can try some more at breakfast,' he suggests.

Paul is quiet for a moment, then drops his spoon onto the table with a clatter.

'Fine,' he snaps, standing up. 'I'm tired anyway. Let's go to bed.'

lundi

I wake up with the birdsong. We slept in Anya's room, in her pink and green sheets embroidered with flowers and lined with soft-toy sentinels. When we'd turned off the light, the room had begun to softly illuminate, as if by bioluminescent fungi: glow-in-the-dark stars and planets stuck to the ceiling; a red ladybird nightlight plugged into the wall. Paul fell asleep without trouble, but I'd found the red glow distracting. Eventually I'd got up and pulled it out of the socket.

Paul dozing next to me looks sweet, peaceful. Last night he'd been frustrated because I was dry again; I told him I was just tired, or dehydrated. He handed me the half-empty bottle of water we'd had in the car all day and told me to sort it out. I tried to apologise but he wouldn't come round; I couldn't see him properly in the dark but he sounded so angry and disappointed that in the end I just crept down and kissed until I felt him go hard. I hated it. I hated myself for hating it. He pressed my head into him and all I could think of was being in an eight-year-old's bed. *Sorry, Anya,* I apologised silently. But once Paul had finished he murmured that I was a miracle, and then I felt the blood rushing back into my body, felt more alive than I had all day.

When I go downstairs, Félix is at the table reading the newspaper with a coffee in hand. 'I've already eaten,' he says. 'But there's bread – help yourself.'

I sit down and tear a hunk off the baguette, smearing it with butter.

'No honey?' Félix says with a half-smile.

I take a bite and shake my head. Not today.

Félix pours me a coffee and pulls out a section of the newspaper.

'There's a good article about storing seeds in Arctic ice,' he says, passing it to me. 'Page six. I'm not much of a morning person.'

He carries on reading, as if my presence has no effect on his behaviour at all. It's a relief. I try to concentrate on the Arctic seed article but feel too on edge. I feel like we are extras waiting for the star to arrive. I don't know how to be when Paul's not here. Everything feels like a question I don't know how to answer.

Then I hear him on the stairs, and he comes in whistling.

'Salut *à* tous!' he says, kissing me on the head.

Félix offers him what's left of the baguette but Paul shakes his head and reaches for the cafetière.

'What time are you setting off?' Félix asks, folding away the paper.

Paul shrugs. 'Whenever.'

I push the crumbs around on my plate, a familiar dread curdling in my stomach. Leaving now means going back to Lazeaux as Paul's lover. I realise, like swallowing a heavy stone, that Lazeaux can never be the same place it was when I arrived, before anything happened with Paul. I wonder absently if there are other options; maybe I could lodge with Patrice, or Marcel and the girls? I could do chores and go on walks and keep to myself. But it wouldn't be the same. I could never go back to being an anonymous guest, welcomed into the village.

I don't know what to do except stall for time, delay as much as possible before leaving with Paul.

'I'd like to see where the bees live,' I say.

'The hives?' Félix asks. 'They're on the hillside of the next valley. We'd have to drive out to them.'

Paul downs the last of his coffee and makes a face, presumably tasting the dregs. 'I've seen plenty of beehives. They're nothing exciting.'

'Well, I've been meaning to check on the queens for a few days,' Félix says. 'I could take Frances and you could stay here. Unless you need help with the car?'

'No.' Paul snorts, as if the idea of him needing help is ridiculous.

'Okay,' Félix says, getting up. 'We'll meet you back here for lunch.'

*

Before we leave, Félix adds a last coat of resin to a beehive he's just built, then loads another onto the back of his pickup truck. It feels strange to get into another man's car, to look at the clutter on a different dashboard, to breathe in unfamiliar scents. Even my noticing these things feels like a kind of betrayal.

On the way to check the hives we chat effortlessly. It turns out Félix worked summers in the UK for a few years, setting up stages and marquees for music festivals.

Before Anya was born he'd been planning to study philosophy at university. I wanted to ask if he had any regrets not going, but decided it might be an insensitive question.

After a short drive we pull over to a grassy verge. The land falls away below, down to the river curving through the trees. Félix points to an unremarkable point in the green and says we'll have to climb down to the ledge the hives are on.

The route is a little tricky, but I make it down without trouble. There's a loud murmur coming from the other side of the trees. Félix pulls his shirt off and hangs it on a nearby branch. I try not to look at his bare chest. Suddenly I realise he hasn't brought any protective clothing.

'Don't we need suits?' I ask.

'These bees have never stung me,' Félix says. 'They're very mild.'

He roots around in his backpack and withdraws a large metal flask attached to bellows. 'We use this to make them drowsy. They'll be even more relaxed soon.'

I follow him through the trees and out onto the ledge.

About fifteen boxes on wooden pallets are scattered around, with a few stray bees buzzing between. Félix beckons me over and reassures me they won't sting.

He opens the nearest box a crack and pumps the bellows a few times, before lifting the lid off altogether. The bees don't rush out but instead crawl sluggishly through the smoke. Inside, three trays of honeycomb are hanging from wooden slats. Félix shows me how to pull one out by pinching the wood firmly at either end. He holds it up to the light to inspect; the honeycomb is so thick with bees that it looks like one living, moving thing. He squints at it closely, seemingly not bothered by the myriad bees centimetres from his face.

'The queen's been doing her work,' he says.

'How can you tell?'

He points to the hexagonal cavities. 'See the tiny white line at the end of the tunnel?' I look, too tentative to get too close. 'Those are eggs,' he says. 'But we still need to find the queen.'

'How?'

'That's easy,' he says, carefully fitting the tray back into the box. 'She's the biggest.'

We begin searching. Within a few minutes Félix has already found a queen in the neighbouring box, and calls me over to spot her. Even with his finger pointing her out, I can barely tell she's bigger than the others.

He tells me I'll get used to it, and proceeds to pick up the queen, holding her thorax gently between his finger and thumb. With his other hand he withdraws a pot of sky-blue nail varnish from his pocket, and asks me to open it. He takes the brush and daubs a spot onto her wiggling, waxy back.

'It's so I can find her easily next time,' he explains. 'And tell how old she is. I used pink last year; now I've switched to blue.'

I nod, finding everything about the process mysterious.

'Do you want to blow on her?'

'What?'

He grins and starts blowing on the nail varnish. 'It'll dry quicker if we both do it,' he says. I roll my eyes and join in. Soon we are both laughing and blowing on the wet blue dot on the queen's back. Does he do this with Hannah, I wonder? With Anya?

We work for another half-hour or so. Félix asks me about university, and I find myself telling him about some apicultural features of the manuscript; the pages for the letter 'A' are filled with illustrations of bees, 'abeilles', that flit in and out of the margins, leading to the pages of 'B'. Some scholars have speculated that the bees are a rebus for the beginning of the alphabet; 'les A–B' is an approximate homophone for 'les abeilles'.

'So will you carry on studying from Lazeaux?' Félix asks with his back to me. He's quickly worked his way round to the other side of the ledge, while I'm only on my third box. I slot the honeycomb I'm holding back into its place; I've spent ten minutes looking for its queen with no luck.

'I don't know,' I say. 'I don't think academia is right for me.'

I turn to watch him slowly pick out the queen and daub

her back with the nail varnish. 'It sounds like it interests you,' he says, blowing on her. 'Why isn't it right for you?'

I gaze past him, out at the green valley. 'Well, it's expensive, for one thing. Competitive. And I don't know if I want to. I've been thinking I might have enough to do just being in Lazeaux. I could look after the garden, help Paul with his book.'

Félix stands up. He puts the lid back on the box and begins to pump smoke into the next one. 'Can I ask you a question, Frances?'

I squint at him, nodding.

'What is it that attracts you to Paul?'

I flounder for a few seconds, surprised by the question. 'I think . . . I think he's interesting.'

'Interesting?'

'Yeah, and – he makes me feel like I'm interesting too.'

Félix nods. 'But before you met him, what were you planning to do?'

'I don't know.'

'You could do anything,' he says. 'You're completely free . . .'

'You mean, why would I want to settle down?'

'Well,' Félix shrugs, 'I wish someone had said it to me when I was your age.'

I stare at him. What did he mean? That he regretted marrying, having a child? I begin to feel the stirrings of resentment. Then, a nagging suspicion that he has touched on some truth I can't yet locate. In the space of a second I flit between the two poles a hundred times, my head spinning.

'But isn't Paul your friend?' I hear myself ask, my voice small and faraway.

Félix's voice is nearer, surer. 'He's been kind to me, yes. But if I was a woman I'd keep my distance.'

Before we leave, Félix calls me over to look at something. He pulls out a frame of honeycomb; it's a little dry looking, most of the cells covered over, scarcely any bees on its surface. Then I notice that the cells aren't blocked with honeycomb to protect the pupae, but instead are stoppered with what look like dead bees. The pupae that never emerged. Others are still moving, though so deformed they look more like a monstrous assemblage of bee parts. Legs and wings poke out of the honeycomb, half fused into the wall, unable to detach themselves without tearing their malformed bodies apart. Some of them have half emerged, but their heads remain stuck inside, facing inwards. It's clearly only a matter of time until their legs stop moving and they go as still as the bees either side of them. The thought is terrifying: your head stuck in a tight space, trying to reverse out into the world, your legs scrabbling for the freedom you'll never see. I ask Félix what had happened to them and he said they must have starved to death; there wasn't enough for them to eat so they tried to survive by licking every last bit of sugar from the bottom of the cell. When that runs out they'll all die head-down, their legs clawing blindly at the air.

We drive back in silence. I have a vague impression that Félix is disappointed in me for being with Paul, which in turn makes me realise how much I had wanted Félix's approval. But mostly I can't shake the last thing he said about Paul. I'm tired of hints and allusions, only getting half answers to my questions. In the end I can't sit on it any longer.

'What did you mean earlier?' I blurt. 'What's so bad about Paul?'

Félix looks over, faintly surprised. 'You don't know?'

My heart begins to pound. 'Know what?'

He bites his bottom lip and looks back at the road ahead. Shadows cast by overhead leaves dapple his face.

'*What?*' I press.

He shifts in his seat. 'It's not my place.'

'Félix, *please.*'

He sighs, and goes quiet for a few moments. 'Okay,' he says eventually. 'But you have to understand first of all that Paul's … complex. Some of the things I know about him make me dislike him, but … I don't think he's *evil.*'

My mouth is completely dry. *Evil.* Why would he use that word?

'Did he tell you why he had to leave the South Pacific?'

My memories crash over each other – conversations with Paul – each eroding the one before it. 'He told me – he told me he was tired of travelling, that he wanted to settle down.'

Félix nods. 'That's partly true. But in a way he had already settled down.'

He pauses. I wait long, slow seconds for him to continue.

'He was married,' he says.

'*Married?* To who?'

He turns to look at me, allowing the shadows to engulf his face. 'A minor. In Tahiti. The French authorities found out. As he was still a citizen they told him to end it and come home, or they'd treat it as a crime.'

My face feels made of stone. 'How old was she?'

Félix clears his throat. 'I can't remember exactly. I think twelve, thirteen . . .'

I nod. It feels like all I can do. I try to add up what Félix has said. I know it's the truth. I know her name was Tehura. But at the same time I don't want to know – part of me resists the knowing.

'Maybe I shouldn't have said anything,' Félix goes on. His voice sounds so far away. 'I just saw how he was with you last night and – well, I thought you should know.'

I nod. I keep nodding.

When we arrive back at the house, Paul is already waiting outside. He's taken his top off and his chest looks even sparer than usual: all sinew and bones. I can't help but think of the starved bees.

'Time to go,' Paul says as Félix gets out of the truck. 'I want to try and miss the evening traffic.'

Félix nods and busies himself with unpacking lengths of wood. It's the first time I've heard Paul say anything about traffic, or planning ahead.

'Ready, Frances?' he calls.

I get out of the truck but stay standing where I am by the door.

'Hold on,' Félix says.

He disappears into the house and returns a few moments later with two jars of honey. He gives one to me – alfalfa – and a darker one to Paul. They talk on the porch for a few minutes; I feel too dazed to try and tune in. Their conversation sounds like a continuation of the bees' buzzing. Soon Félix comes over and we kiss a terse goodbye. I find myself wishing it was longer, slower. I watch his figure shrink from view as Paul and I pull away in his car, by which time I am already half a lifetime deep in my fantasy life as a beekeeper, with Félix, Hannah and Anya, where I am somewhere between daughter and lover.

For the first part of the journey, it seems as though Paul and I have nothing to say to each other. We're finally on our way home, he says. The word 'home' screeches like a siren in my ears. He says when we get closer he'll call Béthanie to let her know. Maybe she'll cook something good for dinner, he says.

The thought of food makes me feel sick. I feel as if my insides are crawling with bees, and have been all along. Paul laid them there, or maybe A.B., and they hatched when I first stepped into Paul's room and set eyes on Tagire. For a while the bees had enough to eat; they ate the mountain and the flowers and the bats' teeth and the festival. I buzzed along happily with them in my stomach. But then the sugar started rotting and the bees had sealed up their mouths. Now they're starving, and the ones that aren't starving are dead. That's why nothing came out when I tried to talk: the bees had begun to feast on my words.

Beyond the window, the Pyrénées loom in full view as we skirt the foothills. Both our windows are wound down and the air is sickly-sweet. We drive over a small stone bridge that makes my stomach leap; the moseying stream is so pictur-esque – blue and yellow wildflowers dappling the banks – that I feel helpless against it; as if a hand on the back of my head is pushing me face-down into the flowers, making sure all I can smell is blossom. It's soporific, this beauty – I can feel it lulling me away from the ugly certainty of what I know must be said. It comes over me in waves – warming, drugging – wearing away anything that isn't total blissful passivity . . .

But then I notice something else – a hint – another whis-pered note in the air. The end of summer, when the flowers are nearing the end of their sex. They know this; they stink of desperation. There's something post-coital about their smell, as if they can't deliver on what they appear to offer. The bees in my mouth stir all the same, giddy – greedy – for the sweetness that will keep them quiet. Would I rather let them starve?

I turn to look at Paul. I see him – shadow with a hot corona – and see A.B. too. As if two stars have collided and created one nebulous, fiery mass. It is so hard to look, so hard to look away. What is it about them that exerts this gravitational pull?

I remember what Patrice said about the magnetic poles and when they would switch; there was no way to predict exactly when it would happen, they just knew, instinctively, when it was time.

The fabric of the bus seat is prickly beneath my thighs. I shift and look out through the grime-streaked window. The scene is anything but inspiring: grey stretches of autoroute cut through straggled fields, billboards for McDonald's in 25 ... 15 ... 5 kilometres. But all the same I feel relieved by their mundanity: I don't want any more mountains, any more flowers. The sun is setting out to the west; the orange rays seem to ignite the dozing bodies of passengers around me. Maybe they'll sleep all the way through the night, and wake up as we pull into Paris tomorrow morning.

In the end it had been easy. I remember keeping my voice very calm as I stared straight ahead and asked Paul: who is Tehura? At first he kept up the pretence but I persisted, gently. I told him I knew Tehura was a girl, a very young girl who he'd known on Tahiti. I asked, had there been other girls? I didn't look at him but felt the density of his body change, as if he had morphed into stone. He said yes. I said, how young? He said he didn't know. He started to cry. He said, things were different there. That Tehura's parents offered her to him, that they were happy about the marriage. He said, it was so hard, that I had no idea how hard it had been for him. Here, it is an affliction, a stigma. But there it is just the way of things, a cultural difference, he said. It was the same with local men and local girls. No one thought he was doing anything wrong.

Then his voice became very thin and small, like a child's. But he was crying with big shudders like an earthquake. He pulled into the next service station and stopped the car. He said, it has been so hard for me, coming back to the West. I said, I know. He said, I am not a bad man. I said, I know. He turned his head toward me – his wet eyes – I didn't want to look. He said that was why he loved me, because I understood him like no one else, because I didn't judge him. That I was special. I said, I'm thirsty. He said, oh, sounded surprised. I turned to look at him then – he looked so small: a clump of cells. I said, I want a Diet Coke. He looked even more surprised, and I saw the thoughts passing through his mind, weighing up his principles versus keeping me happy. He wiped his eyes, patted my thigh and said, okay, coq— before stopping himself.

As soon as he was out of sight I moved like I'd never moved before. I leaped out of my seat and ran round to get my suitcase from the boot. I wheeled it across to the coach a few bays down, the coach that read *PARIS À PERPIGNAN, 24H7*. I paid for a one-way ticket to Paris, then sprinted back to Paul's car to grab my notebook from the dashboard, my sandals smacking over the hot concrete.

'Frances?'

I saw Paul standing outside the main building, watching me. A little tub of silver glinting in his hand. I held my breath, feeling his eyes on me. There were people all around; he wasn't going to do a thing. I began to walk slowly across to the coach. I didn't look back, not as I got on and took my seat, not as the engine started up and we pulled out of the service station and onto the dry, grey road.

Acknowledgements

This novel draws on names, place names and anecdotes found in *Noa Noa: The Tahitian Journal* by Paul Gauguin, first published in 1901.

A first draft of this novel was written between the summers of 2016 and 2017, which wouldn't have been possible without the love and support of several people. I am grateful to Geri Snell and Dec Middleton, who first encouraged me to pursue the project, and to Ryan Edwards, who was always my first reader, and spent a year reading clumsy drafts, giving generous, insightful feedback, and generally cheering me on. Rob Ritchie, Aniela Piasecka, Sophie Collins and Geri Snell all gave their time and thoughts to an early version of the book, and our conversations about it were invaluable to its re-shaping. I am particularly grateful to Zoë Strachan, who gave consistently attentive, thoughtful feedback, and encouraged me to keep writing. Thanks also to Zoë, and to Jo Sharp and Ruth Zadoks, for helping me to secure a PhD scholarship at the University of Glasgow, which gave me the time and financial security to write this novel alongside my research. I am indebted to Sarah Tytler for sharing with me experiences of her time in Tonga, and to Sylvia Whitman and the staff at Shakespeare and Company for their hospitality, which enabled me to live in Paris for a month and undertake vital research for the novel. I am grateful to a friend for suggesting I submit the manuscript to the Society of Authors, which unexpectedly set things in motion. My thanks are due to the judges of the 2019 Betty Trask Prize, who read and shortlisted the manuscript, and particularly to Elanor Dymott, for her encouraging words and guidance. I am grateful for the support of my agent, Karolina Sutton, and for her uncompromising, insightful reading. At Granta I feel blessed to have worked with Ka Bradley, whose diligent and intuitive editing the book has benefitted from greatly.

My thanks are also due to Andy and Alison Piasecka, for their kindness and hospitality, and for helping me out of a tight spot.

All my love to Patrick, who read and recognised the book, just as I was beginning to understand it for myself.